Titles by Anthony Horowitz

The Power of Five (Book One): *Raven's Gate*
The Power of Five (Book Two): *Evil Star*
The Power of Five (Book Three): *Nightrise*
The Power of Five (Book Four): *Necropolis*
The Power of Five (Book Five): *Oblivion*

The Alex Rider series:
Stormbreaker
Point Blanc
Skeleton Key
Eagle Strike
Scorpia
Ark Angel
Snakehead
Crocodile Tears
Scorpia Rising

The Devil and His Boy
Granny
Groosham Grange
Return to Groosham Grange
The Switch
More Bloody Horowitz

The Diamond Brothers books:
The Falcon's Malteser
Public Enemy Number Two
South by South East
Four of Diamonds

WALKER
BOOKS

Based on an idea first published in 1983 as *The Devil's Doorbell*

First published as *Raven's Gate* 2005 by Walker Books Ltd
87 Vauxhall Walk, London SE11 5HJ

This edition with new cover published 2013

2 4 6 8 10 9 7 5 3 1

Text © 2006 Stormbreaker Productions Ltd
Cover illustration and design © 2013 Walker Books Ltd
Power of 5 logo™ © 2006 Walker Books Ltd

The right of Anthony Horowitz to be identified as author of this
work has been asserted by him in accordance with the
Copyright, Designs and Patents Act 1988

This book has been typeset in Frutiger Light and Alternate Gothic

Printed and bound in Great Britain by Clays Ltd, St Ives plc

British Library Cataloguing in Publication Data:
a catalogue record for this book is available from the British Library

ISBN 978-1-4063-5389-1

www.walker.co.uk
www.powerof5.co.uk

CONTENTS

1	The Warehouse	9
2	Broken Glass	21
3	The Leaf Project	32
4	Lesser Malling	46
5	A Warning	56
6	Whispers	71
7	Omega One	84
8	Wet Paint	97
9	Local Affairs	111
10	The Nexus	126
11	A Visitor	139
12	Out of the Fire	152
13	Matt's Story	170
14	Science and Magic	185
15	Unnatural History	203
16	Bones	221
17	Roodmas	234
18	Dark Powers	246
19	Raven's Gate	255
20	The Man from Peru	271

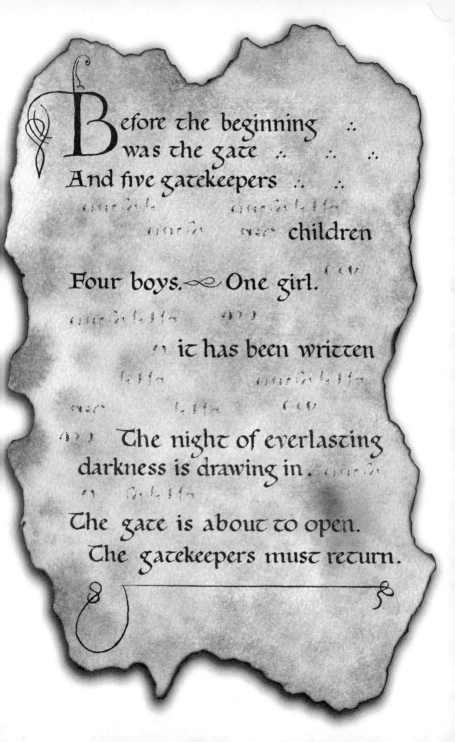

Before the beginning ∴
was the gate ∴ ∴ ∴
And five gatekeepers ∴ ∴

children

Four boys. One girl.

it has been written

The night of everlasting
darkness is drawing in.

The gate is about to open.

The gatekeepers must return.

THE WAREHOUSE

Matt Freeman knew he was making a mistake.

He was sitting on a low wall outside Ipswich station, wearing a grey hooded sweatshirt, shapeless, faded jeans, and trainers with frayed laces. It was six o'clock in the evening and the London train had just pulled in. Behind him, commuters were fighting their way out of the station. The concourse was a tangle of cars, taxis and pedestrians, all of them trying to find their way home. A traffic light blinked from red to green but nothing moved. Somebody leant on their horn and the noise blared out, cutting through the damp evening air. Matt heard it and looked up briefly. But the crowd meant nothing to him. He wasn't part of it. He never had been – and he sometimes thought he never would be.

Two men carrying umbrellas walked past and glanced at him disapprovingly. They probably thought he was up to no good. The way he was sitting – hunched forward with his knees apart – made him look somehow dangerous, and older than fourteen. He had broad shoulders, a well-developed, muscular body and bright blue, intelligent eyes. His hair was black, cut very short. Give him another five years and he could be a footballer or a model – or, like plenty of others, both.

His first name was Matthew but he always called himself Matt. As the troubles had begun to pile up in his life, he had used his surname less and less until it was no longer a part of him. Freeman was the name on the school register and on the truancy list, and it was a name well known to the local social services. But Matthew never wrote it down and seldom spoke it. "Matt" was enough. The name suited him. After all, for as long as he could remember, people had been walking all over him.

He watched the two men with umbrellas cross the bridge and disappear in the direction of the city centre. Matt hadn't been born in Ipswich. He had been brought here and he hated everything about the place. For a start, it wasn't a city. It was too small. But it had none of the charm of a village or a market town. It was really just an oversized shopping centre with the same shops and supermarkets that you saw everywhere else. You could swim in the Crown Pools or you could see movies at the multiplex – or, if you could afford it, there was an artificial ski slope and go-karting. But that was about it. It didn't even have a decent football team.

Matt had just three pounds in his pocket, saved up from his newspaper round. There was another twenty pounds at home, hidden in a box under his bed. He needed money for the same reason as every other teenager in Ipswich. It wasn't just because his trainers were falling apart and the games on his XBox were six months out of date. Money was power. Money was independence. He didn't have any and he was here tonight because he wanted some.

But already he was wishing he hadn't come. It was wrong. It was stupid. Why had he ever agreed?

He glanced at his watch. Ten past six. They had arranged to meet at a quarter to. Well, that was excuse enough. He swung himself off the wall and headed across the station front. But he hadn't taken more than a couple of steps before another, older boy appeared out of nowhere, blocking his path.

"You off then, Matt?" the boy asked.

"I thought you weren't coming," Matt said.

"Oh yes? And why did you think that?"

Because you're twenty-five minutes late. Because I'm cold. Because you're about as reliable as a local bus. That was what Matt wanted to say. But the words didn't come. He just shrugged.

The other boy smiled. His name was Kelvin and he was seventeen, tall and scrawny with fair hair, pale skin and acne. He was dressed expensively in designer jeans and a soft leather jacket. Even when he had been at school, Kelvin had always had the best gear.

"I got held up," he said.

Matt said nothing.

"You haven't had second thoughts, have you?"

"No."

11

"You've got nothing to worry about, Matt, mate. It's going to be easy. Charlie told me…"

Charlie was Kelvin's older brother. Matt had never met him, which wasn't surprising. Charlie was in prison, in a young offenders' institution just outside Manchester. Kelvin didn't often talk about him. But it was Charlie who had first heard about the warehouse.

It was fifteen minutes from the station, in an industrial zone. A warehouse stacked with CDs, video games and DVDs. Amazingly, it had no alarm systems and only one security guard, a retired policeman who was half-asleep most of the time, with his feet up and his head buried in a newspaper. Charlie knew all this because a friend of his had been in to do some electrical work. According to Charlie, you could break in with a bent paper clip and you could probably walk out with a couple of hundred quid's worth of equipment. It was easy, just waiting to be taken.

That was why the two of them had arranged to meet here. Matt had agreed to the idea when they were talking about it, but half of him had thought Kelvin wasn't being serious. The two of them had done plenty of things together. Under Kelvin's guidance, they'd stolen stuff from supermarkets, and once they'd driven off in someone's car. But Matt knew this was much worse. This was serious. It was breaking and entering. Burglary. Real crime.

"Are you sure about this?" Matt asked.

"Sure I'm sure. What's the problem?"

"If we get caught…"

"We won't. Charlie says they don't even have CCTV." Kelvin rested a foot on the wall. Matt noticed he was wearing a pair of brand new Nikes. He had often wondered how Kelvin could afford his clothes. Now, he supposed, he knew. "Come on, Matt," Kelvin went on. "If you're going to be such a wuss, I'm not sure I want to hang out with you. What's the big deal?"

A look of exasperation had crept into Kelvin's face and in that moment, Matt knew he would have to go. If he didn't, he would lose his only friend. When Matt had first started at St Edmund's Comprehensive in Ipswich, Kelvin had taken him under his wing. There had been kids who thought Matt was weird. Other kids had tried to bully him. Kelvin had helped see them off. And it was useful having Kelvin just a few doors away in Eastfield Terrace, where Matt lived with his aunt and her partner. When things were really bad, there was always somewhere to go. And he had to admit that it was flattering, hanging out with someone three years older than him.

"There's no big deal," he said. "I'll come."

And that was it. The decision had been made. Matt tried to damp down the sense of rising fear. Kelvin slapped him on the back. The two of them set off together.

Darkness came very quickly. It was the end of March but there was little sign of spring. It had rained heavily all month and the night still seemed to arrive before it was meant to. As they reached the industrial zone, the street lamps flickered on,

13

throwing pools of ugly orange light on to the ground. The area was fenced off with signs warning that this was private property, but the fence was rusty and full of holes, and the only other barrier was the wild grass and thistles that sprouted all around where the tarmac ended. Railway lines stretched out overhead, high up on a series of brick supports, and as the two boys approached quietly, flitting through the shadows, a train rattled past on its way to London.

There were about a dozen buildings in all. Some had advertisements painted on the side: L for Leather, office furniture. J.B. Stryker Auto Engineering. Spit & Polish Industrial Cleaning. Kelvin's warehouse was unmarked. It was a long, rectangular block with corrugated iron walls and a sloping, tiled roof. It had been built slightly apart from its neighbours, separated from them by a row of bottle banks and a junk heap of cartons and old tyres. There was nobody in sight. The whole area seemed deserted and forgotten.

The main entrance to the warehouse – a large, sliding door – was at the front. There were no windows, but Kelvin led Matt round to a second door at the side. The two of them were crouching now, hurrying through the darkness on tiptoe. Matt tried to relax, to enjoy what they were doing. This was an adventure, wasn't it? An hour from now, they'd be laughing about it with their pockets full of cash. But he was uneasy, and when Kelvin reached into his pocket and produced a knife, his stomach tightened and he felt even worse.

"What's that for?" he whispered.

"Don't worry. It's just to get us in."

Kelvin inserted the point of the blade into the crack between the door and its frame, and began to play with the bolt. Matt watched him without saying anything, secretly hoping that the door wouldn't open. The lock looked secure enough and it seemed somehow improbable that the seventeen-year-old would be able to unfasten it with anything as cumbersome as a knife. But then there was a click and light spilled out as the door swung open. Kelvin stepped back and Matt saw that he was equally surprised, although he was trying not to show it.

"We're in," he said.

Matt nodded. For a moment he wondered if Charlie might have been right after all. Perhaps this was going to be as easy as Kelvin had said.

They went through the door.

Inside, the warehouse was huge – much bigger than Matt had expected. When Kelvin had talked about the place, he had imagined nothing more than a few racks of DVDs in an otherwise empty space. But it seemed to go on for ever, with hundreds and hundreds of shelves numbered and divided into corridors that formed a complex grid system, all lit by vast industrial lights hanging on chains. And as well as the games and the DVDs, there were boxes of computer equipment, Game Boys, MP3 players and even mobile phones, all wrapped in plastic, ready for the shops.

Matt looked up. There were no security cameras – just like Kelvin had said.

"You head that way." Kelvin pointed. "Go for the small, expensive stuff. I'll meet you back here."

"Why don't we stick together?"

"Don't you worry, Matty. I won't leave without you!"

The two of them split up. Matt found himself in a narrow corridor with DVDs on both sides. Tom Cruise, Johnny Depp, Brad Pitt... All the familiar faces in the most recent feature films were there. He reached out and took a handful, not even looking at what he'd chosen. He was sure there were more expensive things in the warehouse but he didn't care. He just wanted to get out.

Everything went wrong at once.

It began with a smell that was suddenly in his nostrils, everywhere, coming from nowhere.

The smell of burnt toast.

And a voice. *"Come on, Matthew. We're going to be late."*

A flash of colour. A bright yellow wall. Pine cupboards. A teapot shaped like a teddy bear.

The smell told him something was wrong in the same way that a dog will often bark before danger actually appears. Matt knew that it was odd but he had never really questioned it before. It was a knack ... a sort of instinct. A warning. But this time it had come too late. Before he knew what was happening, a heavy hand had clamped down on his shoulder, spinning him round, and a voice exclaimed, "What the hell do you think you're doing?"

Matt felt his arms go weak and the DVDs cascaded to the floor, clattering around his feet. He found himself looking into the face of a security guard and knew at once that this wasn't the old codger Kelvin had described. This was a tall, serious man in a black and silver uniform with a radio transmitter attached to some sort of holster on his chest. The man was in his fifties but looked fit, built like a rugby player.

"The police are already on their way," he said. "You set off the alarm when you opened that door. So don't try anything funny."

Matt couldn't move. He was too shocked by the appearance of the guard. His heart was hammering in his chest, making it difficult to breathe. He was suddenly feeling very young again.

"What's your name?" the guard demanded.

Matt said nothing.

"Are you alone?" This time, his voice was a little kinder. He must have seen that Matt was no threat to him. "How many of you are there?"

Matt drew a breath. "I…"

And then, as if a switch had been thrown and the whole world sent into a spin, the real horror began.

The security guard jerked upright, his eyes widening, his mouth falling open. He released Matt and fell sideways. Matt looked past him and saw Kelvin standing there, a dazed smile on his face. At first he didn't understand what had happened. Then he saw the hilt of the knife, sticking out of the guard's back, just above his waist. The security guard didn't look hurt. He just looked surprised. He collapsed slowly, rested on his knees, then pitched forward on to the floor and lay still.

A whole eternity seemed to pass by. Matt was frozen. He felt he was being sucked into some sort of black hole. Then Kelvin grabbed hold of him.

"We've got to move," he said.

"Kelvin...?" Matt fought for control. "What have you done?" he whispered. "Why did you have to do that?"

"What else was I meant to do?" Kelvin demanded. "He'd seen you."

"I know he'd seen me. But you didn't have to stab him! Do you know what you've done? Do you know what you are?"

Matt was speechless, horrified, and before he knew what he was doing, he had thrown himself at Kelvin, hurling him into one of the shelves. Kelvin recovered quickly. He was bigger and stronger than Matt. He coiled forward, then lashed out with a fist, catching Matt on the side of the head. Matt fell back, dazed.

"What's the matter with you, Matt?" Kelvin snarled. "What's your problem?"

"*You* are! You didn't have to do that! You must be out of your mind!" Matt's head was spinning. He didn't know what to say.

18

"I was only thinking of you, mate." Kelvin jabbed at him with his finger. "I only did it for you."

The security guard groaned. Matt forced himself to look down. The man was still alive. But he was lying in a pool of blood that seemed to be spreading with every second.

"Let's go!" Kelvin hissed.

"No. We can't leave him."

"What?"

"Where's your mobile? We have to call for help."

"To hell with that!" Kelvin ran his tongue over his lips. "You stay if you want to. I'm out of here."

"You can't!"

"Watch me!"

And then he was gone, disappearing back up the corridor. Matt ignored him. The security guard groaned a second time and tried to say something. Feeling sick, Matt crouched down beside him and placed a hand on his arm. "Don't move," he said. "I'm going to get help."

But help had already arrived. Matt heard the sirens seconds before the screech of tyres announced that the police had arrived. They must have begun their journey to the warehouse the moment Kelvin forced open the door. Leaving the guard, Matt stood up and walked out into the open. A whole section of the wall suddenly slid aside. Matt could see all the way down the warehouse and out into the darkness, which was flashing black blue black blue. There were three cars parked across the entrance. A set of headlamps came on and a dazzling beam of light shot through the darkness and hammered into his eyes. At the same time, half a dozen figures, no more than silhouettes, moved towards him. He could see that they were all dressed in protective clothing. Some of them were carrying guns.

They had already caught Kelvin. He was being led, squealing and crying, by two armoured men a great deal bigger than him. Then he saw Matt. At once he turned and pointed.

"It wasn't me!" he whined in a high-pitched voice. "It was him! He made me come! And he killed the guard!"

"Don't move!" somebody shouted, as two more men came running towards Matt.

Matt stood where he was. Slowly, he raised his arms. The palms of his hands were caught in the light from the cars and now he saw that they were glistening red, covered in blood.

"He did it! He did it! He did it!" Kelvin screamed.

The two police officers reached Matt and fell on him. His hands were twisted behind his back and cuffed. He heard the click of the metal and knew there was nothing he could do. Then he was jerked off his feet and dragged, silent and unresisting, out into the night.

BROKEN GLASS

They took Matt to a building that wasn't a prison and wasn't a hospital but was something in between. The car drove into a rectangular, tarmac-covered area with high walls all around. As they drew to a halt, a steel door slid across, blocking the way out. The door closed with a loud, electric buzz. Matt heard the locks engage. They seemed to echo inside his head. He wondered if he would ever see the world on the other side of the door again.

"Out!" The voice didn't seem to belong to anyone. It told him what to do and he obeyed. It was drizzling and for a few moments he felt the cold water against his face and was almost grateful for it. He wanted to wash. He could still feel the blood on his hands, behind his back. It had dried and gone sticky.

They passed through a set of double doors into a corridor with harsh lighting, tiles, the smell of urine and disinfectant. People in uniforms passed him by. Two policemen, then a nurse. Matt was still handcuffed. He had seen people being arrested on television but he had never realized what it really felt like, to have his freedom taken away like this. He could feel his arms, pinned behind his back. He was utterly defenceless.

The two policemen stopped in front of a desk, where a third man in a blue jersey made some entries in a book. He asked a few questions but Matt didn't understand what he was saying. He could see the man's mouth moving. He heard the words. But they seemed far away and made no sense.

Then he was on the move again, escorted into a lift that needed a key to be operated. He was taken up to the second floor and down another corridor. Matt kept his head bowed, his eyes fixed on his feet. He didn't want to look around him. He didn't want to know where he was.

They stopped again in an open-plan area, a meeting place of several corridors, painted green, with police information posters on the walls. There was an office with a window that had been wired off and in front of it a table with a computer and two chairs. They went in. The handcuffs were unlocked and he brought his arms forward with a sense of relief. His shoulders were aching.

"Sit down," one of the policemen said.

Matt did as he was told.

About five minutes passed. Then a door opened and a man in a suit and a brightly coloured open-neck shirt appeared. He was black, with a slim figure and kind, intelligent eyes. He looked a bit more friendly than the others and he was also younger. Matt didn't think he could be out of his twenties.

"My name is Detective Superintendent Mallory," he said. He had a pleasant, cultivated voice. Like a newsreader on TV. "Are you all right?"

"I'm all right." Matt was surprised by the question.

Mallory had sat down opposite him at the table. He pressed a few keys on the computer. "What's your name?" he asked.

"Matt."

Mallory's fingers hovered over the keyboard. "I'm afraid you're going to have to tell me your full name. I need it for the report."

Matt hesitated. But he knew he had to co-operate. "Matthew Freeman," he said.

The detective tapped in the letters and pressed ENTER, then watched as a dozen lines of information scrolled up on the screen. "You seem to have made quite a name for yourself," Mallory said. "You live at 27 Eastfield Terrace?"

"Yes." Matt nodded.

"With a guardian. A Ms Davis?"

"She's my aunt."

"You're fourteen."

"Yes."

Mallory looked up from the computer screen. "You're in a lot of trouble," he said.

Matt took a breath. "I know." He was almost afraid to ask, but he still had to know. "Is he dead?"

"The guard you stabbed has a name – Mark Adams. He's

married with two kids." Mallory couldn't conceal his anger. "Right now he's in hospital. He's going to be there for a while. But he won't die."

"I didn't stab him," Matt said. "I didn't know anyone was going to get hurt. That wasn't the idea."

"That's not what your friend Kelvin told us. He said it was your knife and your plan, and it was you who panicked when you were caught."

"He's lying."

Mallory sighed. "I know. I've already spoken to the guard and he's told us what happened. He heard the two of you argue and he knows that you wanted to stay. But you're still responsible, Matthew. I have to tell you that you're going to be charged as an accessory. Do you know what that means?"

"Are you going to send me to prison?"

"You're fourteen. You're too young for prison. But it's quite possible you could be facing a custodial sentence." Mallory stopped. He had seen dozens of kids in this room. Many of them had been thugs, ranging from openly defiant to snivelling and pathetic. But he was puzzled by the quiet, good-looking boy who sat opposite him now. Matt was somehow different and Mallory found himself wondering what had brought him here. "Look, it's too late to talk about this now," he said. "Are you hungry?"

Matt shook his head.

"Is there anything you need?"

"No."

"Try not to be too scared. We'll look after you tonight, and tomorrow morning we'll try to make sense of all this. Right now, you'd better get out of those clothes. I'm afraid someone will have to stay with you while you undress – your clothes are evidence. You can have a shower, and then a doctor will look at you."

"I'm not sick. I don't need a doctor."

"It's just routine. He'll give you a quick examination and maybe something to help you sleep." Mallory glanced at one of the policemen. "All right."

Matt stood up. "Will you tell him I'm sorry," he said. "The security guard. Mark Adams. I know it doesn't make any difference and you probably don't believe me anyway. But I am."

Mallory nodded. The policeman took Matt's arm and led him back down the corridor.

He was taken to a changing room – bare wooden benches and white tiles. His clothes went into a plastic bag that was stapled shut and labelled. Then he showered. He had no privacy, just as he had been warned. There was a policeman in the room with him the whole time but he still managed to enjoy the shower; the rush of water, scalding hot, shuddering down on his head and his shoulders, washing away the blood and the horror of the last hours. It was over all too quickly. He dried himself, then pulled on a grey T-shirt and undershorts that had been laundered and pressed as flat as paper. Finally, he was taken to a room which could have been a ward in a hospital, with four metal beds, four identical tables, and nothing else. The room felt as if it had been cleaned fifty times. Even the air felt clean. It seemed that he was the only occupant.

He climbed into bed, and before any doctor could arrive he was asleep. Sleep came as quickly as a train in a tunnel. He simply lay back and kept on falling.

Meanwhile, in a room downstairs, Stephen Mallory was sitting opposite a crumpled, sullen-looking woman who was managing both to scowl and to yawn at the same time. The woman was Gwenda Davis, Matt's aunt and legal guardian. She was short and drab, with mousey hair and a pinched, forgettable face. She wore no make-up and there were heavy bags under her eyes. She was dressed in an old, shapeless coat. It might have been expensive once but now it was frayed at the edges. Like the woman who was wearing it, Mallory thought. He supposed that she was about forty-five. She seemed nervous, as if it was she, not her nephew, who had been accused of something.

"So where is he?" Gwenda asked. She had a thin, whiny voice that made every question sound like a complaint.

"He's upstairs," Mallory said. "He fell asleep before the doctor could see him but we gave him a tranquillizer anyway. It's possible he's in shock."

"*He's* in shock?" Gwenda laughed briefly. "*I'm* the one who's in shock, I can tell you. Getting a call in the middle of the night like this! Having to come down here. I'm a respectable person. All this business with knives and burglary. I've never heard such a thing."

"I understand you share your house with a partner?"

"Brian." Gwenda noticed Mallory had taken out a pen. "Brian Conran," she continued, and watched as the detective wrote it down. "He's in bed. He's not any relation to the boy. Why should he come out in the middle of the night? He's got to be up first thing in the morning."

"What's his job?"

"What's it to you?" She shrugged. "He's a milkman."

Mallory pulled a sheet of paper out of a file. "I see from Matthew's record that his parents died," he said.

"A car crash." Gwenda swallowed. "He was eight years old. The family was living in London then. His mother and father were killed. But he'd stayed behind."

"He was an only child?"

"No brothers or sisters. No relatives either. Nobody knew what to do with him."

"You were related to his mother?"

"I was her half-sister. I'd only met them a few times." Gwenda drew herself up, crossing her hands in front of her. "If you want the truth, they were never very friendly. It was all right for them, wasn't it. A nice house in a nice neighbourhood. A nice car. Nice everything. They didn't have any time for me. And when they died in that stupid accident... Well, I don't know what would have happened to Matthew if it hadn't been for me and Brian. We took him in. We had to bring him up all on our own. And what did we get for it? Nothing but trouble!"

Mallory glanced again at the report. "He had never been in trouble before," he said. "He started missing school a year after he came to Ipswich. From there it was downhill all the way."

"Are you blaming me?" Two pinpricks of red had appeared in Gwenda's cheeks. "It was nothing to do with me! It was that boy, Kelvin Johnson... He lives just down the road. He's to blame!"

It was eleven o'clock at night. It had been a long day and Mallory had heard enough. He closed the file and stood up. "Thank you for coming in, Ms Davis," he said. "Would you like to see Matthew?"

"There's hardly any point seeing him if he's asleep, is there?"

"Maybe you'd like to come back in the morning then. The social services will be here. He'll also need legal representation. But if you're here at nine o'clock—"

"I can't come at nine o'clock. I have to make Brian his breakfast when he gets in from his rounds. I'll come in after that."

"Right."

Gwenda Davis picked herself up and left the room. Mallory watched her go. He felt nothing for her. But he couldn't avoid a sense of great sadness for the boy who was asleep upstairs.

28

* * *

Matt woke up.

The room with the four metal beds was deserted. No sound came from anywhere in the building. He could feel a pillow cradling the back of his head and he wondered how long he had been here. There was no sign of a clock, but it was pitch-dark outside – he could see the night sky through the barred window. The room was softly lit. They probably never turned off the lights completely.

He tried to go back to sleep but he was wide awake. Suddenly he was seeing it all again, the events of the evening. The images flickered in front of him like cards caught in the wind. There was Kelvin, outside the railway station. Then the warehouse, the DVDs, the guard, the knife, Kelvin again with that stupid smile, the police cars, and his own hands, stained with blood. Matt squeezed his eyes shut, trying to force the memories out of his mind.

It was very warm in the room. The window was shut and the radiators were on. He could feel the heat shimmering around him. He was suddenly thirsty and looked around, wondering if he could call someone. But there was no bell to press and nobody in sight.

Then he noticed a jug of water and a tumbler on a table at the other side of the room. All he had to do was get out of bed and help himself. He lifted a hand to move the bedcovers but they were too heavy. No. That wasn't possible. He flexed his muscles and tried to lift himself. He could hardly move. And then he realized that a doctor must have seen him while he was asleep. He had been injected with something – tranquillized. He couldn't move.

He almost cried out. He felt the panic suffocating him. What were they going to do to him? Why had he gone to the warehouse? How had he allowed all this to happen? He sank back into the pillow, fighting the wave of despair that had risen over him. He couldn't believe that a man had almost died for the sake of a handful of DVDs. How could he have been stupid enough to think of Kelvin as a friend? *"He did it! He did it!"* Kelvin was pathetic. He always had been.

The water…

The room seemed to be getting hotter and hotter, as if the police had turned up the radiators just to torment him. Matt found his whole concentration focused on the jug. He could see the perfect circle made by the water where it touched the edge of the glass. He willed himself to get up, and when that failed, he found himself willing the jug of water to come to him. He ran his tongue over his lips. His mouth was parched. For a moment, he thought he smelled something burning. The jug was so close to him – only a few metres away. He reached out to it, pulling it towards him with his mind.

The jug smashed.

It seemed to explode, almost in slow motion. For a split second the water hung in the air, its tentacles sprawling outwards. Then it splashed down on to the table, on to the pieces of glass.

Matt was stunned. He had no idea what had happened. He hadn't broken the jug. It had broken itself. It was as if it had been hit by a bullet. Yet he hadn't heard a shot. He hadn't heard anything. Matt stared at the glass fragments, scattered over the table with the water pooling around, dripping on to the floor. Had the heat in the room caused it? Or was it him? Had his thirst somehow, in some inexplicable way, smashed the jug?

Exhaustion finally overcame him a second time and he fell into a deep, suffocating sleep. When he woke up the next morning, the broken glass wasn't there. Nor was the spilled water. A single jug and a tumbler stood on the table, exactly where they had been the night before, and Matt decided that the whole experience must have been nothing more than a weird dream.

THE LEAF PROJECT

Matt, dressed in his own clothes, sat in a chair facing the four people who were examining him from the other side of a long wooden table. It was the sort of room where people got married … or perhaps divorced. Not uncomfortable, but spare and formal with wood panelling on the walls and portraits of officials – probably all dead by now – in gold frames. He was in London, although he wasn't exactly sure where. It had been raining too hard to see much out of the car windows, and he had been driven straight to the door and shown up a flight of stairs into this modern, unattractive building. There had been no time for sightseeing.

A week had passed since Matt's arrest, and in that time he had been interviewed, examined, assessed and, for many hours, left on his own. He had filled in papers that were like exams except that they didn't seem to have any point. "2, 8, 14, 20… What is the next number in the sequence?" And: "How many spelling misteaks are their in this sentence?" Different men and women – doctors, psychologists – had asked him to talk about himself. He had been shown blobs on pieces of paper. "What do you see, Matthew? What does the shape make you think about?" And there had been games – word association, stuff like that.

Finally they had told him he was leaving. A suitcase had appeared, packed with clothes that Gwenda must have sent from home. After a three-hour journey in an ordinary car – not even a police car – he had found himself here. The rain was still lashing against the windows, obscuring the view. He could hear it hammering against the glass, as if demanding to be let in. It seemed that the whole outside world had dissolved and the only things remaining were the five people, here, in this room.

On the far left was his aunt, Gwenda Davis. She was dabbing at her eyes with a paper tissue, causing her mascara to smudge – there was a dirty brown streak all the way down one side of her face. Detective Superintendent Stephen Mallory sat next to her, looking the other way. The third person was a woman magistrate. Matt had only met her for the first time today. She was about sixty years old, smartly dressed and a little severe-looking. She wore gold-rimmed spectacles and a look of disapproval that had, over the years, become permanent. The fourth person was Matt's social worker, an untidy, grey-haired woman about ten years younger than the magistrate. Her name was Jill Hughes and she had been assigned to Matt when he was eleven. She had worked with him ever since and privately thought of him as her greatest failure.

It was the magistrate who was talking.

"Matthew, you have to understand that this was a very cowardly crime and one that involved violence," she was saying. The magistrate had a very precise, clipped manner of speaking, as if every word was of the utmost importance. "Your associate, Kelvin Johnson, will be sent to the Crown Court and he will almost certainly be sentenced to imprisonment in a young offenders' institution. He is seventeen. You, of course, are younger. But even so, you are above the age of criminal responsibility. If you went before the court, I suspect you might well be given a Section 91. This means you would be locked up for perhaps three years in either a secure training centre or a local authority secure children's home."

She paused and opened a file that was on the table in front of her. The sound of the pages turning seemed very loud in the sudden silence.

"You are an intelligent boy," she went on. "I have the results of the tests you have been given during the past week. Although your school results have never done you any credit, you seem to have a good grasp of the basic skills – maths and literacy. Your psychological report suggests that you have a positive and a creative mind. It seems very strange that you should have chosen to drift into truancy and petty crime.

"But then, of course, we have to take into account your unfortunate background. You lost your parents suddenly and at a very early age – and this must have caused you enormous distress. I think it's fairly clear to all of us that the problems in your young life may have resulted from this one, tragic event. Even so, Matthew, you must find the strength to overcome these problems. If you continue down the path you have been following, there is a very real chance that you will end up in prison."

Matt wasn't really listening. He was trying to, but the words sounded distant and irrelevant … like an announcer in a station where he didn't want to catch a train. He couldn't believe that this woman was talking to him. Instead, he listened to the rain, beating against the windows. The rain seemed to tell him more.

"There is a new government programme that has been designed specifically for people like you," the magistrate went on. "The truth is, Matthew, that nobody wants to see young people sent into care. It's expensive – and anyway, we don't have enough places. That is why the government recently created the LEAF Project. Liberty and Education Achieved through Fostering. You can think of it, if you like, as turning over a new leaf."

"I've already been fostered once" – Matt glanced at Gwenda, who twitched in her seat – "and it wasn't exactly a success."

"That's certainly true," the magistrate agreed. "And I'm afraid Ms Davis no longer feels able to look after you. She's had enough."

"Really?" Matt said scornfully.

"I did what I could!" Gwenda cried. She twisted the tissue

into her eye. "You were never grateful. You were never nice. You never even tried."

The magistrate coughed and Gwenda glanced up briefly then fell silent. "And I'm afraid your social worker, Miss Hughes, feels much the same," she went on. "I have to tell you, Matthew, that you've left us with no other alternative. LEAF is your last chance to redeem yourself."

"What is LEAF?" Matt asked. He suddenly wanted to get out of this room. He didn't care where they sent him.

"LEAF is a fostering programme." Jill Hughes had taken over. She was a small woman, half-hidden by the table behind which she was sitting. In fact she was the wrong size for her job. She had spent her whole life dealing with aggressive criminals, most of whom were much bigger than her. "We have a number of volunteers living in remote parts of the country—"

"There are fewer temptations in the countryside," the magistrate cut in.

"All of them are well away from urban areas," Jill Hughes continued. "They take on young people like yourself and offer an old-fashioned home environment. They provide food, clothes, companionship and, most important of all, discipline. The L in LEAF stands for Liberty – but it has to be earned."

"Your new foster parent may ask you to help with light manual labour," the magistrate said.

"You mean ... I have to work?" Matt said, his voice full of contempt.

36

"There's nothing wrong with that!" The magistrate bristled. "Working in the countryside is good for your health, and many children would be delighted to be out there with the animals and the crops on a farm. Nobody can force you to join the LEAF Project, Matthew. You have to volunteer. But I have to say, this is a real opportunity for you. And I'm sure you'll find it preferable to the alternative."

"Locked up for three years." That was what she had said.

"How long will I have to stay there?" he asked.

"A minimum of one year. After that, we'll reassess the situation."

"You may like it," Stephen Mallory said. He was trying to sound upbeat. "It's a whole new start, Matt. A chance to make new friends."

But Matt had his doubts. "What happens if I don't like it?" he asked.

"We'll be in constant touch with the foster parent," the magistrate explained. "The parent has to make a weekly report to the police and your aunt will visit you as soon as you feel ready. There'll be a settling-in period of three months, but after that she'll see you every month."

"She'll provide an interface between the foster parent and the social services," Jill Hughes said.

"I don't know how I'll afford it," Gwenda muttered. "I mean, if there are going to be travelling expenses. And who's going to look after Brian while I'm away? I have responsibilities, you know…"

ice trailed away. The room was suddenly silent,
from the sound of the traffic and the rain hitting the
indows.

"All right." Matt shrugged. "You can send me wherever
you want to. I don't really care. Anything would be better than
being with her and Brian."

Gwenda flushed. Mallory cut in before she could speak.
"We won't abandon you, Matt," he promised. "We'll make
sure you're looked after."

But the magistrate was annoyed. "You have absolutely
nothing to complain about," she snapped. She looked at Matt
over the top of her glasses. "Quite frankly, you should be
grateful you're being given this opportunity. And I should
warn you. If your foster parent is unhappy with your progress,
if you abuse the kindness you're being shown in any way, then
you will be returned to us. And then you will find yourself
in an institution. You won't be given a second chance. Do you
understand?"

"Yes. I understand." Matt glanced at the windows. The
light was almost lost behind the grey, endlessly moving curtain
of water. "So when do I get to meet my foster parent?"

"Her name is Jayne Deverill," the social worker said. "And
she should be here any minute now."

They were mending the escalators at Holborn tube station and
as the woman rose up to street level, sparks from the oxy-
acetylene torches flashed and flickered behind her. But Jayne

Deverill didn't notice them. She was standing completely still, clutching a leather handbag under her arm, staring at a point a few metres in front of her as if she was disgusted by her surroundings.

She fed her ticket into the barrier and watched as it sprang open. Someone knocked into her and for a second something dark flashed in her eyes. But she forced herself to keep control. She was wearing ugly, old-fashioned leather shoes and she walked awkwardly, as if, perhaps, there was something wrong with her legs.

Mrs Deverill was a small woman, at least fifty years old, with white hair, cut short. Her skin was not yet withered but it was strangely lifeless. She had hard, ice-cold eyes and cheekbones that formed two slashes across her face. It was hard to imagine her pale lips ever smiling. She was smartly dressed in a grey skirt and matching jacket with a shirt buttoned to her neck. She wore a silver necklace and, on her lapel, a silver brooch shaped like a lizard.

Her progress from Holborn station had been observed.

Mrs Deverill was unaware that she was being followed as she made her way down Kingsway, heading for the offices behind Lincoln's Inn, but the man in the hooded anorak was never more than ten steps behind. He was twenty years old, with greasy blond hair and a thin, unhealthy-looking face. He had recognized the woman as an out-of-towner the moment he had spotted her coming through the ticket barrier. He didn't know who she was and he didn't care. Just two things about her had interested him: the handbag and the jewellery.

He didn't know where she was going but hoped that she would leave the main road with its many pedestrians and occasional policemen and follow one of the quieter streets that twisted away behind. Anyway, it was worth a few minutes of his time to see. He was still with her as she paused at a corner and turned left next to a pub. He smiled. It couldn't have worked out better. Now there were just the two of them, walking down an alleyway that cut through to the legal offices – solicitors' firms and council buildings – which existed in their own quite separate world. He took one quick look around, checking there was nobody in sight, then dug into the pocket of the dirty anorak he was wearing. He took out a jagged knife and turned it in his hand, enjoying the sense of power that it gave him. Then he ran forward.

"You!" he shouted.

The woman stopped, her back towards him.

"Give me the bag, bitch. Now! And I want the necklace…"

There was a pause.

Jayne Deverill turned round.

Ten minutes later Jayne Deverill was sitting, a little breathless, holding a cup of tea that she had been offered. She was in the office of the Family Proceedings and Youth Court, which was where Matt was being held.

"I'm very sorry I'm late," she was saying. She had a deep, rather throaty voice, like someone who had smoked too many cigarettes. "It's very rude of me – and I deplore rudeness. Punctuality is the first sign of good breeding. That's what I always say."

"You had trouble getting here?" Mallory asked.

"The coach was late. I would have called you from the bus station but I'm afraid I don't carry a mobile. We're not as up to date in the Yorkshire countryside as you are down here in London. In fact, there's no signal where I live, so a mobile telephone would be something of a waste of time." She turned to Matt. "I'm very glad to meet you, my dear. I have, of course, heard so much about you."

Matt looked at the woman who had volunteered to be his foster parent in the LEAF Project. He didn't like what he saw.

Jayne Deverill could have stepped out of another century: a time when teachers were allowed to beat children and there were Bible readings before breakfast and tea. He had never met anyone more severe-looking. Jill Hughes had greeted the woman like an old friend, although it turned out that the two had never met – they had only spoken on the phone. Stephen Mallory looked more uncomfortable. He was also meeting Mrs Deverill for the first time, and although he had shaken her hand, he had lapsed into silence and seemed to be lost in his own thoughts. The magistrate was more interested in the paperwork than anything else, in a hurry to get this whole thing over with. Matt examined Mrs Deverill again. She was sipping her tea but her eyes never left him. They were devouring him.

"Do you know Yorkshire at all?" she asked.

It took a moment for Matt to realize that she was talking to him. "No," he said. "I've never been there."

"Lesser Malling is the name of the village. It's a bit out of the way. The nearest town is Greater Malling and nobody's heard of that either. And why should they have? There's nothing there. We're very down-to-earth in Yorkshire. We look after the land and the land looks after us. I'm sure you'll find it very quiet after the city. But you'll get used to it in time." She glanced at the magistrate. "I can really take him with me today?"

The magistrate nodded.

Mrs Deverill smiled. "And when will you make your first visit?"

"Six weeks from now. We want to give Matthew time to settle in."

"Well, after six weeks with me, I can assure you, you won't recognize him." She turned to Gwenda Davis. "You won't need to worry about him, Ms Davis. You can telephone him any time you want and, of course, we'll both look forward to you coming up to visit."

"Well, I don't know about that." Gwenda was still worried. "It's a long way, and I'm not sure my partner..." She fell silent.

"There are some final forms you have to fill in, Mrs Deverill," the magistrate said. "But then the two of you can be on your way. Ms Davis brought in a suitcase with some of

42

Matthew's clothes and things." She turned to Matt. "I expect you'd like a few minutes on your own to say goodbye to your aunt."

"No. I've got nothing to say to her."

"It wasn't my fault," Gwenda said, and suddenly she was angry. "I was never anything to do with your family. I was never anything to do with you. I didn't even want to take you in after what happened to your parents. But I did and you were nothing but trouble. You've got nobody to blame but yourself."

"There's no need for this," Mallory said. "Good luck, Matt, I really hope this works out for you." He held out a hand. Matt hesitated, then shook it. This wasn't Mallory's fault. That much he knew.

"Time to go!" Mrs Deverill said. "We don't want to miss the coach!"

Matt stood up. Mallory watched him with thoughtful, anxious eyes as he left the room.

Two hours later Matt walked across Victoria coach station carrying the suitcase that Gwenda had packed for him. He looked around him at the coaches thundering in and out, the crowds of travellers and the snack and magazine stalls behind the plate-glass windows. It was an unpleasant place: cold and damp with air that smelled of diesel. He could hardly believe he was here. He was free... Finally out of police custody. No. Not free, he reminded himself. He had been handed over to this woman who called herself his foster mother.

"That's our bus." Mrs Deverill pointed to a coach with YORK written across the front.

Matt handed his case to a man, who stowed it in the luggage compartment, then climbed on board. They had reserved seats at the very back. Mrs Deverill allowed Matt to slide in next to the window and then sat down next to him. Soon the coach was full. At one o'clock exactly, the doors hissed shut, the engine started up and they began to move. Matt sat with his forehead pressed against the glass and he watched as they emerged from the coach station and out into the streets of Victoria. It was still raining. The raindrops chased in front of his eyes. Next to him Mrs Deverill sat with her eyes half-closed, breathing heavily.

He tried to concentrate, tried to work out what he was feeling. But then he realized: he felt nothing. He had been sucked into the system. Evaluated. Approved for the LEAF Project. And sent on his way. At least he wasn't going back to Ipswich. That was something to be thankful for. It was the end of six years with Gwenda and Brian. Whatever lay ahead couldn't possibly be worse.

Meanwhile, about five miles away, an alleyway in Holborn was being sealed off by two police cars and an ambulance. A dead body had been found – a young man in a hooded anorak.

The forensic team had only just arrived, but already the photographers and police scientists knew they had stumbled

44

on to something completely bizarre. The man was well known to them. His name was Will Scott and he was a drug addict who had been involved in many muggings in central London. There was a kitchen knife clutched in his hand and it was this that had killed him. But nobody had attacked him. There were no fingerprints. No sign that anyone had come close.

The dead man's mouth was stretched in a hideous smile and there was a look of sheer terror in his eyes. He was holding the knife very tightly. He had taken it and pushed it, inch by inch, into his own heart. It was unclear how he had done it – or why – but the forensic people had no doubt at all.

For some reason, Will Scott had killed himself.

LESSER MALLING

There were two hundred miles of dreary motorway between London and York, and the journey took more than four hours. The coach stopped twice at service stations but neither Matt nor Mrs Deverill left their seats. She had brought sandwiches with her. They were in her handbag, wrapped in brown paper. She took them out and offered one to Matt.

"Are you hungry, Matthew?"

"No, thank you."

"In Yorkshire I'll expect you to eat what you're given. We don't waste food in my house."

She unwrapped one of the bundles and Matt saw two slabs of white bread filled with cold liver. He was glad he hadn't accepted her offer.

"I expect you're wondering about me," Mrs Deverill said, as she began her lunch. She took small mouthfuls and chewed the food with care. When she swallowed, her throat twisted painfully, as if she had difficulty getting the food down. "I am now your legal guardian," she went on. "You are a thief and a delinquent, and the government has given you to me. But I'm willing to forget your past, Matthew. I can assure you it is your future that is of much more concern to me. If you do as you're told, we'll get on. If you disobey me, if you try to defy me, let me assure you that you will be more miserable than you can imagine. Do you understand?"

"Yes," Matt said.

Her eyes slid over him and he shivered. "You have to remember that nobody cares about you. You have no parents. No family. You have little education and no prospects. I don't want to be cruel to you, my dear, but I'm really all you have left."

She turned away from him and continued eating her sandwiches. After that, she took out a farming magazine and began to read. It was as if she had completely forgotten him.

The motorway stretched on. There was nothing to look at out of the window and Matt found himself hypnotized by the white lines and the crash barrier endlessly flashing past. Almost without knowing it he found himself drifting away, neither awake nor asleep but somewhere in between.

He was back in the terraced house in Dulwich, a leafy, friendly suburb of London. This was where he had lived with his mother and father. It had been six years since he had seen them but, staring out of the window, he saw them now.

There was his mother, rushing around the kitchen that was always in a mess, even when it had just been cleaned. She was wearing the clothes she had worn that last day: a pink dress with a white linen jacket. Whenever he remembered her,

47

this was how he saw her. It was a brand new dress that she had bought especially for the wedding. And there was his father, looking uncomfortable in a suit and tie. Mark Freeman was a doctor and he normally went to work in whatever he could find – jeans, a sweater… He didn't like dressing up. But one of the other doctors at his surgery was getting married and it was going to be a smart affair. First the service, then an expensive hotel. His father was sitting at the table, eating his breakfast, and he turned round, tossing his dark hair in the way he always did, and asked, *"Where's Matthew?"*

And then Matthew came in. Of course, he was still Matthew then. Now, six years later, sitting on a coach heading towards a place he had never heard of, Matt saw himself as he had been at that time: a short, slightly plump, dark-haired boy coming into the bright, yellow kitchen. His father at the table. His mother holding a teapot shaped like a teddy bear. And he heard it all again.

"Come on, Matthew. We're going to be late."

"I don't want to go."

"What? What are you talking about?"

"Matthew…?"

"I don't feel well. I don't want to go."

Now, on the coach, Matt put a hand over his eyes. He didn't want to remember any more. Remembering only hurt him … every time.

"What do you mean, you don't want to go?"

"Please, Dad. Please don't make me…"

48

They had argued, but not very much. His parents had only one child and they spoiled him. They had thought he would enjoy the wedding because they had been told there would be other children there and a special marquee with a magician and balloons. And now this! His father made a quick phone call. It wasn't really a big problem. Rosemary Green – their friendly, always helpful neighbour – agreed to take him for the rest of the day. His parents left without him.

And that was why he hadn't been in the car when they had their accident. That was why they had died and he had lived.

Matt lowered his hand and looked out again. The coach had slowed down. He wasn't feeling very well. He was hot and cold, and there was a dull pounding in his head.

"We're here," Mrs Deverill said.

They had arrived at another coach station, this one more modern and smaller than Victoria. The coach stopped and they jostled forward with the other passengers. It was colder out-side than it had been in London but at least it had stopped raining. Matt collected his case, then followed Mrs Deverill across the concourse.

A man was waiting for them, standing next to a beaten-up old Land Rover that only seemed to be held together by the mud that covered it. The man was short and very fat with yellow, greasy hair, watery eyes and a face that seemed to be slowly slipping off his head. He was wearing dirty jeans and a shirt that was too small for him. Matt could see the buttons straining. The man was about forty. He had flabby lips that parted in a wet, unpleasant smile.

"Good afternoon, Mrs Deverill," he said.

Mrs Deverill ignored him. She turned to Matt. "This is Noah."

Matt said nothing. Noah was examining him in a way that made him feel uneasy. "Welcome to Yorkshire," Noah said. "I'm very pleased to meet you." He held out a hand. The fingers were fat and stubby, the nails encrusted with mud. Matt didn't take it.

"Noah works for me on the farm," Mrs Deverill explained. "He has very little conversation, so I wouldn't bother talking to him."

The farmhand was still staring at him. His mouth was open and there was saliva on his chin. Matt turned away.

"Get in the car," Mrs Deverill said. "It's time you saw your new home."

They drove for an hour; first on a dual carriageway, then on a B-road, then on a twisting country lane. The further they went, the bleaker the landscape became. Lesser Malling seemed to be hidden somewhere on the edge of the Yorkshire moors, but Matt didn't see a single sign. He was feeling even sicker than before and he wondered if it was Noah's driving or some sort of virus that he had picked up.

They came to a crossroads – a meeting of five roads, all of them identical. There were trees on every side. Matt hadn't noticed them enter the wood but now it surrounded them, totally enclosed them. The wood had obviously been planted recently. All the trees were the same – some sort of pine. They were the same height, the same colour and they had been set in dead straight lines with an identical amount of space between them. No matter which direction Matt looked, the view was exactly the same. He remembered what his social worker in London had told him. The LEAF Project wanted to keep him out of urban areas, away from temptation. They certainly couldn't have chosen anywhere more remote than here.

A single signpost stood at the intersection but the top had been broken off. A splintered pole was all that remained.

"Lesser Malling is ten minutes up the road," Mrs Deverill said, gesturing to the left. "I'll show it to you when you've settled in a little more. But we live the other way."

Noah twisted the steering wheel and they turned left, following one of the other lanes for about fifty metres until they came to a gateway. Matt just had time to see a name, written in dull brown paint: Hive Hall. Then they were following a gravel drive between two barbed-wire fences that ran down to a courtyard and a complex of barns and buildings. The car stopped. They had arrived.

Matt got out.

It was a miserable place. The bad weather didn't help but even in the sunshine there would have been little to recommend Hive Hall. The main farmhouse was made out of great stone slabs, with a slate roof that was buckling under the weight of a single, large chimney. The barns had been built with wooden planks that were so old and sodden, they were rotting where they stood, with dark green moss spreading across them like a disease. The farmyard itself was an irregular square of land that was as much water as earth and gravel. Chickens limped to and fro; they had scarcely moved to avoid the wheels of the Land Rover. Six pigs stood in the mud, shivering.

"This is it," Mrs Deverill announced as she got out of the car and stretched her legs. "It may not look much but it's my home and it does well enough for me. Of course, there are no computer games here. There's no television. But once you start working, you'll find you're too tired for these things. We go to bed early in the country. You'll get used to our ways in time."

They went into the farmhouse. The front door opened into a long kitchen with a flagstone floor. There was an Aga stove at one end, with pots and pans hanging from the ceiling, and dozens of jars and bottles on wooden shelves. From here, Mrs Deverill led Matt into a living room with old and battered furniture, shelves full of books and, above a massive fireplace, what looked like a portrait of herself, though it must have been painted hundreds of years ago. It had the same cruel eyes, the same sunken cheeks. Only the hair was different, running loose as if caught in the wind.

"My ancestor," Mrs Deverill explained.

Matt looked past the figure in the canvas. She was standing in front of a village. He could see a few desolate buildings behind her. He looked back at the face. And shivered. Nothing had moved, but he could have sworn she had been looking towards the frame, over to the left. Now her eyes were fixed on him. He swallowed hard. His imagination was playing tricks on him. Turning round he saw that Mrs Deverill was staring at him too. He was trapped between the two of them.

Mrs Deverill smiled thinly. "She looks like me, doesn't she? She was also a Deverill. There have been Deverills in this part of Yorkshire for three hundred years. Her name was Jayne, like mine. She burned to death. They say that when the wind blows in the right direction, you can still hear the screams. Let me show you upstairs…"

Matt followed Mrs Deverill up a twisting staircase to the first floor and into a room at the end of the corridor. This was to be his bedroom … and it was the one room he most wanted to see. His headache had got worse. He wondered if he was going to be sick.

The room had a low ceiling, exposed beams and a bare, wooden floor with a small rug in the centre. It looked over the back of the farm, across a field to the wood. The windows were small, set in walls which were at least a metre thick. There was a sagging bed, made up not with a duvet but with blankets and sheets. Opposite the bed was a washbasin and a chest of drawers with a vase of dried flowers. The pictures on the walls showed views of Lesser Malling, painted in watercolours.

"They made me decorate for you," Mrs Deverill remarked

sourly. Of course the LEAF Project would have visited the farm. They would have insisted that the room was clean and comfortable. "I dried the flowers myself. Belladonna, oleander and mistletoe. Three of my favourites. All of them poisonous ... but such lovely colours."

Matt put his case on the bed. At the same time he noticed something sitting between the pillows.

"And this is Asmodeus," Mrs Deverill said. "My cat."

It was a huge black cat with yellow eyes. Its stomach was bulging, as if it had recently eaten, and Matt noticed a patch of grey, where some of the fur had worn away. It was purring lazily. Matt reached out his hand to stroke it. The cat purred more loudly. Slowly, it turned its head and looked Matt in the eyes. Then it sank its teeth into his flesh.

With a cry, Matt pulled his hand back. Bright red blood welled out of a jagged bite in his thumb. A drop fell on to the floor. Mrs Deverill took a step back. Matt saw that her eyes had widened and now, for the first time, she was smiling. All her attention was fixed on the blood on the floor.

It was too much for him.

The room turned. Matt swayed on his feet. He tried to say something but the words refused to come. The walls were spinning. He heard a door boom open. He looked through it and saw – or thought he saw – a circle of huge granite stones. Someone was holding a knife. He could see it hovering over his head, the pointed blade curving towards his eye. The floor seemed to shake and then, one after another, the wooden

54

planks cracked open, splinters exploding all around. Brilliant light streamed through and in the light he thought he saw something like a giant, inhuman hand.

A voice echoed in his ears.

"One of the Five!" it whispered.

The light engulfed him. He felt it sweeping through him, burning the inside of his head. He slammed the heels of his hands into his eyes, trying to block it out. Then he was falling backwards, but he was unconscious long before he hit the floor.

A WARNING

"What's wrong with him?"

"He has pneumonia."

"What?"

"He may die."

"He can't!"

"Cure him, Mrs Deverill. It's your responsibility. See that he lives!"

Matt heard the voices but he wasn't sure who they belonged to. He was lying in bed. He could feel a pillow against the back of his head. But as for the rest of it, he wasn't sure if he was asleep or awake. He propped himself up and half-opened his eyes. Sweat trickled down the side of his face. The single movement had taken all his strength.

The door had just closed. Someone – the last person who had spoken – had left. It was a man, but Matt had been unable to see his face. Mrs Deverill was in the room with Matt, standing next to another woman, also white-haired but with some sort of bright red mark on the side of her face. Noah was lingering in the background, rubbing his hands.

Then the room shimmered and suddenly the curtains were closed. There were flames leaping up, right next to the bed. Was the building on fire? No. They had set up some sort of metal tripod with a brazier filled with coals. The two women were speaking in a language that he didn't understand, whispering to each other as they fed the flames with black- and green-coloured crystals. Matt saw the crystals melt and bubble, and at once the room was filled with yellow smoke. The smell of sulphur crept into his nostrils. Matt choked and his eyes watered. He tried to lick his lips but his mouth was dry.

Noah came forward, holding a dish. The second woman – the one Matt didn't know – was holding a snake. Where had it come from? It was an ugly brown, half a metre long, writhing in front of her. A viper? She had produced a scalpel, the sort of thing a surgeon might use. Matt saw her hold the snake by the head and then slit it open. Dark red liquid oozed out, dripping down into a metal cup. The snake became rigid and still.

Mrs Deverill pulled back the bedcovers. Matt was only wearing underpants and he shrank back as she leant over him. She dipped a finger in the snake's blood, then drew a line down his chest and on to his stomach. The liquid was warm and sticky against his skin. He tried to move, but his body would no longer obey him. He could only watch as Mrs Deverill reached up and made some sort of mark on his forehead.

"Open your mouth," she commanded.

"No…" Matt whispered the single word. He tried to stop himself. But suddenly his mouth was open and Mrs Deverill was feeding him from the cup. He knew that he was drinking blood. It tasted bitter, more horrible than anything in the world. He was going to be sick. He wanted to get it out of his system but instead it slithered into his stomach like the ghost of the snake it had come from. And at the same time he was sucked backwards, into the mattress, into the floor, buried alive until…

He opened his eyes.

Mrs Deverill was in the room, reading a book. There was nobody with her. The window was open, allowing the breeze to come in. Matt swallowed. He was feeling light-headed but otherwise fine.

"So you've woken up at last," Mrs Deverill muttered, closing the book.

"What happened?" Matt asked.

"You've been ill. Nothing very serious. Pneumonia. A touch of pleurisy. But it's all behind you now."

"You gave me something to drink…" Matt tried to remember, even though he didn't want to. The very thought of what had happened repulsed him. "There was a snake," he said.

"A snake? What are you talking about? You've been having bad dreams, Matthew. I would imagine it comes from watching too much television."

"I'm hungry," Matt said.

"I expect you are. You haven't eaten for three days."

"Three days!"

"That's how long you were unconscious." She got up and shuffled over to the door. "I'll bring you up some tea," she said. "You can rest tomorrow but after that I want you up on your feet. The fresh air will do you good. And anyway, it's time you began work."

She took one last look at him, nodded to herself and closed the door.

Two days later Matt stood in the pigsty with stinking mud and filth reaching almost up to his knees. Mrs Deverill had spoken of fresh air but the stench here was so bad, he could barely breathe. Noah had provided him with boots and gloves but he had no other protective clothes. His jeans and shirt were soon dripping with black slime. The disinfectant he had been given burned his throat and made his eyes water.

He reached down with the spade and scooped up another bucketful of muck. It would be lunch soon and he was looking forward to it. Mrs Deverill was, despite everything, a good cook. When Matt had been living with Gwenda Davis, all his meals had come out of the deep freeze straight into the microwave. He preferred the food here: home-baked bread, rich stews and fruit pies with thick pastry crusts.

He had changed. He knew that something had happened to him during his illness, even if he had no idea what it was. It was as if a switch had been thrown inside him. He couldn't explain it but he felt stronger and more confident than ever before.

And that was good because he had already decided. He was going to run away. He still found it incredible that the LEAF Project could have sent him to this godforsaken place and made him the slave of a grim, unsmiling woman. Matt disliked Mrs Deverill, but it was Noah, the farmhand, who really made his skin crawl. Noah was usually out in the fields, bouncing along in an ancient tractor that belched black smoke. But when he was close, he couldn't keep his eyes off Matt. He was always leering at him, as if he knew something that Matt didn't. Matt wondered if he was brain-damaged. He didn't seem to be quite human.

Matt didn't care what happened to him but he knew he couldn't stay at Hive Hall. Not for a year. Not even for another week. He had no money but he was sure he would be able to find some if he looked hard enough. Then he would either hitch-hike or take a train to London. He would lose himself in the capital, and although he'd heard plenty of horror stories, he was sure that somehow he would be able to survive. In just two years he would be sixteen and independent. Never again would any adult tell him what he had to do.

Mrs Deverill appeared at the door of the farmhouse and called out to him. Matt wasn't wearing his watch but guessed it must be one o'clock. She was always punctual. He threw down the spade and climbed out of the sty. In the distance, Noah appeared, carrying two buckets of animal feed. He never ate in

60

the farmhouse. He had a room on the upper floor of the barn and that was where he cooked, slept and presumably washed – although not often, as he smelled worse than the pigs.

Matt took off his boots outside the front door, then went into the kitchen and washed his hands in the sink. Mrs Deverill was already serving vegetable soup. There was bread, butter and cheese on the table. Asmodeus was sitting on the sideboard and Matt shivered. He disliked the cat even more than he disliked Noah – and it wasn't just because of the jagged scar on his hand. Like Noah, the cat was always watching him. It had a way of appearing out of nowhere. Matt would turn his head and there it would be … in the branch of a tree, on a windowsill or a chair, always with its ugly, yellow eyes fixed on him. Normally he would ignore it, but if he came close, the cat would arch its back and hiss.

"Out of the kitchen, please, Asmodeus," Mrs Deverill said. The cat understood her perfectly. It leapt out of a window and was gone.

Matt sat down and began to eat.

"There's something I want you to do for me this afternoon, Matthew," Mrs Deverill said.

"I'm cleaning the pigs."

"I know what you're doing. One day you'll learn that being rude to people who are older and wiser than you won't do you any good. In fact, I have a task for you which you might enjoy. I'd like you to collect something for me from the chemist in Lesser Malling."

"What do you want me to pick up?"

"It's a package, addressed to me. You can go there after lunch." She held a spoonful of soup to her lips. Steam rose up in front of her unsmiling face. "There's an old bicycle in the barn you can use. It belonged to my husband."

"You were married?" That was news to Matt. He couldn't imagine anyone sharing their life with this woman.

"For a short time."

"What happened to your husband?"

"Young people shouldn't ask questions. It's not good for them. However…" She sighed and lowered the spoon. "Henry disappeared. That was his name. Henry Lutterworth. We'd only been married a few months when he went for a walk in the wood and never came back. It's possible that he simply got lost and starved to death. Let that be a lesson to you, Matthew. The woods are very thick around here, and you can easily get swallowed up. It's quite likely that he stumbled into a bog. That's my guess. It would have been a very unpleasant way to die. He'd have tried to swim, but of course the more he struggled, the faster he'd have gone down, and the water and the mud would have risen up over his nostrils, and that would have been the end of him."

Matt wondered if she was telling him the truth. Or was she just trying to frighten him?

"If his name was Lutterworth, how come you call yourself Deverill?" he asked.

"I prefer my own name. The name of my ancestors. There

have always been Deverills in Lesser Malling. Married or un-married, we keep our own name." She sniffed. "Henry left me Hive Hall in his will," she explained. "We used to have bees but they all went away. They often do that, when their owner dies. I inherited all his money. But the point of all this is, my dear, that if I were you, I'd steer well clear of the wood."

"I'll do that," Matt said.

"Remember now. The chemist. Just tell them it's for me."

After lunch, Matt crossed the farmyard and went into the barn. He found the bicycle parked behind an old plough. It obviously hadn't been used for years. But he pulled it out, oiled the chain, pumped up the tyres, and a few minutes later he was able to pedal out of the farm. It felt good, passing through the rusting gates. He was still doing chores for Mrs Deverill. But anything was better than the pigs.

As he went, a car came the other way and for a moment it seemed they were going to collide. The car was a black Jaguar with tinted windows. Everything happened so quickly that Matt didn't even see who was driving. He jerked the handle-bars and the bike veered up a bank of nettles before curving back on to the lane. He came to a halt and twisted round. The Jaguar had driven into the farm. He saw the red glow of its brake lights but then it disappeared behind the farmhouse. He was tempted to go back. It was the only modern car he had seen since he had come to Hive Hall and he wondered if it had come on account of him. Could it be someone from London, from the social services? He hesitated, then continued on his way. This was the first time he had left the farm – his first taste of freedom. He wasn't going back yet.

It was a mile to the village. Matt quickly arrived at the broken sign where the five roads met. The wood was all around him and he was glad that Mrs Deverill had shown him which road to take, as they all looked the same. No cars passed. Nothing moved. Matt had never felt more alone as he pedalled on. The last part of the road was uphill and he had to work to get the bike to the top. Despite the oil, he could hear it groaning beneath him. But ahead of him he could see the outer buildings of Lesser Malling and before long he pulled into the village square.

Mrs Deverill had already warned him that there wasn't much to Lesser Malling and she was certainly right. The village was small and self-contained with a dull, half-dilapidated church, a pub called The Goat and two rows of shops and houses facing each other across an empty, cobbled area. A war memorial stood in the middle, a slab of grey stone engraved with twenty or thirty names. All of the shops looked fifty years out of date. One sold sweets, the next general groceries, another antiques. At the end of the row was a butcher's. Matt could see chickens hanging by their feet, their necks broken. Slabs of meat, grey and sweating, lay spread out on the counter. A large man with a beard and a blood-splattered apron chopped down with an axe. Matt heard the metal as it sliced through bone.

There were quite a few people around and as he rested the bicycle against the war memorial, more of them appeared, coming from all sides of the square. Matt sensed that they had been drawn here because of him. Their faces were more curious than welcoming. He saw them stop, some distance away, and whisper among themselves. It was unnerving, being the centre of attention in this forgotten community. He had no doubt that they all knew exactly who he was and why he was here.

A woman walked towards him and she seemed familiar. She had long white hair, a tiny head and black eyes that could have belonged to a doll. As she came nearer, he saw that she had been disfigured by a birthmark. An ugly mauve blotch covered one side of her face. He thought back to when he was ill. Had this woman been in his room at Hive Hall?

She walked right up to him. "How nice to see you back on your feet, Matthew," she said. She had a squeaky, rasping voice and seemed to strangle the words at the back of her throat. "My name is Claire Deverill. You're staying with my sister."

So he was right. He had seen her before.

"I am the head teacher at the primary school here in Lesser Malling," she went on. "You may be joining us soon."

"I'm too old for primary school," Matt said.

"But too stupid, I'm afraid, for secondary school. I've seen your reports. You've done no work. You know very little. Not a good example for the other children."

Another woman – tall and thin – had appeared, pushing an antique pram. The wheels squeaked as they turned. "Is this the boy?" she demanded.

"It is indeed, Miss Creevy." Claire Deverill smiled.

Matt glanced down at the pram. There was no baby. Miss Creevy was nursing a large china doll. It looked up at Matt with a frozen smile and wide, empty eyes.

"I'm looking for the chemist," Matt said. Suddenly he wanted to be out of here. He was beginning to wish he'd never come.

"It's over there." Claire Deverill pointed. "Next to the sweet shop."

Two more women had appeared on the far side of the village, in front of the church. They looked like ragged scarecrows, their black coats flapping in the breeze. They were identical twins. At the same time, a short, fat man with blue and green tattoos on his arms, face and head stepped out of the pub. He was smoking a clay pipe. He saw Matt and began to laugh. Matt walked away before he could get too close.

It was no surprise really that everyone in Lesser Malling seemed to be a little mad. You'd have to be to live in a place as forlorn as this, Matt thought. There was a pond near the church and he noticed a group of children feeding the ducks. He went over to them but as soon as ie was close he saw that he was going to find no friends here. There was a ten-year-old boy with strange, greenish hair and fat legs bulging out of short trousers. A couple of girls – sisters – stood together in identical, old-fashioned dresses and pigtails. The last boy was about seven and crippled, one of his legs enclosed in a metal calliper. Matt would have felt sorry for him but as he approached, the boy pulled out a BB gun and, smiling, took aim at the ducks. Quickly Matt kicked out, sending loose gravel into the water. The ducks flew away. The boy fired at them and missed.

"What did you do that for?" one of the girls demanded sulkily.

"What are you doing?" Matt asked.

"We feed the ducks and then Freddy kills them," the other girl explained. "It's a game!"

"A game?"

"Sitting ducks!" both girls chorused.

Freddy reloaded the gun. Matt shook his head in disgust. He left the children and walked back to the chemist.

The shop was like nothing he had ever seen before: a dark, evil-smelling place with rows of wooden shelves. There were some boxes of headache pills and a few packets of soap, but mostly the shelves were stacked with old bottles. Some of these were filled with powders, some with dried herbs. Others contained strange, lumpy objects, floating in murky water. Matt read some of the handwritten labels: *Nux Vomica*. Aconite. Wormwood. They meant nothing to him. He found a flask filled with yellow liquid and turned it round, then almost cried out as a severed eye floated to the surface, kissing the edge of the glass. The eye had been taken from a sheep or a cow. It was trailing tissue behind it. Matt felt sick.

"Can I help you?"

It was the chemist; a short, ginger-haired man in a shabby white coat. The hair continued down his neck and there was more of it on the backs of his hands. He was wearing heavy black spectacles, which had sunk into his nose in such a way that Matt wondered if he ever took them off.

"What is this?" Matt demanded.

"An eye."

"Why is it here?"

The chemist turned the jar round and examined the specimen, his own eyes magnified by the lenses. "The vet requested it," he said. He sounded irritated. "He was doing tests."

"I've come to collect something for Mrs Deverill."

"Oh yes. You must be Matthew then. We've all been looking forward to meeting you. We've all been looking forward to it very much."

The chemist produced a small package, wrapped in brown paper and tied with string. "My name is Barker. I hope I'll be seeing more of you. In a village like this, it's always nice to have new blood." He handed the packet over. "Do drop in again any time."

Matt came out of the shop, noticing that more of the villagers had arrived in the square. There were at least a dozen of them, talking among themselves. He hurried over to the bike. There was a bag behind the saddle and he thrust the package in. He just wanted to get back on the road, away from the village. But it wasn't to be. As he wheeled the bicycle round, a hand suddenly appeared, grabbing hold of the handle-bars. Matt followed the arm it belonged to and found himself looking up at a man in his thirties with straw-coloured hair and a round, ruddy face. He was dressed in a baggy jersey and jeans. He was strong. Matt could tell that from the ease with which he held the bike.

"Let me go!"

Matt tried to pull the bike away but the man held on to it. "That's not very friendly," he said. "What's your name?"

"Why do you want to know?"

"You're Matthew Freeman, aren't you?"

Matt said nothing. They were both still holding the bike. It had become a barrier between them.

"They sent you here on this project?"

"That's right. Yes. You all know that – so why ask?"

"Listen to me, Matthew Freeman," he said suddenly. "You don't want to be hanging around this village. You don't want to be anywhere near here. Do you understand me? I shouldn't be talking to you like this. But if you know what's good for you, you'll get away. You'll go as far away as you can and you won't come back. Do you hear me? You need to—"

He broke off. The chemist had come out of his shop and was standing there in the doorway watching the two of them. The man let go of Matt's bike and hurried away. He didn't look back.

Matt got on to the bicycle and pedalled out of the village. Ahead of him, the pine trees waited, black and ominous. Already it was growing dark.

WHISPERS

Matt was standing on a tower of glistening stone. It was the dead of night but somehow he could still see. Far beneath him the waves rolled forward as if in slow motion, thick and oily. There were rocks slanting outwards, each one razor-sharp. The waves hovered, then threw themselves forward, tearing themselves apart. The wind howled. There was a storm raging. Jagged spears of lightning crashed down – but the lightning was black not white – and now he realized that the entire world had been turned inside out, like the negative of a photograph.

In the distance, he could see four people, standing on a grey, deserted beach. Three boys and a girl, all of them about his own age. They were too far away for him to be able to see their faces, but somehow he recognized them and knew they were waiting for him. He had to reach them, but there was no way. He was trapped on his tower of rock. The storm was growing and now there was something dark and terrible stretching out across the sea. A giant wing that was folding around him. The girl was calling to him.

"Matthew! Matthew!"

The wind caught the two words and tossed them aside. The girl pleaded with him but time was running out for her too. The beach cracked and began to break up. Dark crevices appeared, the sand spilling into them. The waves were rushing in. The four of them were trapped, unable to move.

"I'm coming!" Matt called.

He took a step towards them and stumbled, then twisted forward and fell. He cried out. But there was nothing to stop him. Everything spun as he plummeted through the night sky, down towards the sea.

Matt woke up with a start.

He was lying in bed at Hive Hall. He could make out the wooden beams on the ceiling, the dried flowers in their vase on the chest of drawers. There was a full moon, the pale light washing through the room. For a moment he lay still, thinking about his dream. He had dreamt it many times, not just at Hive Hall but before. It was always the same, apart from two things. Each time, the presence he had felt forming itself – the folding wing or whatever it was – had come a little closer to taking shape. And each time, he woke up a few seconds later, a few centimetres nearer the end of his fall. He wondered what would happen if he didn't wake up in time.

He looked at his watch, turning it to the window to check. It was almost midnight. It had been ten o'clock when he went to bed. What had woken him up? He had been exhausted by the day's work and should have slept through.

And then he heard it.

It was faint and far away, and yet still quite clear, carried on the stillness of the night. It came from the wood, sliding over the silver tips of the trees under the moonlight.

Whispering.

At first Matt thought it was nothing more than the wind rustling through the branches, but there was no wind. And as he threw back the cover and sat up in bed, he heard another sound. It was underneath the whispers, constant and un-changing. A soft, electronic hum. The whispers stopped, then started again. The hum went on.

Despite himself, Matt felt the hairs on the back of his neck begin to prickle. The sounds were far away but the horrible thing was that they could have been coming from somewhere inside the building. They were all around him. He got out of bed and went over to the window.

The moon slid behind a cloud and for a moment every-thing was dark. Yet there was a light. In the surrounding darkness, somewhere not far from the edge of the wood, he could see a faint glow. The light was being swallowed up by the trees, hemmed in on all sides. However, some of it had escaped through gaps in the branches and had spread out, the cold white shafts evaporating in the air. It was electric, not the light of a fire. And it seemed to be coming from the same source as the sound.

Who was there? What could be happening in the middle

of a Yorkshire wood – and could it have something to do with the warning he had been given only that afternoon?

"You don't want to be anywhere near here. Do you understand me?"

Suddenly Matt wanted to know – and almost before he had worked out what he was doing he had put on his clothes, opened the door and slipped out. He paused for a moment, listening for any sound within the farmhouse. Mrs Deverill's room was at the end of the corridor. The door was closed and Matt had never seen inside her room. He guessed she would be sound asleep. She always went to bed at exactly half past nine. The last thing he wanted to do was wake her up. Moving more carefully now, he tiptoed down the stairs and into the living room. Again, the portrait of Mrs Deverill's ancestor watched him as he made for the front door. Its eyes almost seemed to follow him. The face was dark and secretive.

It was cold in the yard. Nothing stirred. Matt could hear the whispers more clearly now. They seemed not only louder but closer. He could even make out some of the words – not that they made any sense.

"NODEB ... TEMOCMOD ... EMANY ... NEVAEH ... NITRA."

The strange sounds danced around him as he stood there, alone in the night. They were human whispers. Human and yet at the same time unworldly. He wondered what to do. Part of him wanted to get out the bicycle and try to get nearer.

74

Part of him wanted to go back to bed and forget the whole thing. And then he noticed something that he should have seen straight away.

Mrs Deverill's car wasn't there.

The Land Rover was always parked in the same place, next to the barn, and it had been there at dinner time. Could she have left Hive Hall? Was she somewhere in the wood, part of whatever it was that was going on? Was Matt alone at the farm?

He went back into the living room. The portrait was the first thing he noticed and this time he knew it wasn't his imagination: it had definitely changed a second time. The figure had raised a hand and a skeletal finger was now pointing upwards, as if ordering him to bed. Matt was certain it hadn't been painted that way.

Matt did go upstairs, but not to his own room. He had to know if he was right, even though he dreaded what he must do. He crept to the end of the corridor and knocked gently on Mrs Deverill's door. There was no reply. He knocked a second time, louder. Then he opened the door.

He found himself looking into a cold, empty room with bare floorboards and an iron bed. There was a wardrobe and a chest of drawers but little else. The bed was empty. He was right. Mrs Deverill wasn't here. At last he'd been given the opportunity he needed.

Matt had already decided he was going back to London. Now he knew it was going to happen tonight. By daybreak he would have reached the motorway and he would hitch-hike south. He had no doubt that Mrs Deverill would call the police, but the further away he managed to get, the harder it would be for them to find him. Once he reached London, he would be safe. But he needed cash. Money was the difference between survival and constant danger. He would have to buy food. He'd need to find a room. There must be money in the house. He would find it and steal it now.

He began in the kitchen. No longer caring how much noise he made, he rifled through the drawers and cupboards, opened jars and boxes, trying to work out where Mrs Deverill kept her housekeeping funds. He could still hear the whispering, although it was more intermittent now. Was it coming to an end? He glanced at his watch. A quarter past one. He moved more quickly, afraid that the woman could return at any time. There was no money in the room. He looked for her handbag. A handbag would mean cash and possibly credit cards. But she must have taken it with her.

He tried the living room. Now the portrait seemed to watch angrily as he searched, looking behind the books and under the chairs in the hope that Mrs Deverill might have tucked her purse away. Matt hadn't turned on the lights – Noah might still be in the barn and he was afraid of giving himself away. He was crossing over to look around the fireplace when something screamed at him, sending him back, his heart pounding. It was Asmodeus, Mrs Deverill's cat. It had been asleep on one of the chairs but now it was standing up, as if electrocuted, its fur bristling, its eyes ablaze. It opened its mouth and hissed, revealing a set of white fangs. Matt stood still. The cat was going to attack him. He was sure of it. It was already bracing itself, the claws of its two front paws ripping at the material, practising what it was going to do to his face.

Matt looked around. There was a poker next to the fire; a heavy antique thing. He thought of snatching it up but wasn't sure he could bring himself to use it. The cat's tail whipped briefly. Its eyes had never left him. He had dared to abuse Mrs Deverill's hospitality and now he was going to pay. The cat hissed a second time and leapt.

Matt was ready for it. There was a large basket beside the poker. Normally it would contain logs but for once it was empty. Matt grabbed it and threw it down over the cat even as it left the chair. He heard a terrible screaming and yowling, felt the claws battering desperately at the straw cage. Matt slammed the basket down on to the chair, imprisoning the cat inside. Holding the basket with one hand, he reached out with the other. Mrs Deverill had an old-fashioned sewing machine which was on the floor beside the chair. Using all his strength, Matt picked it up and dropped it on top of the basket. The straw creaked. The cat hurled itself against the side. But the basket held. Asmodeus wasn't going anywhere.

Matt straightened up. He was trembling from the shock of what had just happened. And he was suddenly aware of something else. There was no sound coming from the wood. The whispering had stopped. So far he had found nothing and he was running out of time.

There was just one room left.

He went back upstairs and into Mrs Deverill's bedroom. Surely he would find money here. He opened the wardrobe. Mrs Deverill's clothes hovered in the darkness, suspended from wire hangers with her shoes underneath. Matt was about to close the door when he noticed a cardboard box in the back corner. He leant down and opened it. There was something inside. Not money. Photographs.

He took one of them out and found himself looking at a cemetery. The photograph was black and white, taken with a telephoto lens. There was a crowd of people, dressed in the usual sombre clothes, and in the middle of them, a boy who was eight years old. Matt recognized him instantly and felt a surge of horror and sickness. He was looking at a picture of himself.

This was his parents' funeral.

Six years ago.

But it was impossible. Nobody had taken any photographs. And even if they had, even if a journalist or someone had been there, what was this picture doing here? How had Mrs Deverill got hold of it?

There were two sheets of paper attached to the photograph by a clip. Matt slipped them loose, then turned them round so he could read them. An official police report. Each page was marked CONFIDENTIAL in red letters. In the half-light Matt tried to concentrate on the words:

AND THE WITNESS STATEMENT OF MRS
ROSEMARY GREEN IN RELATION TO
THIS CASE IS NOT TO BE RELEASED
AND WE RECOMMEND A COMPLETE MEDIA
BLACKOUT. THE CHILD, MATTHEW
FREEMAN, IS ONLY EIGHT YEARS OLD
AND HAS DEMONSTRATED PRECOGNITIVE
ABILITIES WHICH WOULD SEEM TO BE
BEYOND...

Precognitive abilities. Matt didn't want to put the words into simple English. Nor did he want to read any more of the report. In that second, he made his decision. He thrust the box back into the corner, closed the wardrobe doors and left. In the living room, the portrait watched silently. Asmodeus slammed itself again and again against the sides of the basket, trying to escape. Matt didn't notice either of them. He threw open the door and ran across the yard.

He hadn't found any money but he would just have to do without it.

It was definitely time to leave.

It took Matt just a few minutes to cycle up to the crossroads. The night had grown colder and his breath frosted as he paused by the broken sign, taking his bearings. He had a choice of five country lanes, each one cutting through the wood in a different direction. He had just taken one from the farm, and he knew that one of them led to Lesser Malling. That left only three. He chose the middle path and set off, grateful for the moon showing him the way. There was no sound coming from the wood. The electric lights had been turned off. His greatest fear was that he could run into Mrs Deverill, returning from wherever she had been. He listened out for the sound of her Land Rover but there was nothing. He was utterly alone.

Matt tried to concentrate on what he was doing. He didn't want to look at the woodland but he couldn't help being aware of it as it pressed in on him on all sides. The trunks of the trees, in their long lines, were silhouetted against the moon. They were like the solid bars of a huge open-air jail. The branches, swaying slightly, cast a thousand shadows over the ground. The pine needles rustled together and almost seemed to be whispering to themselves as he pedalled past.

Matt kept his eyes fixed on the road in front of him. He intended to cycle all night. The discovery of the photograph had made him determined. He was just going to have to chance it in London. Without money. Without anywhere to live. The police would probably find him in the end, but that didn't matter. They could put him in a secure training centre for as long as they liked… Anything, so long as it didn't involve Mrs Deverill or Lesser Malling.

Why did she have a photograph of him in her wardrobe? How had she got her hands on a secret police report? And

80

what did the death of his parents mean to her? It was a horrible thought but he wondered if Mrs Deverill had known about him before he had been introduced to her by the LEAF Project. In which case, could she have in some way chosen him? But that would suggest that she had been planning whatever was going on in Lesser Malling for years and years, and that he had always somehow been part of it.

Well, to hell with the whole lot of them, Matt thought. His aunt, his social worker, Mallory, Mrs Deverill... He had been pushed around for too long. It was time to start looking after himself. He might be able to get a job in a kitchen or a bed and breakfast. He looked old for his age. Grimly, he pushed down on the pedals, urging the old bike forward. He checked his watch again. Two o'clock in the morning! He was surprised so much time had passed since he left the farm.

There was a crossroads coming up ahead of him. Matt slowed down, free-wheeling the last few metres. He looked around him. There was a choice of five directions and a broken signpost without any names. It took him half a minute to work out where he was. Somehow, the lane he had chosen had brought him round in a big circle. He was back exactly where he had begun.

Matt was annoyed with himself. He had wasted time and precious energy. Mrs Deverill might have got back to Hive Hall. She would have found the cat under the basket and checked Matt's room. Perhaps she had already called the police.

Gritting his teeth, Matt chose one of the other lanes and

pedalled forward again. He was beginning to wish he had waited until the morning. No. He would have been set to work on the farm and, between them, Noah and Mrs Deverill always had him in their sight. He concentrated on his rhythm, left foot then right foot, listening to the bicycle chain as it groaned and creaked underneath him. The trees rolled by endlessly. About another twenty minutes passed. Matt was strong and he was fit again after his illness. There was a dull ache in his legs but otherwise he was fine. The road turned a corner.

He stopped.

He was back at the crossroads. It was impossible. The lane he had been following had run straight and he must have covered at least two miles. He gazed at the broken signpost with disbelief. It was the same signpost. There could be no doubt of it.

Now he was angry. For this to happen once was unfortunate. But twice! It was stupid. He jerked the bike round and set off down the fifth lane, the one furthest away. He cycled more quickly this time, using his anger to lend himself strength. The night breeze rushed over his shoulders, cooling the sweat on the side of his head. A cloud covered the moon and suddenly everything was very dark. But Matt didn't slow down. The cloud separated and he lurched to a halt, unable to believe what was happening.

The fifth lane had somehow become the first lane. They had looped him back to the start. The broken signpost stood there, mocking him.

Very well. He set off back the way he had come, passing Hive Hall. This lane had to go somewhere different. He cycled past the gate as quickly as he could. There were no lights visible at the end of the drive, so maybe Mrs Deverill wasn't back yet after all. The lane climbed steeply uphill – but that was good. A hill was something different. None of the other lanes had gone up or down. Matt no longer really cared where he was going, he just wanted to find a main road. He was fed up with the wood, fed up with country lanes.

He reached the top of the hill and stopped. For the first time he was really afraid. He had been cycling for the best part of an hour yet he still hadn't found a way out.

He was back at the crossroads where he had begun.

Matt was breathing heavily. His hands were clutching the handlebars so hard that the blood couldn't reach his fingers. He stopped there for a moment, considering his options. He didn't really have any. Either the night was playing tricks on him or something was happening that he didn't understand. But now he knew that he wouldn't get anywhere, even if he cycled all night.

He would just have to take his chances with Mrs Deverill. He turned the bike round and pedalled slowly back to the farm.

OMEGA ONE

"He was in my room last night," Mrs Deverill said. She was talking on the telephone. The receiver was old-fashioned and heavy, made of black Bakelite. A thick wire coiled out of her hand. "I think he found the photographs."

"It was a mistake keeping them there."

"Perhaps. But there's something else I'm worried about. Matthew is stronger than he was when he first came here. I think he may be starting to work things out. I don't like having him here. If you ask me, we've got a tiger by the tail. We should deal with him before it's too late."

It was a man's voice at the other end of the phone. He spoke in a way that was very cold and deliberate. He had an educated voice. Perhaps he was a headmaster in an expensive private school. "What do you mean?" he demanded.

"Lock him up. There's a crypt in the church. We could put him in there, underground, somewhere nobody would find him. It's only for a few more weeks. And then we'll be done with him."

"No." The single word was final. "Right now the boy

thinks he's ordinary. He has no idea of who or what he is. Bury him alive and you could actually help him discover himself. And what happens if the police or his social worker come calling? How will you explain where he is?"

"Suppose he escapes…"

"You know he can't escape. We have him contained. There's nothing he can do. And very soon we'll be ready for him. All you have to do is watch him. Where is he now?"

"I don't know. Somewhere in the yard."

"Watch him, Mrs Deverill. Don't let him out of your sight."

There was a click and the line went dead. Mrs Deverill weighed the phone in one hand, then lowered it. "Asmodeus!" she called.

The cat, sitting on the arm of a chair on the other side of the room, opened one eye and looked at her.

"You heard what he said," she snapped. "The boy…"

The cat leapt off the chair. With no effort, it sprang up on to a windowsill and then out of the window. Outside, Noah walked past, pushing a wheelbarrow piled high with manure. The cat ran past him and continued up the lane. A moment later it had disappeared from sight.

Matt stood at the edge of the wood, looking down a tunnel of trees. The bicycle lay on its side on a grassy verge beside the road. Five minutes had passed since he had slipped past Noah and made his way out of Hive Hall. But he still couldn't make up his mind.

Once again he was tempted to find his way to London. He must have been confused the night before. He had been unable to see where he was going and had somehow missed his way. But an inner voice warned not to try navigating the lanes again. He didn't want to waste any more time going round in circles, and anyway, there was another way out of this. The LEAF Project was supposed to be voluntary. A single phone call to Detective Superintendent Mallory was all it would take to get him out of this nightmare.

But before he did that, he wanted to know more. What were the sounds he had heard the night before? What was going on in the wood? There was only one way to find out.

Matt had pinpointed the spot from which he thought he saw the light coming. It had to be somewhere in front of him now. And yet he was unwilling to step off the road. It wasn't because of the story Mrs Deverill had told him – he doubted there was any chance of his wandering into a bog. It was the wood itself that scared him: its unnaturalness, the uncompromising lines. Nature wasn't meant to grow like this. How could he possibly find his way when every pine tree looked the same, when there were no hillocks, plants or streams to act as landmarks? And there was something else. The corridors between the trees seemed to go on for ever, stretching into a shadowy universe of their own. The darkness was waiting for him. He was like a fly on the edge of a huge web.

He made up his mind, stepped off the road and took twenty paces forward, following a single path. The pine needles crunched underneath his feet. Provided he didn't turn left or right, he would be fine. He would let the trees guide him. And if he thought he was getting lost, he would simply follow the same path back to the road.

And yet... He stopped to catch his breath. It really was extraordinary. He felt as if he had stepped through a mirror between two dimensions. On the road it had been a cool, bright spring morning. The atmosphere in the wood was strangely warm and sluggish. Shafts of sunlight, a deep, intense green, slanted in different directions. On the road, he had heard the twitter of birds and the lowing of a cow. In the wood, everything was silent ... as if sound were forbidden to enter.

Already he saw that he should have brought a compass with him. At the very least he could have brought something: a knife or a tin of paint to help him find his way back. He remembered a story he'd been told at school. Some Greek guy – Theseus or someone – had gone into a maze to fight a creature that was half-man and half-bull. The Minotaur. He'd been given a ball of wool, which he'd unravelled, and that was how he'd found his way out. Matt should have done the same.

He turned round and, counting out loud, retraced the twenty paces he had taken.

The road wasn't there.

It was impossible. He looked back at the wood. The trees stretched on endlessly. He checked left and right. The same.

He took another five steps. More trees, all of them identical, running as far as the eye could see ... and further. The road had disappeared as if it had never been there. Either that, or somehow the trees had grown. That was what it felt like. The artificial wood encircled him. It had captured him and would never let him go.

Matt took a deep breath, counted twenty paces forward, then turned left and walked another ten. Still no road. No matter where he looked, he saw the same thing: tall, narrow trunks and a million needles. Gloomy corridors between them. A hundred different directions but no real choice. Matt stood still, hoping that he would hear a car on its way to Lesser Malling. That would help him find the road. But no car passed. A single crow cawed, somewhere high above. Otherwise, the silence was as thick as fog.

"Great!"

He shouted out the single word because he wanted to hear the sound of his own voice. But it didn't even sound like him: it was small and weak, muffled by the unmoving trees.

He walked on. What else could he do? His footfall was soft on the bed of needles, measuring out his progress into nowhere. Looking up, he could barely see the sky through the dark green canopy. He was getting sick and tired of all this. The roads had played exactly the same trick on him the night before. But at least they were roads. This was much, much worse.

A glimmer of silver caught his eye, quite unexpected in

the middle of so much green. The sun was reflecting off something behind a wall of trees a short distance away. With a surge of relief Matt turned towards it, leaving one path and following another. But if he thought he had discovered the way out, he was mistaken. There was no way forward. He found himself up against a tall fence, rusting in places but still intact. The silver he had seen was the wire. The fence was at least six metres high and the top was barbed with steel spikes. It ran to the left and to the right, curving in what must be a huge circle.

Behind the fence was a clearing, in the centre of which stood a large building that was at once out of date and yet futuristic. It was divided into two parts. The main part was a rectangular, grey brick structure, two storeys high, with windows – half of them broken – running the full length. Some of the brickwork was cracked, with weeds and ivy eating their way in. It had obviously been there for a long time. Matt reckoned it must be thirty or forty metres long. It would have fitted neatly on to a football pitch.

But it was the second part of the building that drew his attention. Painted white and reaching at least thirty metres high, it looked just like a giant golf ball, sitting on the ground as if it had rolled there. Was it an observatory? No. There was no slit in the dome for a telescope. In fact it didn't have any windows at all. The ball had also been stained by time and the weather. The white paint was discoloured, and in places it looked as if it had caught some sort of disease. But it was still impressive. It was the last thing Matt would have expected to find in the middle of a wood.

A brick passageway with a central door but no windows connected the two parts. Could this be the main entrance? Matt wondered if he could get closer. He had no idea what he was looking at. It would be good to find out.

He turned right and followed the fence for about fifty metres. After a while the wood fell back and he came to a pair of gates, firmly locked together with a heavy padlock on a thick, discoloured chain. On one of the gates was a sign, the words painted in faded red paint on a peeling wooden board:

OMEGA ONE
PROPERTY OF HM GOVERNMENT
TRESPASSERS WILL BE PROSECUTED

Omega One. Now Matt wondered if the building might have some military use. The sign said that it was government property. The Ministry of Defence? Briefly he examined the gates. They were old but the padlock was new, meaning someone had been here recently. There was no way he was going to get it open. He looked up and saw razor wire twisted round the top. So much for that.

With growing curiosity Matt continued round, following the fence, hoping to find a tree he could use to climb over. Instead he found something better. There was a hole in the wire, where several strands had rusted loose, and it was just about big enough to allow him to squeeze through. He glanced at his watch. The morning was wearing on but he still had plenty of time.

He was about to squeeze through when someone grabbed hold of him and spun him round.

"What are you doing?" a voice demanded.

Matt's heart lurched. After his time alone in the wood he hadn't dreamt for a minute that there would be anyone else here. His fist was already curled in self-defence, but then he recognized the fair hair and red face of the man who had approached him in Lesser Malling – the one who had warned him to leave.

"I got lost," Matt said, relaxing slightly. "What is this place?" He gestured at the building on the other side of the fence.

"It's a power station."

Matt studied the man more closely, noticing that he was carrying a shotgun, the two barrels broken over his arm.

"You shouldn't be here," the man said.

"I told you. I got lost. I was looking for…"

"What were you looking for?"

"I saw lights in the forest. Last night. I wondered what they were."

"Lights?"

"And I heard something. Strange noises – a sort of humming. Why don't you tell me what's going on around here? You warned me to go away."

"Why didn't you?"

"I tried." Matt left it at that. He was in no mood to explain what had happened to him on the moonlit roads. "What were you warning me about?" he demanded. "Why is everyone in Lesser Malling so weird? Who are you?"

The man seemed to relax a little – but his eyes remained watchful. He rested a hand on the barrel of his gun. "My name is Burgess," he said. "Tom Burgess. I'm a farmer. I own Glendale Farm, down the Greater Malling road."

"And what are you doing here? Are you guarding this place?"

"No. I'm hunting. These woods are full of foxes. They come for my chickens in the night. I'm out to get a few of them." He patted the gun.

"I didn't hear any shots."

"I didn't see any foxes."

Matt looked back at the building. "You said this place was a power station," he began. Suddenly the shape seemed more familiar. He had seen pictures at school. "Is it a nuclear power station?"

Burgess nodded.

"What the hell is it doing here?"

"It's nothing." The farmer shrugged. "It was experimental. The government put it here a long time ago. It was before they started building the real things. They were looking into alternative sources of energy so they built Omega One, and when they'd finished all their experiments they shut it down again. It's empty now. There's nothing there. Nobody's been anywhere near it for years."

"They were here last night," Matt said. "I heard them. And I saw lights."

"Maybe you were imagining things."

"I don't have that much imagination." Matt was angry. "Why won't you tell me the truth?" he went on. "You warned me I was in some sort of danger. You told me to run away. But I can't run away unless I know what it is I'm running from. Why don't you tell me what you know? We're safe here. Nobody can overhear us."

The farmer was clearly struggling with himself. On the one hand, Matt could see that he wanted to talk. But strong though he was, and armed as well, he was still afraid. "How could you begin to understand?" he said at last. "How old are you?"

"Fourteen."

"You shouldn't be here. Listen to me. I only came to this place a year ago. I was left money. I always wanted to have my own place. If I'd known... If I'd even had the faintest idea..."

"If you'd only known what?"

"Mrs Deverill and the rest of them..."

"What about them? What are they doing?"

There was a rustle in the undergrowth, followed by an angry snarl. Matt turned and saw an animal appear, stepping out of a patch of fern a couple of metres away. It was a cat, its eyes ablaze, its mouth wide open to reveal its fangs. But it wasn't just any cat. He recognized the yellow eyes, the mangy fur...

He relaxed. "It's all right," he said. "It's only the cat. It must have followed me here."

But the farmer's face had turned white. All at once he had snapped the barrel of his gun shut and raised the whole thing to his shoulder. Before Matt could stop him, he pulled the trigger. There was an explosion. The cat had no chance. Tom Burgess had emptied both barrels, and lead pellets tore into its fur, spinning it in a horrible somersault over the grass, a ball of black that spat red.

"What did you do that for?" Matt exclaimed. "It wasn't a fox. It was just a farm cat."

"Just a cat?" The farmer shook his head. "It was Asmodeus, Mrs Deverill's cat."

"But—"

"We can't talk. Not here. Not now."

"Why not?"

"There are things happening ... things you wouldn't believe." The colour hadn't returned to the farmer's face. His hands were trembling. "Listen!" he whispered. "Come to my farm. Tomorrow morning – at ten o'clock. Glendale Farm. It's on the Greater Malling road. Turn left when you come out of Hive Hall. Will you be able to find it?"

"Yes." Then Matt remembered. "No. I've tried finding my way round these lanes but they don't seem to lead anywhere. I just end up where I began."

"That's right. You can only go where they want you to go."

"What do you mean?"

"It's too difficult to explain." Burgess thought for a moment. Then he grabbed hold of a leather cord around his neck. Matt watched as he drew it over his head and held it out. He saw there was a small, round stone – a talisman – dangling from it, and on the stone was a symbol engraved in gold. The outline of a key.

"Wear this," Burgess said. "Don't ask me to explain it, but you won't get lost if you're wearing it. Come to my house tomorrow. I'll tell you everything you want to know."

"Why not now?" Matt demanded.

"Because it's not safe – not for either of us. I have a car. You come to my house and we'll leave together."

Tom Burgess strode away, heading for the line of trees.

"Wait a minute!" Matt called after him. "I don't know how to get out of the wood!"

Burgess stopped, turned round and pointed. "Look under your feet," he shouted. "You're standing on the road." Then he was gone.

Matt examined the ground around him. There was a line of black tarmac, barely visible beneath the weeds and the pine needles. He would have to follow it carefully, but at least it would lead him out. The stone talisman was still in his hand. He ran a finger along the key, wondering if it was real gold. Then he slipped it around his neck, making sure it was hidden under his shirt.

A few minutes later, Matt found himself back on the main road. He examined the entrance to Omega One carefully. It was nothing more than a gap between two trees in a line of several hundred. He had pedalled past without even knowing it was there and it would be almost impossible to find again. He took off his jacket, tore a strip of material from his T-shirt, and tied it in a knot around a branch. Then he stepped back and examined his handiwork. The tiny, pale blue flag he had created would show him the way back if he ever needed it. Satisfied, he put his jacket back on and set off to retrieve his bike.

About forty minutes later Matt arrived back at Hive Hall. It was almost midday. Noah was working on the side of the barn, painting it with creosote. Matt could smell the chemical in the air. Mrs Deverill would be in the farmhouse, making lunch.

Brushing a few needles off his jacket, Matt walked up to the front door. He was just reaching for the handle when he stopped and stepped back with a shiver of disbelief.

Asmodeus was there, sitting on the windowsill, licking one of its paws. The cat wasn't dead. It wasn't even hurt. Seeing Matt, it purred menacingly then suddenly leapt away, disappearing into the house.

WET PAINT

Matt didn't sleep well that night. He had too many unanswered questions in his head, and the fact that Tom Burgess had promised to answer them made him tense and restless. He couldn't wait to find out the truth. But that was exactly what he had to do, tossing around in his narrow bed as the sky became grey, then silver, then finally blue. Mornings on the farm normally began with breakfast at seven o'clock. Mrs Deverill was already in the kitchen when he came down.

"So what happened to you yesterday morning?" she demanded. She was wearing a dull yellow cardigan, a shapeless grey dress and wellington boots. All the clothes she wore at Hive Hall looked as if they had come out of a charity shop.

"I went for a walk."

"A walk? Where?"

"Just around."

Mrs Deverill took a pan off the Aga and spooned thick porridge into two bowls. "I don't remember you asking permission," she said.

"I don't remember you telling me I had to," Matt replied.

Mrs Deverill's eyes narrowed. "I can't say I'm used to being spoken to in that way," she muttered. Then she shrugged as if it didn't matter anyway. "I was only thinking of you, Matthew," she went on. "If you look at the booklets provided by the LEAF Project, you'll see quite clearly that I'm supposed to know where you are at all times. I'd hate to have to report that you've broken the rules."

"You can report what you like."

She placed the two bowls on the table and sat down opposite him. "There's a lot of work to be done today. The tractor needs hosing down. And we could do with some firewood being chopped."

"Whatever you say, Mrs Deverill."

"Exactly." The pale lips pressed together in something like a smile. "Whatever I say."

It was nine o'clock, one hour before Matt had arranged to meet Tom Burgess. Matt was working on the tractor, washing it down. For the fiftieth time he looked around him, and realized he was finally alone. Noah was on the other side of the barn, mending some pipes. Mrs Deverill was feeding the pigs. Neither of them was watching him, nor was there any sign of Asmodeus. Matt dropped the hose, then turned off the tap and waited until the last jet of water had splashed on to the ground. Still nobody came. He had left the old bicycle in the yard, close at hand. He stole over to it and pushed it out of the farm. Pedalling would have made too much noise.

A minute later he was through the gate and on the lane. He looked back with a sense of relief. It had all been much easier than he had thought.

Too easy? Matt remembered the way Mrs Deverill had smiled at him in the kitchen. He had wondered then if she knew more than she was letting on. All the time he had the feeling she was playing with him, and the photograph and police report hidden in her bedroom cupboard had only confirmed it. She knew who he was. He was more sure of it than ever. He had been chosen on purpose.

Matt got on the bike and began to pedal, turning left as Tom Burgess had told him. The last time he had attempted this journey, the lane had simply looped him back to where he had started. But this time was different. He was wearing the talisman that the farmer had given him. He reached up and felt it against his chest. Why a stone with a picture of a key should make any difference was beyond him. It was just one of the many questions he intended to ask.

The lane led uphill but there was no crossroads at the top. Instead the road continued past a series of fields. A low, stone wall rose and dipped ahead. He came to a signpost and this one wasn't broken. It read: GREATER MALLING 4 MILES. Matt stared at it. It was the first reminder he'd had that there was an actual world outside Hive Hall and he had no idea how he'd managed to miss it when he made the journey two nights before.

He found Glendale Farm easily enough. There was a

turning about a quarter of a mile further along, with the name printed in bright blue letters on a white gate. Even as Matt cycled down the flower-bordered drive that led from the main road, he thought how much more welcoming it was than Hive Hall. The barn and stables were clean and ordered, standing next to a pretty pond. A swan glided on the water, its reflection shimmering in the morning sunlight, while a family of ducks waddled across the lawn. In a nearby paddock a cow chewed grass, mooing contentedly.

The farmhouse itself was red brick, with neat white shutters and a grey slate roof. Part of the roof was covered in plastic sheeting, where the farmer had been working on repairs. An old weathervane stood at one corner, a wrought-iron cock looking out over the four points of the compass. Today it was facing south.

Matt got off the bike, crossed the farmyard to the front door and pulled a metal chain to ring a bell in the porch. He was early – it was only half past nine. He waited, then rang again. No answer. Perhaps Tom Burgess was working in the barn. Matt walked over and looked inside. There was a tractor and an assortment of tools, a pile of sacks and a few bales of hay ... yet no sign of the farmer.

"Mr Burgess?" he called.

Silence. Nothing moved.

But the farmer *had* to be there. His car, a Peugeot, was parked in the drive. Matt went back to the house and tried the front door. It opened.

"Mr Burgess?" he called again.

There was no answer. Matt went inside.

The front door led straight into the main room, which had a large fireplace with a gleaming pair of bronze tongs and a small shovel leaning against the grate. The fire had evidently burned during the night, as the ashes were still strewn over the hearth. The place was a mess. Tables had been overturned and books and papers scattered on the floor. All the inside shutters were hanging off, some of them broken in half. Matt's foot caught a stray pot of paint. He picked it up and put it to one side.

The kitchen was in a worse state. The drawers were open and their contents had been thrown everywhere. There were broken plates and glasses and, in the middle of the kitchen table, a half-empty bottle of whisky lying on its side. Matt glanced up. A huge carving knife had been thrust into a kitchen cupboard, its blade penetrating the wood. The handle slanted towards him. It looked odd and menacing.

Every fibre of his being was telling him to get out of here, but Matt couldn't leave now. He found himself drawn to the stairs. Narrow and twisting, they led up from the kitchen and before he knew what he was doing, Matt was on his way up, dreading what he would find at the top but still unable to stop himself. He wasn't expected for another half an hour. Maybe Tom Burgess was still asleep. That was what he told himself. But somehow he didn't believe it.

The stairs led to a landing with three doors. Gently, he

101

opened the one nearest to him.

It led into a bedroom, and this was worse than anything Matt had seen downstairs. The room looked as though a whirlwind had hit it. The bedclothes were crumpled and torn, spread out over the carpet. The curtains had been ripped down and one of the window panes was smashed. A bedside table lay on its side, with a lamp, an alarm clock and a pile of paperbacks thrown on to the floor. The wardrobe doors were open and all the clothes were in a heap in one corner. A tin of green paint had toppled over, spilling its contents into the middle of the mess.

Then Matt saw Tom Burgess.

The farmer was lying on the floor on the other side of the bed, partly covered by a sheet. He was obviously dead. Something – some sort of animal – had torn into his face and neck. There were hideous red gashes in his skin and his fair hair was matted with blood. His eyes were bulging, staring vacantly, and his mouth was forced open in a last attempt at a scream. His hands were stiff and twisted in a frantic effort to ward something off. One of them was smeared with green paint, which had glued his fingers together. His legs were bent underneath him in such a way that Matt knew the bones must be broken.

Matt backed away, gasping. He thought he was going to be sick. Somehow he forced his eyes away and then he saw it, painted on the wall behind the door. In the last moments of his life, the farmer had managed to scrawl two words, using his own hand smeared with paint:

RAVEN'S GATE

Matt read it as he backed out of the room. He shut the door behind him and reeled down the stairs. He remembered seeing a phone in the kitchen. He snatched up the receiver and dialled 999 with a finger that wouldn't stop shaking. But there was no dialling tone. The phone had been disconnected.

He threw down the receiver and staggered out of the house. The moment he reached the yard, he threw up. He had never seen a dead body before, let alone one as twisted and tortured as that of Tom Burgess... He hoped he would never see one again. He found that he was shivering. As soon as he felt strong enough, he began to run. He had forgotten the bicycle. He just wanted to get out of there.

Matt ran back up the drive and on to the main road, heading in the direction of Greater Malling. He must have run for at least half a mile before he collapsed on to a bed of grass and lay there, the breath rasping in his throat. He didn't have the strength to go on. And what was the point? He had no parents and no friends. He was going to die in Lesser Malling and nobody would care.

He didn't know how long he'd been lying there, but at last the sound of an approaching car reached his ears and he sat up and looked down the road. The car was white, a four-wheel drive with a sign attached to the roof. Matt breathed a sigh of relief. It was a police car. For the first time in his life, it was something he actually wanted to see.

He pulled himself to his feet and walked into the centre of the road with his arms raised. The police car slowed down and stopped. Two officers got out and walked over to him.

"You all right?" the first one asked. He was middle-aged and plump, with a high forehead and thinning black hair.

"Shouldn't you be at school?" the other asked. He was the younger of the two, thin and boyish with cropped brown hair.

"There's been a murder," Matt said.

"What? What are you talking about?"

"A man called Tom Burgess. He's a farmer. He lives at Glendale Farm. I've just come from there." The sentences came out short and staccato. Matt was finding it hard to stitch the words together.

The two policemen looked doubtful.

"You saw him?" the senior man asked.

Matt nodded. "He was in the bedroom."

"What were you doing there?"

"I was meant to meet him."

"What's your name?"

Matt felt the impatience rising inside him. What was wrong with these men? He had just found a dead body. What did it matter what his name was? He forced himself to calm down. "I'm Matt," he said. "I'm staying with Jayne Deverill at Hive Hall. I met Tom Burgess. He asked me to visit him. I was there just now. And he's dead."

The older policeman looked more suspicious than ever, but his partner shrugged. "We just passed Glendale Farm," he said. "Maybe we should take a look."

The other man thought for a moment, then nodded. "All right." He turned to Matt. "You'd better come with us."

"I don't want to go back there!" Matt exclaimed.

"You can wait in the car. You'll be all right."

Reluctantly Matt climbed into the back seat and allowed the two officers to take him back the way he had come. He gritted his teeth as they turned into the driveway. The car slowed down, the wheels biting into the gravel.

"It seems quiet enough," the older policeman said. He turned round to face Matt. "Where did you say you saw him?"

"Upstairs. In the bedroom."

"There's someone here," the younger one said.

Matt looked out of the window. The policeman was right. A woman had appeared to one side of the house. She was tall and thin with limp grey hair hanging to her shoulders, and he recognized her. She was one of the women he had met in Lesser Malling. She had been pushing a pram. What was her name? Creasey. Or Creevy. Now she was in Tom Burgess's garden, hanging out a basket of washing. Matt couldn't understand what was happening. She had been inside the house, so surely she had seen the state of the rooms. Hadn't she been upstairs?

The policemen got out of the car. Feeling increasingly

uneasy, Matt followed them. The woman saw them coming and stopped what she was doing.

"Good morning," she said. "How can I help you?"

"My name is Sergeant Rivers," replied the older man. "This is Police Constable Reed. Who are you?"

"I'm Joanna Creevy. I help Tom Burgess with his housework. What's wrong?" She seemed to notice Matt for the first time. "Matthew? What are you doing here?" She scowled. "You haven't got yourself into trouble, have you?"

Matt ignored her.

"This is a little difficult," the sergeant began. "The fact is that we just met this young lad on the road."

"You left your bicycle here, Matthew," the woman said. "I thought you must have been visiting."

"Matthew claims that Mr Burgess might have been involved in some sort of accident," the sergeant went on.

"It wasn't an accident," Matt interrupted. "He's been killed. Cut to pieces. I saw him…"

The woman stared at Matt, then broke into laughter. "That's impossible," she said. "I saw Tom ten minutes ago. You just missed him. He's gone to see to the sheep in the far paddock."

The policemen turned to Matt.

"She's lying," Matt said. "He didn't go anywhere ten minutes ago. I was here just now and he was dead."

"That's a terrible thing to say," Miss Creevy muttered. "Tom is fine. And here I am, hanging out his socks!"

106

"Go and look in the bedroom," Matt said.

"Yes. You do that." The woman nodded – and that was when Matt began to worry. She seemed confident – one step ahead of him.

Sergeant Rivers nodded slowly. "We'd better sort this out," he said.

They went into the house and Matt saw at once. Although it was still untidy, Miss Creevy – or someone – had cleared away most of the evidence. The books and papers had been straightened. The shutters were folded back. And the knife had been taken out of the kitchen cupboard ... but the gash it had left was still there. They continued upstairs.

"You'll have to forgive the mess," Miss Creevy said. "Tom has been redecorating and I haven't had a chance to start work yet."

They reached the landing. The door of the bedroom was closed, just as Matt had left it. He didn't want to go in. He didn't think he could bear to look at the body a second time. But he couldn't back out now.

Sergeant Rivers opened the door.

There was a man working in the room, wearing a pair of white overalls that were flecked with green paint. Everything was different. The sheets and blankets had been removed from the floor and the bed was propped up on its side against the wall. The curtains had been hung up and although one of the windows was still broken, there was no sign of any broken glass. The scattered clothes had disappeared. So had the body of Tom Burgess. The man saw the two policemen and stopped work.

"Good morning," he said.

"Good morning, sir." The sergeant took a quick look around. "May I ask who you are?"

"Ken," the man replied. "Ken Rampton." He was in his twenties, scrawny with a sly, crumpled face and curly fair hair. He smiled and Matt saw that one of his front teeth had been chipped diagonally in half. "Can I help you?"

"How long have you been here?"

"All morning. I got here about half eight."

"Do you work for Tom Burgess too?"

"I'm helping him out with the decorating."

"Have you seen him today?"

"I saw him about a quarter of an hour ago. He looked in to see how I was getting on, then he left… Something to do with his sheep."

"That's what I just told you," Miss Creevy said.

Matt felt the blood rush to his cheeks. "He's lying," he insisted. "They both are. I know what I saw." Suddenly he remembered. "Tom Burgess left a message," he said.

He swung round and pushed the door shut to reveal the wall behind it. But the wall, which had been off-white before, was now green. And the words that the farmer had painted had gone.

"Be careful," Ken Rampton warned. "Wet paint…"

Sergeant Rivers came to a decision. "We won't waste

108

any more of your time, sir," he said. He grabbed hold of Matt, his hand tightening on his shoulder. "As for you, I think we should have a word outside."

Miss Creevy followed them back downstairs and out into the yard. Matt wondered if the policemen were going to arrest him. In fact, he suddenly realized, that was exactly what he hoped would happen. If they arrested him, maybe he would be taken back to London. Maybe this sort of behaviour would mean that he could kiss the LEAF Project goodbye. But before anyone could say anything, Miss Creevy stepped forward. "I wonder if I could have a private word with you, officer?"

They spoke for about two minutes. The sergeant glanced his way a couple of times and nodded, while Miss Creevy shrugged and spread her hands. Finally he walked back over to them.

"You ought to know that wasting police time is a very serious business," he said.

"I'm telling the truth."

"Let's not have any more of that, thank you."

The policeman had made up his mind. Matt could see that. He bit his tongue.

"I understand you've been in trouble a few times before," Sergeant Rivers continued. "You're with the LEAF Project, is that right? You ought to count yourself lucky. Personally I don't believe in all this do-good stuff, to tell you the truth. You're a thief, and the best thing for you would be to be birched and locked up where you can't do any more harm. But

[]109

that's not my decision. The courts have sent you here and if you had any sense, you'd be grateful and stop trying to draw attention to yourself. Now, we'll say no more about this nonsense. But I don't want to see or hear from you again."

Matt watched as the two policemen drove away. Then he turned round. Miss Creevy was smiling at him, her long grey hair flapping in the breeze. There was a movement at the door and Ken Rampton appeared with the paintbrush still clutched in his hand. He said nothing. But he too was smiling.

"Go back to Hive Hall," Miss Creevy said. "Mrs Deverill is waiting for you."

"To hell with her!" Matt shouted.

"You can't escape from us, Matthew. There's nowhere you can go. Surely you can see that by now."

Matt ignored her and grabbed the bike.

"There's nowhere you can go." The woman echoed the words in a high-pitched voice.

Ken Rampton began to laugh.

Matt pedalled away as fast as he could.

LOCAL AFFAIRS

Greater Malling had once been a small, attractive village but it had grown into a large, unattractive town. There were still a few reminders of what it had once been: a pond, a row of almshouses and a lopsided sixteenth-century pub. But the roads had come, cutting in from every side and joining together at noisy intersections. New houses had elbowed out the old. Offices and car parks had sprung up, joined by cinemas, supermarkets and a clattering bus station. Now it was very ordinary. Somewhere to pass through on the way to somewhere else.

It had taken Matt an hour to cycle here from Glendale Farm. He had been afraid that the road would play another trick on him and deposit him somewhere he didn't want to be. But he was still wearing the stone talisman that Tom Burgess had given him. Somehow the little golden key had unlocked the maze of country lanes and allowed him to find his way.

Matt parked the bike outside a launderette. It occurred to him that someone might steal it but he didn't care. He wouldn't be needing it again.

He was looking for a railway station and a train to London. That was the decision he had made: to get as far away as possible from Yorkshire and never come back. Unfortunately, there was no station. The line to Greater Malling had been closed down years ago, and if he wanted a train he would have to go all the way to York. He found a traffic warden and asked about buses. There were two a day. The next one wouldn't be leaving until three o'clock. That left three hours to kill.

Matt walked aimlessly down the high street and found himself facing a library – a modern building that already looked down-at-heel, with shabby, pebbledash walls and rusting window frames. He thought for a moment, then went in through a revolving door and up a staircase that was signposted REFERENCE. He found himself in a wide, brightly lit room with about a dozen bookcases arranged along the walls, a bank of computers and an enquiry desk, where a young man sat reading a paperback.

Something nasty, something very dangerous, was going on in the village of Lesser Malling. Somehow it involved many of the villagers, Mrs Deverill, an abandoned nuclear power station and something called Raven's Gate. It also involved Matt. That was what unnerved him most of all. He had been chosen. He was sure of it. And before he left Yorkshire, he was determined to find out why.

Raven's Gate. It was the only clue he had, so that was where he decided to begin.

He started with the books in the local history section. The library had about a dozen books on Yorkshire and half of them made brief references to Greater and Lesser Malling. But not one of them mentioned anything by the name of Raven's Gate. There was one book that seemed more promising and Matt carried it over to a table. It was called *Rambles Around Greater Malling* and had been written – some time ago to judge from the old-fashioned cover and yellowing pages – by a woman named Elizabeth Ashwood. He opened the book and ran his eye down the contents page. He had found it. Chapter Six was entitled *Raven's Gate*.

Matt turned the pages and found Chapter Seven. He went back and found Chapter Five. But Chapter Six wasn't there. A jagged edge and a gap in the binding told their own story. Someone had torn out the whole chapter. Was it just a random act of vandalism or had it been done deliberately? Matt thought he knew.

But the library offered more than books.

Matt went over to the man at the enquiry desk. "I need to use the Internet," he said.

"What for?" the librarian asked.

"It's a school project. We've been told to find out something about Raven's Gate."

"I've never heard of it."

"Nor have I. That's why I want to go on the Internet."

The man pointed and Matt went over to the nearest computer. There was a girl clicking away with the mouse at the next desk but she ignored him. He called up a search engine, then typed in:

RAVEN'S GATE

He remembered the words scrawled on the farmer's wall in green paint. Once again he saw the dead man, his body torn apart, his eyes wide and empty.

He pressed ENTER.

There was a brief pause and then the screen came up with a list of results. Matt saw that his search had listed over twelve thousand possible sites relating to ravens and to gates, but none of them were even slightly relevant. There was an American football team, the Baltimore Ravens, whose players had walked out of the gate. There was a Golden Gate park, also in America, where birdwatchers had spotted a variety of ravens. Apparently ravens were also nesting in the Kaleyard Gate in Chester. But there was no Raven's Gate... Not on the first page, not on the second, not even on the third. Matt realized he would have to scroll through all twelve thousand entries. It would take him hours. There had to be another way.

He was about to give up when a pop-up window suddenly appeared on the computer screen. Matt looked at the three words, floating in the white square:

>Who are you?

There was no way of knowing who they had come from.

He didn't quite know how to answer, so he typed back:

114

>Who r u?

There was a pause. Then:

>Sanjay Dravid

Matt waited a moment to see what would happen next.

>You have made an enquiry about Raven's Gate. What is your field of research?

Field of research? Matt didn't know how to reply. He leant forward and typed again:

>I want to know what it is.
>Who are you?
>My name is Matt.
>Matt who?
>Can you help me?

There was a long pause and Matt began to think that the person at the other end – Sanjay Dravid – had gone away. He was also puzzled. How had Dravid known that he was making the search to begin with? Had his enquiry triggered some sort of alarm on the Net?

Then the window flickered again:

>Goodbye

So that was it. Nothing more happened inside the pop-up window and after a while Matt gave up. He went back to the enquiry desk.

"Yes?" The librarian looked up from his paperback.

"Is there a newspaper office in Greater Malling?"

"A newspaper...?" He considered. "There's the *Gazette*. I'd hardly call it a newspaper. They never print any news. Otherwise there's the *Yorkshire Post*."

"Where's the *Yorkshire Post*?"

"It's in York. If you want a local newspaper office, you'll have to try the *Gazette*. They're in Farrow Street. But I doubt they'll be able to help you with any school project."

It took Matt a moment to work out what the man was talking about. Then he remembered the lie he had told to get on to the computers. "I can try," he said.

Farrow Street was a leftover from medieval times. It was very narrow and quiet, crammed with dustbins full of bottles and cans. As he turned off from the main road Matt thought that the librarian had made a mistake. It seemed the last sort of place you'd want a newspaper office, cut off from the rest of the town in this dirty and forgotten corner. But about halfway down he came to a row of shops. First there was an undertaker. Then a travel agency. And finally a crumbling red-brick building on three floors that advertised itself with a plastic sign next to the door: GREATER MALLING GAZETTE.

Matt entered an open-plan area with a young, frizzy haired girl sitting behind a desk, eating a sandwich, typing on a computer and talking into a headset that was plugged into her phone. She seemed to be both the receptionist and the

116

secretary for the three journalists who were sitting at desks behind her. There were two women and a man, and Matt was struck by how bored they all looked. One of the women was yawning continuously, scratching her head and staring into space. The other woman was half-asleep. The man was fiddling with a pencil and gazing at his computer screen, as if he hoped that whatever story he was working on would write itself.

"Can I help you?" It was the receptionist who had spoken. Matt thought she was talking into the mouthpiece but then he saw that she was looking at him.

"Yeah. I want to talk to someone who knows about local affairs."

"Do you live around here?"

"I'm staying in Lesser Malling."

The girl leant back. "Richard!" she called. She had a nasal, rather whiny voice. "There's someone here for you."

The man who had been playing with the pencil looked up. "What?"

"This kid here – he wants to see you."

"Yeah. All right."

The man stood up and sauntered over to Matt. He was in his twenties, dressed in a striped shirt and loose, faded jeans. He had a serious, intelligent face … the sort of face Sherlock Holmes might have had when he was young. His hair was short, blond and scruffy. He hadn't shaved for the last couple of days. Nor, from the look of it, had he changed his shirt.

Everything about him was crumpled: his hair, his clothes, even the way he stood.

"What do you want?" he asked.

"I need help," Matt replied.

"What sort of help?"

"I'm trying to find out about something."

"Why?"

"It's for a school project."

"What school do you go to?"

That took Matt by surprise. "I go to school in Lesser Malling," he lied. He didn't even know the school's name.

"And you're doing a school project?"

"Yes."

"Try the library."

"I have. They sent me here."

"Sorry, I can't help you." The journalist shrugged. "I'm busy."

"You don't look busy," Matt said.

"Well, I was busy until you arrived."

"Busy doing what?"

"Busy being busy. All right?"

Matt forced himself to keep his temper. "OK, maybe I can help you," he said. "You're a journalist. Maybe I've got a story."

"A story?"

"I might have."

"All right. Come upstairs."

The journalist led Matt up to the first floor and into a conference room that looked out on to Farrow Street. It wasn't much of a room, but it was already obvious to Matt that this wasn't much of a paper either. There were eight seats arranged around a wooden table, a presentation board and a water cooler.

"Thirsty?" the journalist asked.

Matt nodded.

He took out a plastic cup and filled it. Matt saw a single bubble of air rise up inside the water. He took the cup. The water was lukewarm.

"My name is Richard Cole," the journalist said, sitting down at the table. He produced a notepad and opened it at a blank page.

"I'm Matt."

"Just Matt?"

"That's right."

"You said you were staying at Lesser Malling."

"Yes. Do you know it?"

Richard smiled humourlessly. "I've been through. I'm meant to cover it. Me, Kate and Julia – they're the girls you saw downstairs – we all have our own territories. I got Lesser Malling. Lucky me!"

"Why lucky you?"

"Because nothing ever happens. I'm twenty-five years old. I've been working in this dump for eighteen months. And do you know the biggest news event I've had to cover so far?

119

BAD EYESIGHT KILLS OLD LADY."

"How can bad eyesight kill you?"

"She fell in the river. We had a dog show in Greater Malling last week. The fleas were more interesting than the dogs. I got a parking ticket once. I almost put that on the front page." He threw down the notepad and yawned. "You see, Matt, this is one of the most boring places in England ... possibly in the whole world. It's just a poxy little market town that doesn't even have a market. Nothing ever happens."

"So why are you here?"

"That's a good question." Richard sighed. "Three years at York University. All I ever wanted to be was a journalist. I did a course in London. I thought I'd get on to the *Mail* or the *Express* or else I'd just freelance. But there are no jobs around. I couldn't afford to live in London so I thought I'd come back north again. Maybe get a job on the *Yorkshire Post*. I live in York. I like York. But the *Yorkshire Post* wouldn't have me. I think I made a bad impression at my interview."

"What happened?"

"I ran over the editor. It wasn't my fault. I was late. I was reversing and I heard this thump. I didn't realize it was him until I met him ten minutes later." Richard shrugged. "Then I heard there was a place going here and, although Greater Malling was obviously a dump, I thought I'd take it. I mean, it was a job. But nobody reads the *Gazette*. That's because – apart from adverts – there's sod all in it. LOCAL VICAR OPENS FETE. That's one week. Then, a week later ... LOCAL

120

SURGEON OPENS VICAR. It's pathetic. And I'm stuck here until something else comes along, but nothing else has come along so I'm ... stuck!" Richard pulled himself together. "You said you had a story." He reached for his notepad and opened it. "That's the one thing that'll get me out of here. An old-fashioned scoop. Give me something I can put on the front page and I'll give you any help you need. Right, so you're staying in Lesser Malling?"

"I told you..."

"Where exactly?"

"A farm. A place called Hive Hall."

Richard scribbled down the name. "So what's the story?"

"I'm not sure you'll believe me."

"Try me." Richard had perked up. He was looking more interested and alert.

"All right." Matt wasn't sure about this. He had only come to the *Gazette* to ask about Raven's Gate. But there was something about the journalist that seemed trustworthy. He decided to go ahead.

And so he told Richard everything that had happened since his arrival in Lesser Malling. He described his first visit to the village and the chemist shop, his meeting with Tom Burgess, the lights and whispering in the wood, his time with Mrs Deverill, his second meeting with the farmer and his discovery of the dead body in the bedroom.

"...and that's why," he concluded, "I'm trying to find out who or what this Raven's Gate is. It's obviously something

121

important. Tom Burgess died trying to warn me."

"He died – but his body disappeared."

"Yes."

There was a brief silence and in that moment Matt knew it had been a waste of his time. The journalist had been making notes when he started talking but after a while he had stopped. He glanced at the notepad, at the half-empty page with a doodle of a dog and a flea at the bottom. It was obvious that Richard hadn't believed a word he'd said.

"How old are you?" Richard asked.

"Fourteen."

"Do you watch a lot of TV?"

"There is no TV at Hive Hall."

Richard thought for a moment. "You never told me how you got there," he said. "You just said that this woman – Jayne Deverill – is looking after you."

That was the one part of the story that Matt had left out: the wounding of the security guard and his involvement with the LEAF Project. He knew that if he told the journalist who he was, he would end up on the front page of the *Gazette* … but for all the wrong reasons. It was the last thing he wanted.

"Where are your parents?" Richard asked.

"I don't have any," Matt said. "They died six years ago."

"I'm sorry."

Matt shrugged. "I've got used to it," he said, although he never had.

"Well, look…" Richard was less certain now. Either he

122

felt sorry for Matt and didn't want to say what he was about to say. Or he was simply trying to find a nicer way to say it. "I'm sorry, Matt. But everything you've told me is complete…"

"What?"

"Crap. Lanes that loop round in circles. Strange looks from the villagers! Farmers that are dead one minute and disappear the next! I mean, what do you expect me to say? I know I said I wanted a story. But I didn't mean a fairy story!"

"What about the lights in the power station?"

"OK. Yes. I've heard about Omega One. It was built about fifty years ago as a sort of prototype … before they built nuclear power stations in other parts of the country. But they shut it down before I was born. There's nothing there now. It's just an empty shell."

"An empty shell that Tom Burgess was guarding."

"That's what you say. But you don't know for sure."

"He knew something. And he was killed."

There was a long silence.

Richard threw down his pen. It rolled around the table and came to rest next to the notepad. "You seem like a nice kid, Matt," he said. "But the police came and there was nothing there and maybe, just maybe, you sort of imagined the whole thing."

"I imagined a dead body? I imagined the words written on the wall?"

"Raven's Gate? I've never heard of Raven's Gate."

"Well, if you haven't heard of it, it obviously can't exist!" Matt snapped sarcastically. Once again he was angry. "All right, Mr Cole. I can see I wasted my time coming here. It's like you say. Nothing ever happens in Lesser Malling. But I get the feeling that if it did happen, you wouldn't notice. I don't know what I've got myself involved in, but everything I've told you is true and, to be honest, I'm getting scared. So maybe one day, when I turn up floating face down in a local river, you might decide it's worth investigating. And I'm telling you now, I won't have died of bad eyesight."

Matt got up and stalked out of the conference room, slamming the door behind him. The frizzy-haired girl was climbing the stairs and she looked at him, surprised. He ignored her. Coming to the newspaper had been completely pointless. He still had two hours until the bus left for York. It was time to work out how to get enough money to pay for the fare.

He burst out on to Farrow Street and stopped.

There was a car parked in front of him, blocking the entrance. A Land Rover. He recognized it even before he saw Noah sitting in the front seat, his hands resting on the wheel. The back door opened and Mrs Deverill got out. She looked angry. Her eyes were ablaze and her skin seemed to have tightened. Although she was only two or three inches taller than Matt, she loomed over him as she stepped forward.

"What are you doing, Matthew?" she demanded.

"How did you know I was here?" he asked.

"I think you'd better come back with us, my dear. You've already caused quite enough trouble for one day."

"I don't want to come with you."

"I don't think you have any choice."

Matt thought of refusing. She couldn't force him into the car, not right in front of a newspaper office in a busy market town. But suddenly he felt exhausted. Mrs Deverill was right. He didn't even have enough money for a bus. He had nowhere to go. What else could he do?

He got into the car.

Mrs Deverill climbed in after him, closing the door.

Noah rammed the car into gear and the three of them set off.

THE NEXUS

The sun had just dipped below the horizon and night was closing in once again. Mrs Deverill had lit a fire. She was sitting in front of the burning logs with a knitted shawl on her shoulders and Asmodeus curled up on her lap. To look at, she could have been anybody's grandmother. Even the portrait of her ancestor seemed more friendly than usual. The hair was neater. The eyes were perhaps a little less cruel. Matt was standing in the doorway.

"I think you and I need to have a talk, Matthew," she said. "Why don't you sit down?"

She gestured at the armchair opposite her. Matt hesitated, then sat down. Six hours had passed since she had found him in Greater Malling. There had been no work that afternoon. The two of them had eaten dinner together in silence. And now this.

"You and I don't seem to quite understand each other," Mrs Deverill began. Her voice was soft and reasonable. "I get the feeling that you're against me. I don't know why. I haven't hurt you. You're living in my house. You're eating my food.

126

What exactly is wrong?"

"I don't like it here," Matt replied simply.

"You're not meant to like it. You were sent here as a punishment, not because you deserved a holiday. Or maybe you've forgotten that."

"I want to go back to London."

"Is that what you told the people in Greater Malling? The people at the newspaper? Just what *did* you tell them?"

"The truth."

A log collapsed in the hearth and a flurry of sparks leapt up. Asmodeus purred and Mrs Deverill reached down, running a single finger down the animal's back.

"You shouldn't have gone there. I don't like journalists and I don't like newspapers. Busying themselves in other people's affairs. What were you thinking of, Matthew! Telling stories about me, about the village... It won't do you any good. Did they believe you?" Matt didn't answer. Mrs Deverill drew a breath and tried to smile, but the hardness never left her eyes. "Did you tell them about Tom Burgess?" she asked.

"Yes." There was no point denying it.

"Well, that's precisely the point I'm trying to make. First you get the police involved. Yes ... I heard what happened from Miss Creevy. And when that doesn't work, you go running to the press. And all the time you're completely mistaken. You actually have no idea what's going on."

"I know what I saw!"

"I don't think you do," Mrs Deverill replied. "In a way, it's

127

my own fault. I got you to clean out the pigs and I didn't realize... Some of the chemicals we use are very strong. They have
a way of getting up your nose and into your brain. An adult
like Noah can cope with it. Of course, he didn't have much
brain to begin with. But a young boy like yourself..."

"What are you saying?" Matt demanded. "Are you saying
I imagined what I saw?"

"That's exactly what I'm saying. I think you've probably
been imagining all sorts of things since you arrived here. But
don't worry. You're never going to have to clean out the pigs
again. At least, not with disinfectant. From now on, you're
going to use only soap and water."

"You're lying!"

"I won't have that sort of language in my house, if you
don't mind, young man. It may have been allowed with your
aunt in Ipswich, but it won't do with me!"

"I know what I saw! He was dead in his room and the
whole place had been torn apart. I didn't imagine it. I was
there!"

"What would it take to persuade you otherwise? What
would it take to make you believe me?"

The telephone rang.

"Exactly on time," Mrs Deverill said. She didn't move from
her seat but waved with a single hand. "I think you'll find it's
for you."

"For me?"

"Why don't you answer it?"

With a sinking feeling, Matt got up and went over to the telephone. He lifted the receiver. "Hello?"

"Matthew – is that you?"

Matt felt a shiver work its way down his spine. He knew it was impossible. It had to be some sort of trick.

It was Tom Burgess.

"I wanted to say I'm sorry," the farmer said. No. It wasn't the farmer. It was the farmer's voice. Somehow it had been duplicated. "I'm afraid I missed you this morning. I had to go down to a market in Cirencester. I'm going to be away for a couple of weeks but I'll come round and see you when I'm back…"

Was it Matt's imagination or had it suddenly become very cold in the living room? The fire was still burning but there was no warmth from the flames. He hadn't said a word to whoever – or whatever – it was at the other end of the line. He slammed down the phone.

"That wasn't very friendly," Mrs Deverill said.

"That wasn't Tom Burgess."

"I asked him to call you." The firelight danced in her eyes. Matt glanced at the portrait and shivered. It was smiling at him, just like the woman who was sitting beneath it. "I thought it was best that he spoke to you himself."

"How did you…?" Matt began.

But there was no point asking questions. He remembered the roads that led round in impossible circles, the cat that had been shot and come back to life. And now there was a farmer who had been dead but was somehow phoning from Cirencester. Matt was in the grip of a power much stronger than himself. He was helpless.

"I hope this is the end of the matter, Matthew," Mrs Deverill was saying. "And I think you should be careful before you tell any more of these stories. Anybody who knows anything about you is unlikely to believe you. And I would have said that the last thing you need is to get into any more trouble with the police."

Matt didn't hear her. He had stopped listening. Silently he walked upstairs to his room. He was defeated – and he knew it. He undressed, slid under the covers and fell into a restless sleep.

The building was in Farringdon, close to the centre of London. It was two storeys high, Victorian, a survivor in a street which had been bombed in the Second World War and redeveloped ever since. It looked like a private house or perhaps a solicitor's office. There was a single black door with a letter box, but the only letters that were ever delivered were junk mail. Once a month the doormat was cleared, the letters taken away and burned. Lights came on and off inside the building but they were on time switches. Nobody lived there. Despite the high cost of property in London, for most of the year the building was unused.

At eight o'clock in the evening, a taxi drew up outside and a man got out. He was Indian, about fifty years old, dressed in a suit with a light raincoat draped around his shoulders. He paid the driver and waited until the taxi had driven away. Then, taking a key out of his pocket, he walked over to the door and unlocked it. Briefly, he glanced up and down the pavement. There was nobody in sight. He went in.

The narrow hallway was empty and spotlessly clean. Ahead, a flight of stairs led up to the first floor. The man had not been here for several months and he paused for a moment, remembering the details of the place: the wooden steps, the cream-coloured walls, the old-fashioned light switch next to the banister. Nothing had changed. The man wished he hadn't come here. Every time he came, he hoped he would never have to return.

He went upstairs. The top corridor was more modern, expensively carpeted, with halogen lighting and a swivelling security camera at every corner. There was another door at the far end, this one made of darkened glass. It opened electronically as the man approached, then closed quietly behind him.

The Nexus had come together again.

There were twelve of them – eight men and four women. They had travelled here from all parts of the world. They only saw each other very occasionally but they were always connected, communicating with each other by phone or email. All of them were influential. They were linked to government, to the secret service, to business, to the Church. They had told nobody that they would be here tonight. Very few people outside the room even knew that their organization existed.

Apart from the table and twelve leather chairs, there was very little else in the room. Three phones and a computer sat next to each other on a long wooden console. Clocks showed the time in London, Paris, New York, Moscow, Beijing and – curiously – Lima, in Peru. Various maps of the world hung on the walls, which, although there was no way of knowing it, were soundproofed and filled with sophisticated surveillance equipment to prevent the room from being bugged.

The Indian man nodded and sat down in the last empty seat.

"Thank you for coming, Professor Dravid." The speaker was sitting at the head of the table. It was a woman in her late thirties, dressed in a severe black dress and a jacket fastened at the neck. She had a thin, chiselled face and black hair, cut short. Her eyes were strangely out of focus. She didn't look at the professor as she spoke. She couldn't look at anyone: she was blind.

"I'm very glad to see you, Miss Ashwood," Dravid replied. He spoke slowly. His voice was deep, his accent very precise. "As a matter of fact, I was in England anyway. I'm working at the Natural History Museum. But I'm grateful to everyone else for coming. This meeting was called at short notice and I know some of you have travelled a long way." He nodded at the man sitting next to him, who had flown in from Sydney, Australia. "As you are all aware, Miss Ashwood called me three nights ago, requesting an emergency session of the Nexus. Having spoken with her, I agreed that it was critical we

132

should meet straight away. Again, I thank you for coming."

Dravid turned to Miss Ashwood. "Tell them what you told me, Miss Ashwood," he said.

"Of course." Miss Ashwood glided her hand to a glass in front of her and took a sip of water. "Seven months have passed since we last met," she began. "At that time I told you that I was aware of a growing danger, a sense that something was very wrong. We agreed that we would continue to monitor the situation, as we have always done. We are the eyes of the world. Although I, of course, have other ways of seeing."

She paused.

"The danger has become more acute," she continued. "For weeks now I've been thinking I should call you and I've spoken several times with Professor Dravid. Well, I can't leave it any longer. I am certain, in my heart, that our worst fears are to be realized. Raven's Gate is about to open."

There was a stir around the table. But several of them were looking doubtful.

"What evidence do you have, Miss Ashwood?" one of the men asked. He was tall and olive-skinned. He had travelled from South America to be here.

"You know my evidence very well, Mr Fabian. You know why I was invited to join the Nexus."

"Even so... What have you been told?"

"I haven't been told anything. I wish it were as simple as that. I can only tell you what I feel. And right now, it's as if there's poison in the air. I'm aware of it all the time and it's getting worse. The darkness is coming. It's taking shape. You have to trust me."

"I hope that isn't why you've brought us all here tonight." An elderly man had spoken. He was a bishop, dressed in a clerical collar with a gold cross around his neck. He took off his spectacles and cleaned them as he continued. "I'm very well aware of your abilities, Miss Ashwood, and I have great respect for them. But can you really ask us to accept that something is the case just because you believe it to be so?"

"I thought that was what faith was all about," Miss Ashwood retorted.

"The Christian faith is written down. Nobody has ever written a history of the Old Ones."

"That's not true," Dravid muttered. He raised a single finger. "You're forgetting the Spanish monk."

"St Joseph of Cordoba? His book has been lost and he himself was discredited centuries ago." The bishop sighed. "This is very difficult for me," he said. "You have to remember that, officially, the Church does not believe in your Old Ones any more than we believe in demons or devils or all the rest of it. If it was known that I was part of the Nexus, I would have to resign. I am here only because you and I have the same aims. We are all afraid of the same thing, no matter what we choose to call it. But I cannot accept – *will* not accept – guesswork and superstition. I'm sorry, Miss Ashwood. You have to give us more evidence."

"Maybe I can be of assistance," another man said. He was

a policeman, an assistant commissioner based at Scotland Yard. "I did notice something very recently that might be of interest. It was very minor, so I didn't report it to you, but in the light of what you are saying now…"

"Go on," Professor Dravid said.

"Well, it concerns a petty criminal, a drug addict by the name of Will Scott. He was last seen following a woman into an alleyway not very far from here, in Holborn. Presumably she would have been his next victim. He had a knife. And a record of armed violence."

"What happened?"

"It wasn't the woman who ended up as the victim. She disappeared. It was Scott who was found dead. He killed himself. He pushed the knife into his own heart."

"What's so strange about that?" one of the women asked.

"He did it in broad daylight in the middle of London. But it wasn't just that. I saw his face…" The policeman paused. "I knew at once that this was something completely abnormal. The look of terror. It was as if he had tried to fight it. As if he didn't want to die. It was horrible."

"The power of the Old Ones," Miss Ashwood whispered.

"Why should one death in Holborn have anything to do with the Nexus?" the bishop insisted.

"I agree with you," Dravid said. "One isolated incident. A possible suicide. But there is something else, and it happened only this morning. That in itself is rather strange, because of course I knew I was coming here tonight. But I was at my office, in the museum, and I was online. This was around lunchtime. And my computer picked up an enquiry into Raven's Gate." He hesitated. "I have a program," he explained. "Whenever anybody, anywhere, puts those words into a search engine, I get to hear about it. It's only happened twice in the last year – both times academics. But this was different. I managed to instant-mail the person at the other end. And I have a feeling it was a teenager or maybe even a child."

"Did he say so?" the policeman asked.

"No. But he used the letters r and u instead of writing 'are you'. That's very much the sign of a young person. He called himself Matt."

"Just Matt?"

"He gave no surname. But here's something else that's interesting. The enquiry came from a computer in the library at Greater Malling."

The statement caused another stir around the table. This time, even the bishop looked concerned.

"Shouldn't you have contacted us straight away, Professor?" the South American asked.

"I hardly had time, Mr Fabian. As I told you, this only happened today and I knew we would all meet this evening anyway. On its own, it might not have been significant. A schoolboy might have stumbled across Raven's Gate and made enquiries about it for no particular reason. But given Miss Ashwood's feelings and what we've just heard…" He let the sentence hang in the air. "Maybe we should try to find this 'Matt' and discover how much he knows."

"And how are we meant to do that?" a silver-haired man with a French accent asked. His name was Danton and he was connected in some way to military intelligence. "Give me a full name and we could find him in seconds. But Matt? Short for Matthew? Or he could be from my country... Matthieu. Or he could even be a girl... Matilda."

"He'll find us," Miss Ashwood said.

"You think he'll just walk in here?" the bishop asked. He shook his head. "It seems obvious to me. If you really think something is happening in Yorkshire, we should go there and try to prevent it. We should be there now."

"We can't," Dravid said. "It would be far too dangerous. We don't know what we're looking for. And anyway, we agreed from the start that we cannot become personally involved. That's not our role. We exist to watch, to share information and – when the time comes – to fight back. That's when we'll be needed. We cannot do anything that will put us at risk."

"So we sit back and do nothing?"

"He will find his way to us," Miss Ashwood said. "You have to remember. It is meant to happen. Everything in the history of the world has been preparing itself for this moment, for the return of the Five and the final struggle. There is no coincidence. Everything is planned. If we don't see that, we lose one of our greatest weapons."

"Matt." The Frenchman spoke the single word. He didn't sound too impressed.

Miss Ashwood nodded slowly. "Let's just pray he finds us soon."

A VISITOR

Matt was chopping wood again. There were blisters on his hands and the sweat was running down his back, but the pile never seemed to get any smaller. Noah was sitting a few paces away, watching him. Matt split another log apart and threw down the axe. He wiped his forehead with the back of his hand.

"How long have you been here, Noah?" he asked.

Noah shrugged.

"Where did Mrs Deverill find you? Were you born here or did you escape from the local lunatic asylum?"

Noah glared at him. Matt knew he had difficulty understanding sentences with more than four or five words. "You shouldn't make fun of me," Noah replied at last, scowling.

"Why not? It's the only fun I have." Matt picked up a handful of wood and dumped it in the wheelbarrow. "Why don't you go anywhere?" he asked. "You're always hanging around. Don't you have a girlfriend or anything?"

Noah sniffed. "I don't like girls."

"Do you prefer pigs? I think one or two of them fancy you."

139

Matt leant forward to take the axe and as he did so Noah's hand shot out, grabbing hold of him. "You don't know," he rasped. He was so close that Matt could smell the rotten food on his breath. His fat lips twisted in an unpleasant smile. "Sometimes Mrs Deverill lets me kill one," he said. "A pig. I put the knife in and I listen to it squeal. We'll do the same to you…"

"Let me go!" Matt tried to pull away but Noah was incredibly strong and his fingers were clamped on to Matt's arm in a vice-like grip.

"You laugh at Noah. But when the end comes, it'll be Noah who laughs at you…"

"Get off me!" Matt was afraid his bone was going to break.

Just then a car pulled into the yard. Noah released his hold and Matt fell back, cradling his arm. There were four welts where the fingers had held him. The car was a Honda Estate. The door opened and a man got out, dressed in a suit and white shirt but no tie. Matt recognized him at once. It was Stephen Mallory, the detective who had interrogated him after the Ipswich break-in.

Noah had seen him too. As Mallory looked around him, the farmhand scurried away, disappearing behind the barn. Matt walked over to the detective. He could feel a sense of excitement stirring inside him but tried not to show it. Although Mallory was partly responsible for sending him here, he was exactly the man Matt most wanted to see.

140

"Matthew!" The detective nodded. "How are you?"

"I'm fine."

"You don't look it. You've lost a lot of weight."

"What are you doing here?" Matt was in no mood to talk.

"I've been to a conference in Harrogate. It's not that far away so I thought I'd look in and see how you were getting on." Mallory stretched. "I have to say, it wasn't an easy place to find."

"If you think it's hard getting in, you should try getting out."

"What?"

"Nothing." Matt glanced over Mallory's shoulder. Mrs Deverill was somewhere inside the house. He knew she'd come into the yard at any moment and he wanted to talk before she arrived. "I was going to phone you," he said.

"Why?"

"I don't want to stay here. You told me that the LEAF Project is voluntary. Well, I'm volunteering myself out. I don't care where you send me. You can lock me up in Alcatraz if you want to. But this place sucks and I want to go."

The detective looked at him curiously. "What were you doing when I arrived?" he asked.

"What does it look like?" Matt spread his hands, showing the red calluses and blisters. "I was chopping wood."

"Have you started school yet?"

"No."

141

Mallory shook his head. "This is all wrong," he said. "This shouldn't be happening."

"Then do something about it. Get me out of here."

There was a movement in the doorway behind them. Mrs Deverill had appeared and Noah along with her. She had put on a brightly coloured apron and was holding a basket of apples. Matt wondered if they were for Mallory's benefit, just like the suit she had worn when she went down to London.

"Don't say anything," Mallory muttered quietly. "Leave this to me."

Mrs Deverill came over. She seemed surprised to see someone there. "Can I help you?" she asked.

"You don't remember me? Detective Superintendent Mallory. We met in London. I'm with the LEAF Project."

Mrs Deverill nodded. "Of course I remember you, Mr Mallory," she said. "And it's a great pleasure to see you, although it might have been a courtesy to let me know you were coming. If I recall correctly, you were supposed to give me twenty-four hours' notice of any official visit."

"Do you have something to hide, Mrs Deverill?"

"Of course not." The hard eyes blinked. "You're welcome any time."

"The fact is that I picked up a report from the local police," Mallory said. "Something about a false alarm at a place called Glendale Farm. Matthew was involved."

"Oh yes." Mrs Deverill rearranged her features into a look of concern. "Matthew and I have already spoken about that.

142

I was very sorry that he wasted the policemen's time. Still, in the end there was no harm done. I think we've both put it behind us."

Matt wanted to speak but Mallory warned him with his eyes.

"Why isn't Matthew at school?" he asked.

"It's my feeling that it's too early," Mrs Deverill replied. "I have discussed the matter with my sister. She happens to be the head teacher. We both agree that he would be a disruptive influence. We'll send him to school as soon as he's ready." Mrs Deverill smiled. She was doing her best to appear friendly. "Why don't you come inside, Detective Superintendent? I'm not sure we should be discussing this in front of the boy. Perhaps I could offer you a cup of tea?"

"No, thank you, Mrs Deverill." Mallory looked around him a second time. "I haven't seen very much," he went on, "but it seems obvious to me that living conditions on this farm are entirely inadequate for Matthew's needs—"

"We were examined before he came," Mrs Deverill interrupted.

"And frankly I'm appalled by Matthew's physical condition. He looks as if he's been worked to the bone. You've actually broken the law by keeping him out of school."

"The boy's been perfectly happy here. Haven't you, Matthew!"

"No." Matt was glad he'd been given a chance to speak. "I hate it here. I hate this farm. I hate you, most of all."

"Well, that's gratitude!" Mrs Deverill snapped.

"I'm going back to London," Mallory said. "And I want you to know that I'll be contacting the LEAF committee the moment I arrive. I'll be recommending that Matthew is removed from your care with immediate effect."

Mrs Deverill's face darkened. Her eyes were like razors. "I wouldn't do that if I were you."

"Are you threatening me, Mrs Deverill?"

There was a long pause.

"No. Why would I want to do that? I'm a law-abiding person. And if you really think that Matthew would be better off locked up in some sort of juvenile institution, that's your business. Nevertheless you aren't meant to be here, Mr Mallory. You weren't invited, and this visit of yours is a violation of our agreement. You make your report, if you want to. But you'll be the one who ends up with the red face."

She turned on her heels and walked back into the farmhouse. Matt watched her go with a sense of elation. Mallory had defeated her. For the first time, he could see an end to his ordeal.

Mallory leant towards him. "Listen to me, Matt," he said. "I'd put you in the car and take you with me if I could—"

"I wish you would," Matt said.

"But I can't. I don't have any right and technically I'd be breaking the law. Mrs Deverill could even say I'd abducted you and in the long run I might be doing more harm than good. But give me twenty-four hours and I'll be back. And then we'll get you out of this dump. OK?"

"Sure." Matt nodded. "Thanks."

Mallory sighed. "If you want the honest truth, I was always against the LEAF Project," he said. "It's just a gimmick ... another bit of government spin. They don't really want to help kids like you. They're only interested in massaging the figures, reducing the number of children behind bars." He walked over to his car and opened the door. "Well, as soon as I've put in my report, they'll have to listen to what I say. And whatever happens, I promise you Mrs Deverill will never get custody of anyone ever again."

Matt watched him go. Then he turned and looked at the farmhouse. Mrs Deverill was standing in the doorway. She had taken off the apron and was now dressed all in black. She too had seen the detective leave, but said nothing. She stepped back, disappearing into the house. The door slammed shut behind her.

It was dark by the time Stephen Mallory reached the motorway and the fast route back to Ipswich. He was deep in thought as he steered his Honda Estate into the outside lane.

He hadn't told Matt the whole truth. There never had been any conference in Harrogate.

Stephen Mallory specialized in juvenile crime. He had met many young delinquents, some only ten or eleven years old, and, like so many of them, it seemed to him that Matt wasn't so much a criminal as a victim. He had already spoken to

Kelvin, who was in a remand centre awaiting trial. He had met with Gwenda Davis and her partner Brian. He had read all the reports. But even so, he felt that there was something missing. The boy he had met was nothing like the one he'd been reading about.

And so, immediately after he had handed Matt over to Mrs Deverill, he had decided to see if he could fill in the missing pieces. He was in London anyway. Nobody would know, or care, how he spent the afternoon.

He had taken a taxi to a police records office in south London. Everything he needed was there in a cardboard box, one of about a hundred, filed away with a reference number and a name: FREEMAN M.J. There were articles cut out of the local newspaper in Ipswich, reports from both the local and the metropolitan police, a post-mortem report and a psychiatric assessment from a doctor who had been attached to the case. The story was exactly as he had been told. A road accident. The parents killed. An eight-year-old boy left behind. Adoption by an aunt in Ipswich. Mallory had read all of it before. But then, at the very bottom of the box, he had stumbled on a witness report that he hadn't seen. It changed everything.

It was a signed statement by the woman who had been living next door to Matthew at the time of the accident; she had in fact been looking after him when it happened. Her name was Rosemary Green. Mallory read it twice, then ordered a taxi to take him to Dulwich. It was four o'clock in the afternoon. He doubted she would be in.

But he had been in luck. Rosemary Green was a teacher and arrived home just as he stepped out of the cab. He talked to her outside her small Victorian house with pink and white honeysuckle trailing all the way up the front wall. It was strange to think that Matthew Freeman had once played in the garden next door. It couldn't have been a more different world from the one he would later inhabit in Ipswich.

Mrs Green didn't have much to add to what she had already said. Yes, she agreed that her story didn't seem likely, but it was true. She had explained it to the police at the time and she stood by it now, six years later.

Mallory had drunk two miniature bottles of whisky on the train back to Ipswich. A copy of Matthew's file was on the table in front of him, as well as the late edition of the *Evening Standard*. The newspaper belonged to one of the passengers sitting opposite him. Mallory had almost snatched it out of the man's hand when he saw the story on the front page.

A bizarre suicide in Holborn. A twenty-year-old criminal called Will Scott had been found dead in a street close to Lincoln's Inn Fields. The cause of death was a knife wound to the heart, which police believed to be self-inflicted. Scott had a record for aggravated burglary and assault, and was a known drug dealer. Three witnesses had seen him following a middle-aged woman, dressed in a grey suit with a silver brooch shaped like a lizard. Police were urging her to come forward.

A coincidence?

Mallory remembered the brooch Mrs Deverill had been wearing. She had arrived late to the meeting, and she might well have come through Lincoln's Inn Fields. He felt certain she must be the woman referred to in the article, although he had no idea how she could have been involved in Will Scott's death. But from that moment on Mallory had been worried. He had found himself thinking more and more about Matthew and he was certain that the boy shouldn't be in her care.

Then, only a few days later, he had intercepted a routine transmission from a police station in York: something about another death, one that had been reported by a fourteen-year-old boy from the LEAF Project. It had been enough for Mallory. He had cleared a space in his diary and headed north.

Now, driving back from Lesser Malling, he was very glad he'd done it. What he had seen had been a disgrace. The boy looked ill. More than that, he looked traumatized. And Mallory had quickly noticed the welts on his arm. Well, he would soon put a stop to it. He would hand in his own report the very next day.

He checked his speedometer. He was doing exactly seventy miles an hour. He had moved into the central lane and cars were speeding past him on both sides, all of them break-ing the speed limit. He watched the red tail lights blur into the distance. It was raining again, tiny drops splattering against the windscreen. Was it his imagination or had it become very cold inside the car? He turned on the heater. Air pumped out of the ventilation grilles in the dashboard, but it didn't seem to make any difference. He switched on the windscreen wipers. The road ahead shimmered and bent as the water swept over the glass.

Mallory glanced at the clock. It was half past nine. He was at least another two hours away from Ipswich – it would be midnight before he was home. He turned on the radio to listen to the news. The voices would help keep him awake.

The radio was tuned to BBC Radio 4 but there was no news. At first Mallory thought there was nothing on the radio at all and wondered if it had broken ... like the heating. It really was very cold. Perhaps one of the fuses had blown. He would have to take the car into the garage when he got back. But then it came on. There was a burst of static and, behind it, something else.

A faint whispering.

Puzzled, he leant down and pressed the button that was preset to Classic FM. Mallory liked classical music. Maybe there would be a concert. But there was no music. Once again, all he could hear was the strange whispering. They were definitely the same voices. He could even make out some of the words they were saying.

"EMANY ... NEVAEH ... NITRA ... OH ... WREHTAF..."

What the hell was going on? Frantically Mallory pressed button after button, his eyes never leaving the road. It was impossible. The same voices were being transmitted on every station, louder now, more insistent. He turned the radio off.

But the whispering continued. It seemed to be everywhere, all around him in the car.

The cold was more intense. It was like sitting in a fridge – or a deep freeze. Mallory decided to pull over on to the hard shoulder and stop. The rain was coming down harder. He could barely see out of the windscreen. Red lights zoomed past. Blinding white lights sped towards him.

He pressed his foot on the brake and signalled left. But the indicator had failed and the car wouldn't slow down. Mallory was beginning to panic. He had never been afraid in his life. It wasn't in his nature. But he was afraid now, knowing that the car was out of control. He stamped his foot down more urgently on the brake. Nothing happened. The car was picking up speed.

And then it was as if he had hit some sort of invisible ramp. He felt the tyres leave the road and the whole car rocketed into the air. His vision twisted three hundred and sixty degrees. The whispering had somehow become a great clamour that filled his consciousness.

Mallory screamed.

His car, travelling at ninety miles an hour, somersaulted over the crash barrier. The last thing Mallory saw, upside down, was a petrol tanker hurtling towards him, the driver's face frozen in horror. The Honda hit it and disintegrated. There was a screech of tyres. An explosion. A single blare from the loudest horn in the world. Then silence.

*   *   *

Matt was sound asleep when the covers were torn off him and he woke up in the chill of the morning to find Mrs Deverill in a black dressing gown, looming over his bed. He looked at his watch. It was ten past six. Outside, the sky was still grey. Rain pattered against the windows. The trees bent in the wind.

"What is it?" he demanded.

"I just heard it on the radio," Mrs Deverill said. "I thought you ought to know. I'm afraid it's bad news, Matthew. It seems there was a multiple pile-up on the motorway last night. Six people were killed. Detective Superintendent Mallory was one of them. It's a terrible shame. Really terrible. But it looks as if you won't be leaving after all."

OUT OF THE FIRE

The next few days were the worst Matt had experienced since he had arrived in Yorkshire.

Mrs Deverill worked him harder than ever and Noah never left his side. The hours passed in a tedious procession of cleaning, painting, chopping, mending and carrying. Matt was close to despair. He had tried to escape to London and he had failed. He had gone looking for clues in the wood but had found almost nothing. Two people had tried to help him and they had both died. Nobody else cared. A sort of fog had descended on his mind. He had given in. He would remain at Hive Hall until Mrs Deverill had finished with him. Maybe she planned to keep him there all his life and he would end up hollowed out and empty, like Noah, a dribbling slave.

Then, one evening – Matt thought it was a Saturday, although all days had become very much the same – Mrs Deverill's sister Claire came to dinner. He hadn't seen the teacher since his encounter with her in Lesser Malling. Sitting next to her at the kitchen table, he found it hard to keep his eyes off her birthmark, the discolouration that covered most of her face. He was both drawn to it and repulsed at the same time.

"Jayne tells me that you have been missing school," she remarked in her strange, high-pitched voice.

"I haven't been to school because she won't let me go," Matt replied. "I have to work here."

"And yet when you were at school, you regularly missed class. You played truant. You preferred shoplifting and loitering on motorway bridges, smoking. That's what I heard."

"I never smoked," Matt growled.

"Modern children have no real education," Jayne Deverill remarked. She was serving some sort of stew out of a pot. The meat was thick and fatty, and came in a rich, blood-coloured gravy. Road kill in a primeval swamp. "You see them in the street in their shapeless clothes, listening to what they call music but what you or I would call a horrible noise. They have no respect, no intelligence, no taste. And they think the world belongs to them!"

"They'll soon find out..." Claire Deverill muttered.

There was a knock at the door and Noah appeared, dressed in what might have passed for a suit except that it was about fifty years old, faded and shapeless. He wore a shirt buttoned to the neck, but no tie. He looked to Matt like an out-of-work funeral director.

"The car's ready," he announced.

"We're still eating, Noah." Jayne Deverill scowled. "Wait for us outside."

153

"It's raining." Noah sniffed the food hopefully.

"Then wait in the car. We'll be out soon."

Matt waited until Noah had gone. "Are you going out?" he asked.

"We might be."

"Where?"

"When I was young, a child never asked questions of his elders," Claire Deverill said.

"Was that before or after the First World War?" Matt asked.

"Pardon?"

"Forget it…"

Matt fell silent and finished his meal. Jayne Deverill stood up and went over to the kettle. "I'm making you a cup of herbal tea," she explained. "I want you to drink it all, Matthew. It has a restorative quality and it seems to me that you've been rather on edge since the death of that poor detective."

"Are you going to arrange for him to phone me tomorrow?"

"Oh no. Mr Mallory won't be coming back." She poured steaming water into a squat black teapot, stirred it and then poured out a cup for Matthew. "Now you get that down you. It'll help you relax."

"It'll help you relax."

Maybe it was the way she spoke the words. Or maybe it was the fact that Mrs Deverill had never made tea like this before, but suddenly Matt was determined not to touch the liquid he was being offered. He cupped it in his hands and sniffed. It was green and smelled bitter.

"What's in it?" he asked.

"Leaves."

"What sort of leaves?"

"Dandelion. Full of Vitamin A."

"Not for me, thanks," Matt said. He tried to sound casual. "I've never been that crazy about dandelions."

"Nonetheless, you will try it. You're not leaving the table until you do."

Claire Deverill was watching him too carefully. Matt was certain now: if he drank the tea, the next thing he knew it would be the morning of the next day.

"All right." Matt lifted the cup. "If you insist."

"I do."

The question was – how to get rid of it?

Finally, it was Asmodeus who helped him out. The cat must have crept into the kitchen while they were eating. It jumped up on to the sideboard and caught a jug of milk with its tail, causing it to topple and break. Both sisters turned round, their attention momentarily diverted. Instantly Matt reached down and up-ended his cup under the table. When the two women turned back again, he was cradling the cup in his hand as if nothing had happened. He just hoped they wouldn't notice the steam rising out of the damp carpet.

He pretended to drink until the cup was empty, then set it down on the table. Something stirred in Jayne Deverill's eyes and he knew she was pleased. Now to see if his theory was right. He yawned and stretched his arms.

"Tired, Matthew?" She spoke the words too quickly.

"Yes."

"No need to help with the dishes tonight then. Why don't you go up to bed?"

"Yes. I'll do that."

He stood up and went to the stairs, making his movements deliberately slow and heavy. He didn't turn on the light in his room. Instead he lay down on the bed and closed his eyes, wondering what would happen next.

He didn't have long to wait. The door opened and light spilled into the room.

"Is he asleep?" It was Claire Deverill's voice.

"Of course. He'll sleep twelve hours and wake up with a chainsaw of a headache. Are you ready?"

"Yes."

"Then let's go."

Matt heard the women leave. He listened to their footsteps on the stairs. The front door opened and closed. The engine of the Land Rover started and the headlights swung round as it turned in the yard and then set off up the drive. Only when he was sure they weren't coming back did he sit up on the bed. Everything had happened just as he had anticipated. He was alone at Hive Hall.

Half an hour later the lights came back on at Omega One. Matt had been expecting that too.

Dressed in black jeans and a dark shirt, he grabbed the bike and pedalled away from the farm.

It was time to go back into the wood.

It didn't take Matt long to find the entrance. The little flag he had made from his T-shirt was still there, tied round a branch. Grateful for the pine needles underfoot, he made his way along the corridor of trees, making sure he didn't stray off the tarmac strip that Tom Burgess had shown him the last time he was here. The moon was behind the clouds but he used the glow from the power station to guide him. When he looked back, the wood was pitch-black. An owl cried out. There was a scurry of leaves as some night creature batted its way up towards the sky.

Matt heard the villagers before he saw them. There was the sound of crackling and a murmur of voices. They were very close. He pulled aside a pair of low branches and realized that he was back at the fence that surrounded the power station. He knelt down and looked through the wire. An incredible sight met his eyes.

The flat circle of land surrounding the power station was bustling with activity. A huge fire blazed outside the sphere, throwing out vivid snakes' tongues of flames. Thick black smoke curled into the air. Four or five people were throwing armfuls of twigs and shrubbery on to the fire, the damp wood hissing and snapping as it was consumed. Overhead, a line of arc lamps cast a brilliant glare over the field. It was a strange mixture: the building, with its electric lights, was modern, industrial; the bonfire, with the shadowy figures of people grouped around, reminded him of a scene from primitive times.

There was a car parked between the fire and the fence – Matt thought it might be a Saab or a Jaguar. A man got out but he was silhouetted against the light and Matt couldn't make out who he was. The man raised a hand and the gold signet ring he was wearing momentarily flashed red, reflecting the light of the fire.

He had given a signal. A lorry that was parked on the other side of the clearing immediately began to reverse right up to the corridor that joined the giant sphere of Omega One to the rest of the building. As Matt watched, the doors of the lorry were thrown open and several men emerged, dressed in strange, cumbersome clothes. They congregated together, then lifted something: a large silver box about five metres long. It was obviously heavy. They took a lot of time lowering it to the ground.

Matt couldn't quite see what was going on. He had to get closer. He followed the fence back to the gap he'd discovered the last time he was here and waited, making sure nobody was looking in his direction. But all the villagers were concentrating on the lorry. Matt chose his moment, then dived forward, head first. He felt the jagged edge of the wire tear his shirt and scrape his back, but he was lucky. He hadn't drawn blood. He landed face down on the grass and lay still.

A large, bearded man walked across the clearing, heading towards the lorry. It was the butcher from Lesser Malling. The ginger-haired chemist was there too. And Matt also recognized Joanna Creevy, the woman who had been at Glendale Farm when he returned with the police. She was talking to Jayne Deverill. Matt looked back at the bonfire. The village children were standing round, poking sticks into the flames, making the sparks leap up. There were forty or fifty people at Omega One and suddenly Matt knew that he was spying on the entire village. Young or old, every one of them had made the journey into the forest. They were all in on it.

All his instincts screamed at him to slip away before he was spotted. But at the same time he knew that what he was seeing was important. He just had to work out what these people were doing, why they were here. And what was inside the silver box? The men had disappeared inside. The villagers were queuing up, about to follow them. The man with the signet ring began talking to Mrs Deverill. Matt was desperate to hear what they were saying.

He crawled over the ground, keeping low, hardly daring to raise his head. The closer he got, the greater the chance of his being seen. He hoped the long grass would provide some sort of cover, but the light of the flames seemed to be reaching out to him, eager to show that he was there. He could even feel the warmth of the fire on his shoulders and head. He heard laughter. The man with the ring had cracked a joke. Matt wriggled further forward. His hand caught something and pulled it away. Too late he saw the thin plastic wire that ran along the ground. Too late he realized that he should never have touched it.

The stillness of the night was shattered by a siren. The villagers spun round, staring out over the field. Three men ran forward, shotguns appearing in their hands. The children dropped their sticks into the fire and ran over to the lorry. The man with the signet ring slowly passed through the crowd, his eyes scanning the ground. Matt clutched the earth, burying his face in the grass. But there was no use trying to hide.

Mrs Deverill was standing beside the bonfire. She shouted a brief sentence in a strange language and took something out of her pocket. Then she waved her hand over the flames. It was trailing a cloud of white powder, which hung for a moment in the air before falling.

The flames exploded, leaping almost as high as the power station itself, bright red light flooding the field. Something black began to take shape within them, moulding itself out of the shadows. In seconds the blackness had solidified and now it sprang – seemingly in slow motion – out of the fire and on to the ground beyond. It was some sort of animal and, moments later, a second one appeared, bounding forward to join it. Behind them the bonfire shrank back to its normal size. The wail of the alarm stopped abruptly.

They were dogs, but like no dogs Matt had ever seen.

They were huge, two or three times bigger than Rott-weilers – and more savage too. The flames of the fire that had

160

given birth to them still flickered in their black, shark-like eyes. Their mouths hung open, with teeth like two lines of kitchen knives jutting out beyond their lips. Their heads were high and uneven, their bulging skulls topped by two tiny ears, like horns. Slowly, one of them turned its ugly snout up to the sky and uttered a ghastly howl. Then, as one, they padded forward, their heads slanting unnaturally to one side as if listening to the ground.

Matt had no choice. He had to get away. If the dogs found him, they would tear him apart. No longer caring if he was seen or not, he stumbled to his feet and began to run. His legs were as heavy as lead but desperately he forced them to carry him. The fence was still about ten metres away. Arms out-stretched, he raced towards it, not wanting to look behind him. But he couldn't stop himself. He had to know. Where were the dogs? How near were they? With a grimace, he looked back over his shoulder. And regretted it.

The first of the creatures had already halved the distance between itself and Matt, yet it didn't seem to be moving fast. It hovered in the air between each bound, barely touching the grass before jumping up again. There was something hideous about the way it ran. A panther or a leopard closing in for the kill has a certain majesty. But the dog was deformed, lopsided, ghastly. The flesh on one of its flanks had rotted and a glisten-ing ribcage jutted out. As if to avoid the stench of the wound, the animal had turned away, its head hanging close to its front paws. Strings of saliva trailed from its mouth. And every time its feet hit the ground, its whole body quivered, threatening to collapse in on itself.

Matt reached the fence and clawed at it with his hands, crashing his fingers against the wire. He thought he had run in a straight line, following the way he had come, but he seemed to have got it wrong. He couldn't find the gap. He looked behind him. Two more bounds and the dogs would reach him. There was no doubt that they would tear him apart. He could almost feel their teeth tearing into him, ripping the flesh away from his bones. He had never seen anything so ferocious … not in a zoo, not in a film, not anywhere in the real world.

Where was the gap? In blind panic he threw his whole weight against the fence, almost crying with relief as the edge buckled, revealing the jagged hole. Without hesitating he dived forward. His head and shoulders went through but this time the wire hooked into his trousers. Thrashing out with his arms, expecting to feel the jaws of the dog close on his leg at any moment, he struggled like a fish in a net. Out of the corner of his eye he saw a huge black shape plummeting towards him. He gave a last frantic heave. His jeans ripped and he fell through, rolling into a ball on the other side.

Blood oozed out of a gash in his leg, but he was safe … at least for the moment. He struggled to his feet, then staggered back as one of the dogs lunged at th fence, its mouth foaming, its teeth gnashing at the wire. The two creatures were trapped. The hole had barely been big enough for Matt to pass through and they were bigger and more awkwardly built than him. But then, even as he watched, the dogs began pounding at the earth, raking the soft soil with their claws. They weren't going to allow the fence to stop them. They were going to burrow their way under it.

Matt fled into the wood. Low-lying branches whipped into his body. Pine needles cascaded on to his hair and into his face. He blinked, trying to keep them out of his eyes. There was nowhere to hide, no way of knowing if he had taken the right path. He was trapped in a vast grid system where every direction looked exactly the same. But the dogs had the advantage. They didn't need to see him. They would smell him out.

Matt didn't care where he was going. His only thought was to get away, to put as much space as he could between himself and the two dogs. How long did he have? Thirty seconds? A minute or two at the most. Then they would emerge from the ground on the other side of the fence as if rising out of a grave. They would stalk him through the wood, outrun him and rip him to shreds.

He crashed into the trunk of a tree and reeled away, spinning round. The lights from the power station were already a long way behind him, barely visible through the branches. Matt was exhausted but he couldn't let himself rest. He needed to find a stretch of water, a river or a stream. Maybe he could throw the dogs off his scent. But there was no such thing in this artificial wood. It stretched on endlessly, with not a glimpse of water in sight.

He paused to catch his breath, his chest and throat rasping, his head pounding. At that moment a terrible baying broke through the air. It was a howl of triumph. The dogs were through the fence. Matt almost gave up. He felt a shiver of despair travel through his body. It was all-consuming. He would just stand here and wait for them to come. All he could do was hope his death would be quick.

No. He forced himself to snap out of it. He wasn't dead yet. Gathering up his last reserves of strength, he forced himself on, desperately twisting between the trees.

Only the sudden stamping of his feet on hard concrete after the soft silence of the pine needles told him that he was out of the wood. Incredibly, he had broken out on to a road – but it wasn't the road to Lesser Malling. It was wider and there were white markings down the centre. For a moment Matt felt relief. He was back in the modern world – a car might come. He looked left and right. Nothing. And suddenly he knew that this was the worst place for him to be. He was out in the open, with no cover, nowhere to hide from the dogs.

Where could he go? The strip of concrete divided two worlds. Behind him was the wood. Ahead was some sort of moorland, wild and open. He remembered what he had been thinking. A river or a stream. Matt crossed the road and plunged into the wild grass. He could tell at once that the ground was damp. He could feel it, soft and sticky under his feet. He ran on and as he ran he became aware that the ground was getting wetter. Cold water slid over his trainers and on to his feet.

He was only conscious of the danger when it was too late. He staggered to a halt and at that same moment the ground gave way altogether and he found himself being sucked down, unable to move.

A bog. He had blundered right into it.

Matt screamed. He was being pulled under incredibly fast. He felt mud and slime rising up over his knees and thighs, then his waist. He flailed about but the effort only speeded things up. The bog gripped him around his stomach and he could already imagine what was about to happen next, during the last, horrific moments of his life. The bog would rise over his face and he would give one last scream. But there would be no sound. He would be silenced for ever as stinking mud rushed into his mouth and down his throat.

Matt forced himself to stay calm. He knew that struggling would only make the end come faster. He almost smiled. At least he had cheated the dogs. He had found the one place where they could never reach him. And if he had to die, perhaps it would be better to go this way.

He relaxed and in that instant he thought he could smell something … very close and yet distant. The smell of burning. The bonfire? No, that was too far away. Could there be someone else out there on the moor? His hopes were raised, only to be dashed again. There was no one there. The smell disappeared. It had been just his imagination.

The bog bubbled around him and rose to his armpits. Its touch was cold, final. A stench of mud and rotting leaves reached his nostrils. Matt closed his eyes and waited for the end. But now the bog was toying with him, creeping upwards centimetre by centimetre, lovingly drawing him into its embrace.

The beam of light hit him before he even heard the noise of the engine. Out of nowhere a car had appeared. It had veered off the road and now it was parked right on the edge of the bog. A man got out, barely visible behind the glare of the headlamps.

"Don't move!" a voice commanded. "I've got a rope."

But the bog, as if afraid it was going to lose its victim, tightened its hold. Greedily it clung to Matt, its hands spreading over his shoulders, pushing him down.

"Hurry!" Matt shouted.

The mud was touching his chin. He forced his head up despairingly, staring up at a pale moon that had at last come from behind the clouds. Only seconds remained.

The bog pulled. The stagnant water rose over his head, up his nose, into his eyes. Now only his hands remained above the surface. But then he was struck by the flying edge of a rope. Smothered, blind, he groped for it. And found it. He held his breath and tightened his grip.

And then he was being hauled up towards the surface. His lungs were bursting. With a cry, he opened his mouth and sucked in. And breathed air. The man pulled on the rope and he felt himself being dragged forward. His waist cleared the edge of the bog with a loud, sucking noise. He kicked out with his legs, still clinging on to the rope. A strong hand grabbed him and pulled him clear. Exhausted, he collapsed on to firm ground.

For a moment he lay there, retching, getting the filthy water out of his system. Then he looked up. And recognized Richard Cole, the journalist from the *Greater Malling Gazette*.

"You!" he gasped.

"What the hell…?" Richard was equally surprised.

"How…"

"What are you doing?"

The broken questions hung in the air.

Then Matt took control of the situation. "Not now," he said. He was thinking about the dogs. They might have lost his scent when he was in the bog, but they would find it again soon enough. "We have to go."

"All right. Can you get into the car?" Richard leant down and helped Matt to his feet. Matt could feel the slime dripping off him. He wondered what he must look like.

The car was standing near the side of the road with its engine running. Richard rested Matt against the bonnet, then went round to open the passenger door. There were piles of old newspapers and magazines on the front seat and he began throwing them into the back to clear a space. Matt was edging round to get in when he saw them.

The dogs had emerged from the wood. They were in the middle of the road. Watching. Waiting.

"There…" Matt whispered.

"What?"

Richard turned and saw them. The dogs were just ten metres away. Their tongues were hanging out. Their breath rose in white clouds. Their eyes flickered. Richard held up a hand. "Nice dogs! Stay!" he muttered. He reached into the car and pulled out a can. "Get in," he said to Matt.

"What are you…?"

"I'm going to put them down."

Painfully, Matt eased himself into the front seat, his eyes fixed on the waiting dogs. Water oozed out underneath him and dripped on to the carpet. Richard fumbled in his pocket and produced a handkerchief. Slowly, forcing himself not to panic, he unscrewed the lid of the can and pushed the handkerchief into its neck. Matt smelled petrol fumes. Richard found a lighter. The dogs crept forward, suddenly suspicious, and Matt knew they were preparing themselves for the final leap. Richard flicked the lighter against the handkerchief and hurled the can towards them.

The first dog had just left the ground when the can hit it and exploded into flame. Burning petrol sprayed over the second dog, instantly setting it alight. The fire roared around them. With an unearthly howl, the dogs fell back, one curling itself into a ball, the other snapping at its own hide in a vain attempt to devour the cause of its agony. Fire had been their creator. Now fire destroyed them.

Richard slid over the bonnet and landed next to the driver's door. He got into the car, slammed the door, threw the gears into reverse and stamped on the accelerator. The back wheels spun, then found a grip, rocketing the car backwards. Matt felt a thump as they drove over the body of one of the dying creatures. But where was the other? He looked around, then yelled out as, still blazing, it slammed into the windscreen, launching itself out of nowhere. For a few seconds it was in front of him, its dreadful teeth centimetres from his face. Then Richard changed into first gear and wrenched the wheel. The dog spun away. Matt looked out of the back window. The flickering remains of one carcass lay in the middle of the road. The second had got snarled up in the wheels, but as the car sped forward it fell free and was tossed to one side.

They drove through the night for half a mile without speaking. The car was filled with the smell of the bog. Water was dripping out of Matt's clothes, on to the seat and on to the floor. Richard pulled a face and opened the window. "So, do you mind telling me what that was all about?" he demanded.

Matt didn't know where to begin. "I think something is happening in Lesser Malling," he said.

Richard nodded. "I think you could be right."

MATT'S STORY

Richard Cole lived in the very centre of York. He had rented a flat above a souvenir shop in one of the city's most famous medieval streets: a pretty, cobbled passageway called The Shambles. The flat was arranged over three floors, a series of oddly shaped rooms piled on top of each other like children's building bricks. A kitchen and a living room took up the first floor. Then, above, there was a bedroom and a shower. And finally a narrow flight of steps twisted round to a spare room built into the roof.

The place was in a shambles itself. All the furniture looked as if it had been rescued from a skip – as indeed much of it had. There were old clothes everywhere, unwashed plates piled high in the sink, CDs, books, magazines and half-written articles shuffled together in a way that would surely make it impossible to find anything. The walls were covered with posters, mainly old American films. Richard's laptop was on the kitchen table, next to a box of Weetabix, a half-eaten can of baked beans with the fork still sticking out, and two pieces of very cold toast.

Matt had felt awkward as they climbed to the first floor and it was worse now that he was in the flat itself. He was very aware that he stank. Richard left him in the kitchen and came back with a large towel.

"We can talk later," he said. "Right now you need a shower. And we'll have to get rid of those clothes."

"Have you got a washing machine?"

"Are you kidding? The washing machine hasn't been built that could handle all that muck. They can go in the bin and we'll buy you some more tomorrow. I'll find you some of mine to wear in the meantime." Richard pointed upstairs. "You'll find the shower easily enough. Are you hungry?"

"Starving."

"Well there's no food in the house. I'll go out and get something while you get changed."

Half an hour later the two of them were sitting in the living room, surrounded by Chinese food from the takeaway at the end of the street. Matt had spent twenty minutes in the shower, only coming out when he had washed away all traces of the bog. He was now wearing an old York University T-shirt with a towel wrapped round his waist and nothing on his feet. He hadn't been aware how hungry he was until he had begun eating. Now he was feeling stuffed.

"Nice place," he said, looking around.

"I was lucky to get it," Richard said. "It's very cheap. Not that I'm here very much. I normally eat at the pub..."

"Do you live on your own?"

"I had a girlfriend until about a week ago. Unfortunately she took a liking to classical music."

"What's so bad about that?"

"Now she's going out with an opera singer." Richard went to the fridge and took out a can of beer. "You want anything to drink?"

"I'm all right." There was a brief silence while Richard sat down again. Matt knew that they both had a lot to explain. "How did you find me tonight?" he asked.

Richard shrugged. "There's not much to tell. After you left the office, I thought about some of the things you'd said. It all sounded pretty stupid, to tell the truth. But there were parts of your story… Well, I couldn't get them out of my head. And I had nothing else to do."

"So you went to look at Omega One?"

"Let's just say I happened to be passing."

"You knew where it was?"

Richard nodded. "The man who built it still lives in York. He was a scientific adviser to the government back in the sixties but he's retired now. Name of Michael Marsh."

"Did you meet him?"

"About six months ago. He got a knighthood from the Queen and I had to do a story about him. He's an unbelievably boring man. Lives in a big house near the river. He collects matchbox labels. If the worst comes to the worst, I may give him a call and we can go and see him. He may be able to help."

"So you decided to visit Omega One in the middle of the night…"

"It was on the way home from the pub. What's the big deal? I was near by so I thought I'd drive past. And then I heard someone shouting for help and that was how I found you."

"That's not possible." Matt thought back. "I didn't shout for help."

"I heard you."

"I may have yelled once. But I didn't even hear your car. You were suddenly just there."

"Maybe you shouted without realizing it, Matt. I mean, you were panicking. You were probably out of your mind. I know I would have been."

"How fast were you driving?"

"About fifty. I don't know."

"Were the car windows open?"

"No."

"Then even if I had shouted, how could you have heard my voice? It's not possible."

"You have a point," Richard admitted. "But then how do you explain that I swerved off the road in exactly the right place and came straight to you?"

"I can't," Matt said, in a quiet voice.

"Look, I heard someone. All right? I pulled over and there you were, up to your neck in—" He broke off. "You're just lucky I hadn't decided to stay for another pint. But now you're here, maybe you should tell me a bit more about yourself."

"Like what?"

"I don't even know your full name. You say your parents are dead but you never told me how you ended up living with this woman ... Mrs Deverill." Matt looked away. "You might as well tell me now," Richard went on. "It might help me work out what we're going to do."

"Are you going to put me in the newspaper?"

"That's the general idea."

Matt shook his head. "You can forget it. I don't want anyone writing about me. I don't want anyone to know about my life."

"I think you're forgetting something, Matt. You were the one who came to me. You told me you had a story..."

"I needed your help."

"Well, maybe we need each other."

"I don't want to be in the papers."

"Then you shouldn't be in my flat." Richard put down his can of beer. "All right," he said. "That's not fair. I'm not going to throw you out. Not tonight, anyway. But to be honest with you, I don't really need a fourteen-year-old in my life. So I'll tell you what I'll do. Tell me your story and I promise I won't publish it until you say. OK?"

"That'll never happen," Matt replied. But he nodded. "All right."

Richard reached for a notebook and a pen, just as he had when they first met at the newspaper office. He sat, waiting.

"I don't really know where to start," Matt said. "But since

you asked, my full name is Matthew Freeman. I was sent to stay with Mrs Deverill because of something called the LEAF Project."

"The LEAF Project?" Richard had heard the name before. "Isn't that one of the government's big ideas? Some sort of crazy scheme for dealing with juvenile offenders?"

"That's right. That's what I am. I was arrested for breaking into a warehouse. A man got stabbed."

"You stabbed him?"

"No. But I was there when it happened. I was to blame." Matt paused. "Maybe now you won't be so keen to help me."

"Why not? I don't give a damn what you've done. I just want to know why you did it." Richard sighed. "Why don't you try starting at the beginning? You may find it easier."

"All right." Matt didn't want to do this. His social worker, Jill Hughes, had always tried to make him talk about himself. *"You have to take responsibility for who you are."* That was one of the things she had always said. But the more she had pressed him, the more reluctant he had become, until their relationship had dissolved into a hostile silence. And now this journalist was asking him to do the same. Had he finally found an adult he could really trust? Matt hoped so, but he wasn't sure.

"I don't remember very much about my parents," Matt said. "I thought I would. They only died six years ago, but bit by bit they've just sort of … faded away. There's not much of them left.

175

"I think we were happy. We lived in a pretty ordinary sort of street in Dulwich. Do you know it? It's in south London. My dad was a doctor. I don't think my mum worked. We had a nice house, so I suppose there was a bit of money around. But we weren't that rich. The last time my parents took me on holiday we went camping in France. I must have been about seven then."

"Do you have any brothers or sisters?"

"No. There were just the three of us. And there wasn't much family. My dad was actually born in New Zealand and most of his family's still over there. My mum had a half-sister called Gwenda who lived in Ipswich. She visited us a few times but they didn't get on. Gwenda was nothing like her. When I was small, I used to think she was really boring. I never dreamt…"

Matt drew a breath.

"Anyway, my mum and dad were killed. They were driving to a wedding in Oxford, which was about two hours away. I was meant to go too, but at the last minute I didn't feel well so I stayed behind with a neighbour."

Matt stopped. Richard knew that he wasn't telling the whole truth about the wedding. He could see it. But he didn't interrupt.

"There was an accident," Matt continued. "A tyre burst while they were crossing a bridge. My dad lost control of the car and they went over the side and into the river. They were drowned." Matt paused. "The first thing I knew about it was when the police came to the house. I was only eight years old but I knew straight away.

"After that it's all quite jumbled. I spent quite a bit of time – it must have been three or four weeks – living in a sort of hostel. Everyone was trying to help but there was nothing anyone could do. The real trouble was that there was nobody to look after me. They tried to get in touch with my dad's family out in New Zealand but nobody wanted to know.

"And then my mum's one relation turned up. Gwenda Davis, from Ipswich. She was sort of my aunt. We met and she took me out for lunch. We went to a McDonald's. I remember that because my dad never let me eat fast food. He used to say it was the worst thing anyone could eat. Anyway, she bought me a burger and chips, and there we were, sitting in the middle of the noise and the plastic tables, with a big clown looking down at us, and she asked me if I wanted to move in with her. I said I didn't. But in the end what I wanted didn't make any difference because it had all been decided already. I moved in with her" – he paused – "and Brian."

Matt looked Richard straight in the eyes. "Promise me you won't write about this," he said.

"I've already said. I won't write about anything unless you let me."

"I won't let you. I don't want people to know."

"Go on, Matt…"

"Gwenda's house was really gross. It was terraced and it was half falling down and it had a tiny garden that was full of bottles. Brian was a milkman. The whole place smelled. All the pipes leaked, so the walls were damp and half the lights never worked. Gwenda and Brian had no money. At least, they had no money until I came along. But that's the point, you see. My mum and dad had left everything they owned to me, and Gwenda got control of the money. And of course she spent it. The whole lot."

Matt stopped. Richard could see him looking back into his own past. The hurt was right there, in his eyes.

"The money ran out pretty fast," he went on. "The two of them spent it on cars and holidays and that sort of thing. And when it was gone, that was when they turned nasty. Brian especially. He said it would have been better if I'd never come in the first place. He started finding fault with everything I did. He'd yell at me and I'd yell back. And then he started bashing me around a bit too. He was always careful not to leave bruises. Not ones that showed.

"And then I met Kelvin, who lived down the road from me, and he became my mate. Kelvin was always in trouble at school. He had a brother who was in prison and people were scared of him. But at least he was on my side – or that's what I thought. It felt good having him around.

"But in the end he only made things worse. I started missing a lot of school and even the teachers who'd been trying to help gave up on me. We used to go shoplifting together and of course we got caught, and that was when I had to start seeing a social worker. We used to take things from supermarkets. It wasn't even things we needed. We just got a buzz out of doing it. Kelvin used to like scratching new cars. He'd run his key ring up the paintwork … just for the hell of it. We did all sorts of stuff together. And then one day we broke into this warehouse to nick some DVDs and we were caught by a security guard. It was Kelvin who stabbed him, but it was my fault as much as his. I shouldn't have gone there. I shouldn't have been there. I just wish I'd tried to talk him out of it."

Matt rubbed his eyes.

"Anyway, you know the rest. I got arrested and I thought I'd be sent to prison, but in the end I didn't even have to go to court. They sent me to Lesser Malling as part of this thing called the LEAF Project. Liberty and Education … that was what it's meant to stand for. But since I arrived it's been more like Lunatics and Evil Freaks. I've already told you about Mrs Deverill and all the rest of it, and you didn't believe me. I suppose that's fair enough. I wouldn't have believed any of it either. Except I've had to live it. And what I told you, at the paper – it's all true."

"Why do you think she wants you?" Richard asked.

"I don't know. I haven't got the faintest idea. But I think I know what she is. I think I know what they all are."

"And what's that?"

"You'll laugh at me."

"No, I won't."

"I think they're witches."

Richard laughed.

"You saw the dogs!" Matt protested. "You think they came out of Battersea Dogs' Home? I saw how she made them. She sprinkled some sort of powder on the flames and they just appeared. It was like … magic!"

"It was an illusion," Richard said.

"Richard, this wasn't like something on TV. There wasn't a girl there in spangly sequins. I saw the dogs. They came out of the fire. And what about this?"

Matt was still wearing the stone talisman. He tore it off and threw it on to the table. The golden key lay face up in the light.

Richard looked at it. "Yeah. All right," he said. "Witches! Yorkshire used to be full of them, it's true. But that was five hundred years ago."

"I know. She's got a picture in her house … some sort of ancestor. And Mrs Deverill said she got burned. Maybe she was burned as a witch!" Matt thought for a moment. "If there were witches five hundred years ago, why can't there be witches now?"

"Because we've grown up. We don't believe in witches any more."

"I don't believe in witches. But the cat was killed and it came back. Tom Burgess died but I heard his voice on the phone. And there was a detective from Ipswich…"

"What?"

"His name was Mallory. He said he was going to help

me. He argued with Mrs Deverill. And the next thing I knew, he was dead too. He was killed on the motorway."

There was a brief silence. Then Richard spoke again.

"They're not witches, Matt," he said. "They may think they're witches. They may act like witches. They might have made you believe they're witches. But whatever's going on at Lesser Malling, it's real. It's something to do with the power station. And that's science, not magic."

"What about the dogs?"

"Genetically modified. Mutants. I don't know. Maybe they'd been exposed to some sort of radiation."

"So you don't believe in magic?"

"I enjoy Harry Potter, like everyone else. But do I believe in it? No."

Matt stood up. "I'm tired," he said. "I want to go to bed."

Richard nodded. "You can have the spare room upstairs."

The spare room was built into the roof of the house. It was filled with junk. Richard used it as a dumping ground for anything he no longer needed. Matt was lying on a sofa bed, tucked under a duvet and feeling warm and drowsy. He was gazing up at the ceiling that slanted over his head, when there was a knock at the door and Richard came in.

"I just wanted to check you were all right," he said.

"I'm fine." Matt turned on to his side to face him. "What are you going to do?" he asked. "How long can I stay here?"

"I don't know. A couple of days, maybe." Matt's face

fell. "I told you, Matt. You can't stay with me. It's just not right. I don't even know you. But I do want to help you." Richard sighed. "I must be crazy, because the last two people who tried to help seem to have ended up dead – and, personally, I had other plans. But at least we can take a look into Omega One. I mean, forget witches and all that stuff. The old power station seems to be at the heart of whatever it is that's going on."

"You said you knew the man who built it."

"I'll call him tomorrow. All right?"

Matt nodded.

"Goodnight then." Richard turned to go.

"Wait!" Matt said. "There was something I didn't tell you."

Richard hovered once again in the doorway.

"You said you wanted to know who I am, so you might as well know all of it. My mum always used to say I was strange. All my life, I've been involved in a lot of strange things. Mrs Deverill and all the rest of it … I sometimes think it was *meant* to happen. I'm meant to be here. I don't know why.

"The night before my mum and dad were killed, I had a bad dream. I often had dreams but this was something else. I saw the bridge. I saw the tyre burst. I even saw the water, flooding in through the windows, filling the car. It was like I was in the car with them and it was horrible. I couldn't breathe." He stopped. He had never told anyone this before. "And when I woke up the next morning, I knew they would

182

never get to the wedding. I knew the accident was going to happen exactly the way it did…"

Matt hesitated. This was the difficult part.

"My dad was like you. He didn't believe in stuff like witches and magic, and things he couldn't understand. I suppose it was because he was a doctor. And I knew that if I told him about my dream, he'd just get angry. It had happened before … once or twice, when I was very young. Dad would say I was just being silly, letting my imagination run away with me. And maybe he was right. That's what I told myself. *It's just a dream. It's just a dream. Everything's going to be all right. Don't get into trouble with Dad…*

"So I said nothing.

"But I was too scared to get in the car. I pretended I was ill. I threw a tantrum and made them leave me with Mrs Green, next door. I was only young. I didn't know what was going on. I still don't. But I know that I'm different. Sometimes I seem to be able to do things that are impossible. You won't believe me, Richard. But I can break a jug just by looking at it. I can do it! I *have* done it! I know when something bad is going to happen before it does. When I was in the warehouse, I *knew* the guard was there. And tonight! Maybe I managed to call to you – when I was in the bog – without opening my mouth. I don't know. It's like I've got some sort of power but I can't control it. It just flickers on and off by itself."

Matt yawned. Suddenly he was exhausted. He'd had enough.

183

"I told Mrs Green," he said. "I told her that my mum and dad weren't going to come back from the wedding. I told her about the tyre. I even knew about the bridge and the river underneath. She got very angry with me. She didn't want to hear all this stuff. And what was she meant to do? She couldn't ring my parents and tell them not to go to the wedding. In the end, she told me to go out and play in the garden. She didn't want to hear any more.

"I was still out in the garden when the police arrived. And I'll never forget the look on her face. She was horrified. More than that. She was actually sick. And it wasn't just because of what had happened to my parents. She was horrified and sick because of me.

"And the thing is, Richard, I didn't believe in magic either. I didn't believe in myself. And almost every hour of every day since then, I've asked myself why I didn't try to warn my mum and dad. I could have saved their lives. But I said nothing. I just let them drive off by themselves. Every day I've woken up knowing that I'm to blame. It's my fault they're no longer here."

Matt turned over and lay still.

Richard looked at the sleeping boy for a long time. Then he turned out the lights and crept quietly downstairs.

SCIENCE AND MAGIC

Matt woke up slowly and with a sense of reluctance. It had been the best sleep he'd had for weeks – and for once there had been no dreams.

It took him a few moments to get used to the unfamiliar surroundings and remember where he was. His eyes took in a slanting roof, a narrow window with the sun already shining brightly through, a box of old paperbacks and an alarm clock showing ten o'clock. Then he remembered the events of the previous night. The power station, the dogs, the chase through the wood. He had told Richard Cole everything, even the truth about the way his parents had died. For six years he had managed to live with the knowledge of what he'd done.

I could have warned them. I didn't.

And finally he had unburdened himself to a journalist who probably hadn't believed him anyway. He wished now that he hadn't. He felt embarrassed. He remembered how Richard had dismissed his theories about witchcraft and magic. It wasn't surprising. If it had been the other way round, he wouldn't have believed it himself.

And yet…

He knew what had happened. He had lived through it. The dogs *had* come out of the flames. Tom Burgess *had* died trying to warn him.

And then there was the question of his own powers.

He had seen the car accident that had killed his parents before it happened. It was the reason he was still alive. And there had been other things too. The jug of water that had smashed in the detention centre. And the night before, the way he had somehow managed to get Richard to stop his car.

Suppose…

Matt lay back against the pillows.

…suppose he did have some sort of special ability. The police report he had found in Mrs Deverill's bedroom had mentioned his precognitive abilities. By that they meant his ability to see the future. Somehow Mrs Deverill had got hold of a copy and that was why she wanted him. Not because of *who* he was. Because of *what* he was.

But that was ridiculous. Matt had seen *X-Men* and *Spider-Man* at the cinema. Superheroes. He even liked the comics. But was he really pretending that he had some sort of superpower too? He had never been bitten by a radioactive spider or zapped by a mad scientist inside a space machine. He was just an ordinary teenager who had got himself into trouble.

But he had broken the jug of water in the detention centre. He had gazed at it across the room and it had shattered.

There was a glass vase on the windowsill. It was about fifteen centimetres high, filled with pens and pencils. Matt found himself gazing at it. *All right. Why not?* He began to concentrate, breathing slowly and evenly, his back supported by the pillows. Without moving, he focused all his attention on the vase. He could do it. If he ordered the vase to smash itself, it would explode then and there. He had done it before. He would do it now. Then he would do it again for Richard, and after that the journalist would have to believe him.

He could feel the thought patterns emanating from his head. The vase filled his vision. *Break, damn you! Break!* He tried to imagine the glass blowing itself apart, as if by imagining it he could make it happen. But it didn't move. Matt was gritting his teeth now, holding his breath, desperately trying to make it break.

He stopped. His chest fell and he turned his head aside. Who did he think he was kidding? He wasn't an X-man. More like a zero kid.

There were new clothes piled at the bottom of the bed: jeans and a sweatshirt. Richard must have come in some time earlier that morning. And although he had threatened to throw them away, he'd also washed Matt's trainers. They were still damp but at least they were clean. Matt got dressed and went downstairs. He found Richard in the kitchen, boiling eggs.

"I was wondering when you'd get up," Richard said. "Did you sleep OK?"

"Yes, thanks. Where did you get the clothes?"

"There's a shop down the road. I had to guess your size."
He pointed at the bubbling saucepan. "I'm just making breakfast. Do you like your eggs hard or soft?"

"I don't mind."

"They've been in twenty minutes. I have a feeling they'll
be hard."

They sat down at the table and ate together. "So what
happens now?" Matt asked.

"Right now we have to be careful. Mrs Deverill and her
friends will be looking for you. They might even have called
the police and reported you missing, and if they find you with
me, we'll both be in trouble. You can't just pick up fourteen-
year-old kids these days and hang out with them. Not that
I intend to hang out with you. As soon as we've found out
what's going on, it's goodbye. No offence but there's only
room in this place for one."

"That's fine by me."

"Anyway, I've been busy. While you were asleep, I made
a few calls. The first one was to Sir Michael Marsh."

"The scientist."

"He's agreed to see us at half past eleven. After that,
we're going to Manchester."

"Why?"

"When you came to the newspaper office you told me
about a book you'd found in the library. Written by someone
called Elizabeth Ashwood. She's quite well known. This will
probably grab you, Matt. She writes about black magic and

witchcraft … that sort of stuff. We've got a file on her at the *Gazette* and I managed to get hold of one of our researchers. She gave me an address for her. No phone number, unfortunately. But we can drive over and see what she has to say."

"That's great," Matt said. "Thank you."

"Don't thank me. If this leads me to a story, I'll be the one thanking you."

"And if it doesn't?"

Richard thought for a moment. "I'll throw you back in the bog."

Sir Michael Marsh looked very much like the government scientist he had once been. He was elderly now, well into his seventies, but his eyes had lost none of their intelligence and seemed to demand respect. Although it was a Sunday morning, he was formally dressed in a dark suit with a white shirt and blue silk tie. His shoes were highly polished and his fingernails manicured. His hair had long ago turned silver but it was thick and well groomed. He was sitting with his legs crossed, one hand resting on his knee, listening to what his visitors had to say.

It was Richard who was talking. He was more smartly dressed than usual. He had shaved and put on a clean shirt and a jacket. Matt was next to him. The three of them were in a first-floor sitting room with large windows giving an uninterrupted view of the River Ouse. The house was Georgian, built to impress. There was something almost stage-like about the room, with its polished wooden desk, shelves of leather-bound books, marble fireplace and antique chairs. And Richard had been right about the matchbox label collection. There were hundreds of them, displayed in narrow glass cases on the walls. They had come from every country in the world.

Richard had given a very cut-down version of Matt's story. He hadn't told Sir Michael who Matt was or how he had arrived at Lesser Malling but had concentrated instead on the things Matt had seen at Omega One. At last Richard came to a halt. Matt waited to hear how Sir Michael would react.

"You say that there were electric lights at the power station," he began. "And the boy heard a humming sound?"

"Yes, sir."

"He saw a lorry. Unloading some sort of box?"

"Yes."

"And what conclusion have you drawn from all this, Mr Cole?"

"Matt couldn't see very much in the darkness, Sir Michael. But he said that the people carrying the box were wearing strange, bulky clothes. I wondered if they might have been radiation suits."

"You think that somebody is trying to start up Omega One?"

"It is a possibility."

"An impossibility, I'm afraid." He turned to Matt. "How much do you know about nuclear power, young man?"

"Not a lot," Matt answered.

"Well, let me tell you a bit about it. I'm sure you don't want a physics lesson, but you have to understand." Sir Michael thought for a moment. "We'll start with the nuclear bomb. You know, of course, what that is."

"Yes."

"A nuclear bomb contains devastating power. It can destroy an entire city as it did, in the last war, at Hiroshima. In tests in the Nevada Desert, a small nuclear bomb blew out a crater so deep, you could have fitted the Empire State Building into it. The power of the bomb is the energy released in the explosion. And that energy comes from splitting the atom. Are you with me so far?"

Matt nodded. If he had been at school his attention would have wandered already, but this time he was determined·to keep up.

"A nuclear power station works in much the same way. It splits the atom in a metal called uranium but instead of producing an explosion, which is uncontrolled, the energy is released gradually in the form of heat. The heat is fantastic. It turns water into steam, which then drives the turbines of an electricity generator and out comes electricity. That's all a nuclear power station does. It turns heat into electricity."

"What's wrong with coal?" Matt asked.

"Coal, gas, oil... They're all too expensive. And one day they'll run out. But uranium is incredible stuff. One tiny piece of it, a piece you could hold in your hand, has enough power to keep a million electric heaters running non-stop for twenty-four hours."

"Except it would kill you … if you held it in your hand," Richard added.

"Yes, Mr Cole. The radiation would indeed kill you. Which is why, when uranium is moved, it is carried in heavy, lead-lined boxes."

"Like the box I saw!" Matt said.

Sir Michael ignored him. "At the heart of any nuclear power station is a nuclear reactor," he continued. "The re-actor is basically a massive concrete box – and it is in here that our controlled explosion takes place. The uranium is surrounded by long sticks called control rods. When you lift up the control rods, the explosion starts. And the higher you lift them, the more powerful the explosion becomes.

"The reactor is the most dangerous part of the sta-tion. You have to remember what happened at Chernobyl, in Russia. One mistake here and you risk what is known as an excursion, an explosion which might kill hundreds or even thousands of people and which would destroy a vast area of land for years."

Was that what they were planning, Matt wondered. Did Mrs Deverill and the other villagers want to commit some sort of act of terrorism? No. It made no sense. If that was the case, what did they want with him?

Sir Michael Marsh continued. "When the government began to think about building nuclear stations, fifty years ago, they set up a number of experimental stations where they could study reactors in action and make sure they were safe. Omega One was the first of these experiments and I helped design and build it. It ran for less than eighteen months. And after we'd finished with it, we shut it down and left it to rot in the pine forest that surrounds it."

"Maybe someone wants to get it running again," Richard persisted.

"They couldn't – for all sorts of reasons." Sir Michael sighed. "Let's start with the uranium. As I'm sure you know, you can't just buy uranium. Even dictators in countries like Iraq have found it impossible to get supplies. Let's suppose these villagers of yours owned a uranium mine. It still wouldn't help. How would they process the stuff? Where would they get the technical know-how and the resources?"

"But Matt saw something…"

"He saw a box. For all we know, it could have contained a picnic." Sir Michael glanced at his watch. "I last visited Omega One about twenty years ago," he said. "And there's nothing left inside. We removed anything that could possibly be dangerous when we dismantled the place. It was quite a job, I can tell you, transporting everything out of the wood."

"Why did you build it there?" Richard asked.

The scientist seemed momentarily thrown. "I beg your pardon?"

"Why did you build it in the middle of a wood?"

"Well, it had to be somewhere out of the way. And

there's an underground river that runs through the wood. That was the main reason. A nuclear power station requires a constant supply of water, you see."

There was nothing more to be said.

"I'm sorry, Sir Michael," Richard said, as he got to his feet. "It seems that we've been wasting your time."

"Not at all. I've found what you and your young friend had to tell me most disturbing. At the very least, it would seem that somebody is trespassing on what is still government property and I shall certainly contact the appropriate authorities." He stood up. "Personally I wanted to knock the building down when we'd finished with it, but it was too expensive. As the minister put it, nature is the best demolition expert. However, let me assure you, you probably couldn't spark a decent fire in that damp old place, let alone a nuclear reaction."

Sir Michael showed them to the door. But before he opened it, he turned to Matt. "Are you interested in phillumeny?" he asked.

"In what?" Matt didn't know what he was talking about.

"The collecting of matchbox labels. I have almost a thousand of them." He pointed at a case on the wall. "The Tekka brand, made in India. And those are Russian. I think it rather wonderful that anything so ordinary can be so beautiful."

He opened the door.

"Do let me know how you get on," he said. "And I'll call when I've spoken to the police and tell you if there's any news."

*　*　*

Elizabeth Ashwood, the author of *Rambles Around Greater Malling*, lived in Didsbury, a suburb of Manchester. The address that Richard had been given took them to a detached house in a wide, leafy street. A gate and a path led through a garden that was perfectly neat, with an array of spring flowers. On the front door was a knocker shaped like a hand. Richard lifted it and let it fall. A hollow boom echoed through the house, and a minute later the door opened.

A thin, dark-haired woman stood there, not looking at them but past them, her eyes covered by two circles of black glass. Matt guessed she must be about thirty-five. He had never met a blind person before. He wondered what it must be like, living in perpetual night.

"Yes?" she asked impatiently.

"Hi." Richard smiled, unnecessarily. She couldn't see him, of course. "Are you Elizabeth Ashwood?" he asked.

"I am Susan Ashwood. Elizabeth was my mother."

"Was?" Richard couldn't keep the disappointment out of his voice.

"She died a year ago."

So that was it. They had come all this way for nothing. Matt was ready to turn round and go back to the car, but suddenly the woman spoke again. "Who are you?"

"My name is Richard Cole. I'm a journalist from the *Greater Malling Gazette* in Yorkshire."

"There are two of you."

195

"Yes."

How had she known? Matt hadn't made any sound.

"A boy…" Her hand reached out and somehow caught hold of Matt's arm. "Where have you come from?" she demanded. "Why are you here?"

Matt squirmed, embarrassed to be held by her. "I've come from Lesser Malling," he said. "We wanted to know about a book your mother wrote."

"Come into the house," the woman said. "I can help you. But you must come in."

Matt glanced at Richard, who shrugged. The two of them went inside.

Miss Ashwood led them into a wide, airy corridor. The house was Victorian but had been carefully modernized with oak floors, concealed lighting and floor-to-ceiling windows. There were paintings on the walls – mainly expensive abstracts. Matt couldn't help wondering for whose benefit they were, since the owner couldn't see them. Of course, it was always possible that the woman had a husband and family. And yet at the front door he had got the impression that this was someone who was always alone.

She led them into a living room with low leather sofas and gestured at them to sit down. A polished grand piano, brilliant black, stood in the corner.

"Which of my mother's books brought you all this way?" she asked.

"It was a book about Lesser Malling," Richard said.

Matt decided to cut straight to the point. "We need to know about Raven's Gate."

The woman became very still. It was hard to read her emotions behind the black glasses but Matt could sense her excitement. "So you've found me…" she whispered.

"Do you know what it is?"

Susan Ashwood made no reply. The two black circles were fixed on Matt and he felt uncomfortable, wanting to move. He knew she could see nothing at all and wished she wouldn't stare at him in this way. "Is your name Matt?" she enquired.

"Yes."

"How did you know that?" Richard asked.

"I knew you would come," Miss Ashwood said. She was ignoring Richard. All her attention was focused on Matt. "I knew you would find me. It was meant to happen this way. I'm just glad you've arrived in time."

"What are you talking about?" Richard was getting angry. "I think we're at cross purposes," he went on. "We came to see your mother…"

"I know. She told me you'd seen her book."

"I thought you said she was dead?"

For the first time she turned to Richard. "You don't know who I am?"

"Sure." Richard shrugged at Matt. "You're Susan Ashwood."

"You haven't heard of me?"

"I don't mean to be rude, but should I have? Are you

famous? What do you do? Do you play the piano?"

By way of an answer, the woman fumbled on a table beside the sofa. She picked up a business card and handed it to Richard. He turned it over and read:

Susan Ashwood ....
.... *Psychic & spiritualist*

A link with the other side

"You're a medium."

"What?" Matt asked.

"Miss Ashwood talks to ghosts," Richard explained. "Or that's what she believes."

"I talk to the dead in just the same way that I am talking to you now. And if you could hear them, you would know that there is a great upheaval in the spirit world. Terrible things are about to happen. Indeed they are already happening. That is what brought you here to my house."

"What brought me to your house," Richard said, "was the M62 motorway from Leeds. And it looks to me like I was wasting my time." He stood up. "Let's go, Matt!"

"If you leave this room without hearing what I have to say, you will be making the greatest mistake of your life."

"That's what *you* say!"

"You are involved in something bigger and more incredible than anything you could imagine. Like it or not, you have begun a journey without knowing it, and there can be no going back."

"I'm going back right now," Richard said.

"You can make light of it, but you have no idea what is happening. I feel sorry for you, Mr Cole. Because, you see, there are two worlds. The world you understand and the world you don't. These worlds exist side by side, sometimes only centimetres apart, and the great majority of people spend their entire lives in one without being aware of the other. It's like living on one side of a mirror: you think there is nothing on the other side until one day a switch is thrown and suddenly the mirror is transparent. You see the other side. That was what happened to you the day you heard about Raven's Gate. Nothing can be the same for you any more. It's as I say. You have begun a journey. You must continue to the end."

"What exactly is Raven's Gate?" Matt asked.

"I can't tell you. I know how unreasonable it must sound, but you have to understand." Miss Ashwood took a deep breath. "I belong to an organization," she continued. "I suppose you might say we're a secret society. But I'd put it another way. I'd say we were a society that looks after secrets."

"You mean ... like MI6?" Richard muttered.

"We call ourselves the Nexus, Mr Cole. And if you knew more about us, who we are, what we represent, perhaps you'd be a little less sarcastic. But as much as I want to, I can't speak to you on my own. You have to come with me to London. There's a man you must meet. His name is Professor Sanjay Dravid."

"Dravid!" Matt knew the name. He'd heard it somewhere before.

"This is ridiculous," Richard insisted. "Why do you have to drag us all the way to London? Why can't you tell us what we want to know here and now?"

"Because I swore an oath that I would never talk about this with anyone. We all did. However, if you come with me to London, if you meet the Nexus, then we can help you. You want to learn about Raven's Gate? We'll tell you everything you want to know … and more."

"And how much money will it cost us to join this Nexus?" Richard demanded.

Miss Ashwood sat upright in her chair and Matt could sense how angry she was. Her fists were clenched. When she spoke, her voice was utterly cold. "I know what you think of me," she began. "You imagine I'm some sort of con artist. I sit in this house and I try to frighten people, to cheat them out of money. I call myself a psychic so I must be a fraud. I tell stories about ghosts and spirits, and weak, gullible people believe me." She paused. "But the boy understands," she continued. She turned to face Matt. "You believe me, don't you, Matt? You know about magic. I felt your power the moment you came here. I have never felt such strength before."

"Where is Professor Dravid?" Matt asked.

"In London. I told you. If you won't come with me, at least give me your telephone number. Let him speak with you."

"I'm not giving my number to anyone," Richard said. "And I don't care what you say, Miss Ashwood. We came here with a simple question. If you're not going to give us an answer, we might as well leave."

"Professor Dravid is at the Natural History Museum in South Kensington. That's where you'll find him."

"Sure. We'll send you a postcard." Richard stood up and more or less dragged Matt out of the room.

The car was parked opposite the house. They got in and Richard searched in his pockets for the keys. Matt could see that he was rattled.

"Actually, a man called Dravid contacted me," he said.

"What?"

"When I was at the library in Greater Malling. I was on the Internet and he popped up. You know … in a pop-up window."

"What did he say?"

"I was doing a search on Raven's Gate and he wanted to know why."

"What did you tell him?"

"I didn't tell him anything."

"Well you can forget about seeing him." Richard had found the key. He started the car and they drove off. "We're not going to London, Matt. I can't believe I drove all the way here from York just to talk to a woman who was obviously out of her tree. You're not going to tell me you believed her, are you?"

Matt looked back and watched as the house disappeared behind them. "I wonder..." he said.

UNNATURAL HISTORY

The taxi dropped them off at the Natural History Museum in west London. Richard paid the fare.

"I don't know how I let you talk me into this," he said.

"I didn't say anything," Matt protested.

"You were the one who wanted to see Dravid."

"You were the one who called him."

It was true. When they had got back to York, Richard had checked Dravid out on the Internet. It turned out that the professor had an international reputation. Born in the Indian city of Madras, he had become a world expert on anthropology, ethnology, prehistory and a dozen other related areas. He had written books and presented television programmes. There were over a hundred web sites featuring his name, the most recent of which concerned an exhibition about dinosaurs. It was opening at the museum in less than a week's time. Dravid had organized it and written the catalogue.

In the end Richard had decided to call him. He'd expected to be given the brush-off. Perhaps he'd even hoped that would happen. But Dravid had been eager to meet them.

They'd made an appointment for the following day – at six o'clock, after the museum closed.

Matt examined the grand Victorian building. It looked like something out of a fairy tale with its terracotta and blue bricks, its Gothic towers and its menagerie of carved stone animals poking out of every nook and corner. There was a stream of people pouring out of the main entrance, down the curved walkways, past the line of wrought-iron lamps and on to the lawns on either side.

"Let's go in," Richard said.

They went up to the gate, where a security guard stood, blocking their way. "I'm very sorry," he said. "You're too late for today…"

"We have an appointment with Professor Dravid," Richard told him.

"Professor Dravid? Yes, sir. Of course. You can ask at the enquiries desk."

They climbed the steps and went in. There were certainly plenty of dinosaurs. As Matt entered the museum he was greeted by the black skull of a huge creature. The skull was at the end of an elongated neck, suspended from an arch that swept over the entrance. He looked around him. The dinosaur skeleton was the centrepiece in a vast hall which – with its many arches, its glass and steel roof, its broad staircase and mosaic floor – looked like a cross between a cathedral and a railway station.

They went to the enquiries desk, which, like the rest of

the museum, was just closing.

"My name is Richard Cole. I'm here to see Professor Dravid."

"Ah, yes. The professor is expecting you. His office is on the first floor."

A second guard pointed at a stone staircase that led up to a balcony overlooking the main entrance hall. They walked towards it, passing many other dinosaur skeletons, some in glass cases, others standing free. A few last remaining visitors went by, on their way out. The museum seemed bigger and somehow more mysterious now that it was empty. They climbed the stone stairs and continued along a corridor to a solid wooden door. Richard knocked and they went in.

Professor Sanjay Dravid was sitting in the middle of a room stacked high with books, magazines, files and loose bundles of paper. The walls were covered with charts, graphs and maps. He was typing something into a laptop, working at a desk which was itself crowded with more papers, dozens of specimens in glass cases, bits of bone, and pieces of crystal and stone. He was in his late forties, Matt thought. His hair was black and neatly brushed and he had dark, tired eyes. His jacket hung over the back of his chair.

"Professor Dravid?" Richard asked.

The man looked up. "You're Richard Cole?" He finished typing his sentence, pressed ENTER and closed the laptop. "Susan Ashwood telephoned me after she met you." His voice was warm and cultured. "I'm glad you decided to get in touch."

"How do you know Miss Ashwood?"

"We've known each other for many years." Dravid turned to Matt, examining him minutely. "You must be Matt. Nobody's told me your full name."

"I'm just Matt."

"Well, please sit down. I'm sorry I can't offer you any refreshments. There is a café here, although of course it's closed now. But perhaps you ate on the train..."

Richard and Matt sat down in front of the desk. "What's the exhibition about?" Richard asked.

"It is without question the most remarkable exhibition of dinosaur fossils ever assembled in London," Dravid replied. "You saw the diplodocus as you came in?" He spoke very quickly and all the time his eyes never once left Matt. Matt could feel himself being weighed up, assessed. "Very hard to miss it. It's about one hundred and fifty million years old and probably the longest land animal that ever lived. Shipped all the way from the United States, bone by bone, just for the exhibition. And then there's a first-rate ceratosaurus – a recent find. It would tear you apart in seconds if it were still alive. And then there are the museum's own specimens, including a virtually intact paracyclotosaurus skeleton. It resembles a crocodile, although in fact it's no relation."

He stopped suddenly.

"But of course that's not why you're here."

"We want to know about Raven's Gate," Richard said.

"So Miss Ashwood told me."

"She wouldn't tell us anything. She said we had to meet you."

"Do you know what it is?" Matt asked.

"Raven's Gate? Yes, I do."

"Can you tell us?"

"That depends. I'm not entirely sure…"

Matt ran out of patience. "Why is it that nobody wants to help me?" he demanded. "You sit here, tapping away at your laptop and talking about dinosaurs. You don't know what I've been through. I've been dumped in Yorkshire. I've been pushed around and terrorized, and the only people who have tried to help me have ended up dead. Richard doesn't want me hanging around with him, and now we've come all the way down here and you're not saying anything either. You were the one who wanted to see us. Why won't you tell us what we want to know?"

"He's right," Richard agreed. "We've spent hours on a train to King's Cross, not to mention the price of the tickets. You've got to make it worth our while."

Dravid had sat silently through all this. Now he looked at Matt more carefully. "Matt… I take it you were the boy on the Internet."

"In the library at Greater Malling. Yes." Matt nodded. "How did you know I was searching for Raven's Gate?"

"Thanks to a simple piece of software. Whenever anyone, anywhere in the world, enters those two words, I am informed at once."

"Why?"

"I can't tell you that. Yet. And I apologize for mistrusting you, Matt. We live in a world with so many dangers that we have to be careful whom we trust. Please bear with me for a moment. There are things I need to ask you." He paused. "You were in Greater Malling. Is that where you live?"

"No. I'm living in Lesser Malling. It's a village—"

"I know Lesser Malling," Dravid interrupted. "How long have you been there?"

"I don't know. Two or three weeks."

Dravid pressed his hands together underneath his chin. "You must tell me everything," he said. "I want to know everything that has happened to you. I need to know exactly what brought you to me here today." He leant back in his chair. "Begin at the beginning and don't leave anything out."

There was only one guard on night shift at the museum. There should have been four but, like many of London's institutions, a shortage of funds had led to cutbacks. Two of the men had been laid off and one was sick. The one remaining guard was in his twenties. He had only recently come to England, from Bulgaria. He didn't speak much of the language but he was learning. He liked London, although he could have done without the job.

He found it creepy patrolling the museum. There were all the dinosaur bones … they were bad enough. But the creatures in the glass cases were even more horrible: stuffed rats and leopards, eagles and owls. Spiders and scorpions and huge winged beetles. He could feel their eyes following him as he did his rounds. He should have got a job at McDonald's or KFC. The pay would have been only fractionally worse.

He had just come out of the main door and was walking towards the gate when he heard a soft sound like the breaking of a twig. What now? It was getting dark and there was no moon tonight.

"Who is it?" he called out.

He looked up and smiled to himself, turning the torch off again. One of the ornate lamps, illuminated for the night, had blown a bulb. That was what he had heard.

"I am scared," he muttered to himself. It was a phrase he had learned at foreign-language school only the day before. "You are scared. He is scared."

A second bulb blinked out. Then a third and a fourth. Rapidly the darkness made its way along the whole line of lamps, squeezing the life out of the bulbs until none of them remained alight. The guard rubbed his shoulders. It suddenly felt much colder. He breathed out and saw his own breath frost. It was crazy. It was almost the end of April but it seemed that winter had just returned.

He pressed the switch of his torch. The bulb exploded in his hand, grey smoke curling beneath the glass. That was when the guard decided to call it a night. The museum had its own sophisticated alarm system. It could look after itself. And if he was fired, what did he care? He could always get that job at KFC.

The guard unlocked the gate and scurried through, then crossed the road, dodging the traffic through to South Kensington tube station. He didn't see the shadows reaching out to enclose the museum or the soft, white mist that trickled over the grass. All he knew was that he wanted to get away. He didn't once look back.

Matt finished his story. He shivered in the sudden cold but neither Richard nor the professor seemed to notice it.

"Well, what do you think?" Richard asked.

Professor Dravid turned on his desk lamp. "It's almost impossible to believe," he said. "From a warehouse in Ipswich to Lesser Malling and then to here. Nobody would believe it. Even to you it must seem incomprehensible. But let me tell you straight away, Matt, that you are *meant* to be here. There are no coincidences. It's all happening the way it was meant to be."

"But what *is* happening?" Matt asked. "What are Mrs Deverill and the rest of them doing in Lesser Malling? What is Raven's Gate?"

"We're not leaving until you tell us," Richard added.

"Of course I will tell you." Dravid looked at Matt and there was something strange in his eyes; a sense of puzzlement and wonder. It was as if Dravid had been waiting to meet him all his life.

"If I told anybody else what I'm about to tell you now,"

he began, "my reputation – everything I've worked for – would disappear overnight. It makes no sense. Not in the real world, anyway. Susan Ashwood may have seemed eccentric to you. You might have thought she was a fraud. However, I'm telling you she was right. There *is* another world. We are surrounded by it. There is an alternative history as alive in the streets of twenty-first-century London as it was many thousands of years ago, when it all began. But only cranks and lunatics are meant to believe in it because, you see, that way everyone feels safer...

"Raven's Gate is at the very heart of that alternative history. Few people have even heard of it. Look for it on the Internet, as you did, and you won't find anything. But that doesn't make it any less real. It is the reason why you are here now. It may even be the reason why you were born."

Dravid stopped. The room seemed to be getting darker and darker. The desk lamp had only pushed back the shadows a little way. They were still there, waiting.

"Raven's Gate was the name given to a strange circle of stones that stood, until the Middle Ages, outside Lesser Malling. It was mentioned by name in Elizabeth Ashwood's book – the only occasion, to my knowledge, that it has ever appeared in print. Standing stones are by no means unique to Lesser Malling. There are at least six hundred examples in Britain. The most famous of them is Stonehenge in Wiltshire.

"You have to remember how mysterious all these stone circles are. Consider Stonehenge. No one is quite certain why it was built. There must have been a purpose. After all, it took a million and a half man-hours to construct. The stones, some of them weighing up to fifty tons, were carried all the way across England, and actually constructing the circle required a fantastic knowledge of engineering. Obviously it wasn't put there just for decoration.

"Some say that Stonehenge is a temple. Some say it's a sort of stone computer or even a magical tape recorder. Some believe it's an observatory and that it can calculate the exact time of a solar eclipse. There are dozens of different theories. But the thing is, even in the twenty-first century, with all our knowledge and science, nobody knows for sure."

"But *you* know," Richard said.

Dravid nodded gravely. "Yes." He leant forward. "Stonehenge is four or five thousand years old. But it wasn't by any means the first stone circle ever built. In fact it was nothing more than a copy of one that had been around a lot longer. Raven's Gate was the first stone circle and all the later ones were nothing more than imitations."

"But where is it?" Matt asked. "What happened to it?"

"A great many of the stone circles in Britain have been destroyed over the years. Some were pulled down by farmers who needed the land for agriculture. The spread of towns and cities finished off others. A few simply collapsed or crumbled away over the years.

"But something very strange happened to Raven's Gate. At some time in the Middle Ages it was deliberately taken down and smashed. More than that. Each and every one of its stones was ground to powder. The powder was loaded on to carts and carried to the four corners of Britain: north, south, east and west. Then it was poured into the sea. Something about the circle seemed so frightening, so evil, that the people who set about this fantastic task were determined that every grain should be separated. Nobody ever spoke of it again. It was as if Raven's Gate had never existed."

"So how did you hear of it?" Richard asked. It seemed to Matt that he still sounded doubtful.

"You're a journalist, Mr Cole. You obviously think that if something hasn't been written down, then it can't possibly be true. Well, there have been some written records. The diary of a Spanish monk. A carving on a temple. A few letters and other documents. And of course there has always been a strong oral tradition. How did I hear of it?" Dravid half-smiled but his eyes were dark and serious. "I belong to an organization – you might call it a secret society – and we have kept the story alive for centuries. We have passed it from generation to generation.

"That society is called the Nexus."

There was a jug of water on the desk. Dravid reached out and poured himself a glass. He drank half of it, then continued.

"There are twelve members of the Nexus, as there always have been. Incidentally, a nexus means a connection – and we are, I suppose, connected by what we know. Susan Ashwood is a member and there are ten others apart from myself from all over the world. In due course you will meet them, Matt. They will certainly want to meet you. The whole purpose of the Nexus, the reason that it exists, is to help you with what you have to do."

"What do I have to do?" Matt asked. "You're talking about stuff that happened thousands of years ago. Why are you telling me this now?"

"I'm about to explain. But it isn't easy. I can understand how hard it must be for you to take all this on board."

Professor Dravid finished his water while he collected his thoughts.

"There are some who believe that a great civilization existed on this planet before the Greek empire of 600 BC. Even before the Egyptians, who had flourished two thousand years earlier. I'm talking about the time of Atlantis, perhaps as long ago as ten thousand years. In a way, I suppose, I'm talking about the beginning of the world as we know it today.

"This first civilization was destroyed ... slowly and deliberately. Creatures of unimaginable power and evil arrived in the world. They were called the Old Ones and their only desire was to see pain and misery all around them. The Christian Church talks about Satan, Lucifer and all the other devils. But these are just memories of the greatest, original evil: the Old Ones. They thrived on chaos. Once they had gained a foothold on the planet, they started a war. Torturing, killing, spreading mass destruction everywhere they went. That was their only pleasure. If they'd had their way, they would have reduced

214

the whole world to an empty swamp.

"But according to the stories, there was a miracle, and it arrived in the shape of five young people: four boys and a girl.

"Nobody knows where they came from. They have no names. They have never been described. But together they organized the resistance against the Old Ones. What was left of humanity joined together behind the Five and there was a single, final battle in which the future of the world would be decided.

"The five children won that battle. The Old Ones were expelled, sent to another dimension, and a barrier, a magical gate, was built to make sure they could never come back. This gate took the form of a stone circle and later on it came to be known as Raven's Gate."

"Wait a minute," Richard cut in. "You said Raven's Gate was destroyed because it was evil."

"I said it was destroyed because the people *thought* it was evil," the professor corrected him. "They were mistaken. They gave it a name, Raven's Gate, because the raven has always been associated with death. They had a memory that connected the stones with something horrible... But after all the years that had passed, they had forgotten what it was. And in the end they came to think that it was the stones themselves that were evil. So they tore them down."

"So the gate was destroyed!" Matt exclaimed.

Professor Dravid shook his head. "The *stones* were

destroyed, not the gate," he said. "How can I explain it to you? It's like an idea. If you write something down on a sheet of paper and then burn the paper, do you burn the idea? Of course not! The stones are gone, but the gate is still in place."

Richard sighed. "Let me get this straight, Professor," he said. "A very long time ago, the world was ruled by evil creatures called the Old Ones. However, five kids appeared and threw them out. These kids then built a barrier, which came to be known as Raven's Gate. Unfortunately the stones that marked the gate were knocked down by medieval peasants who didn't know any better. But it doesn't matter that much because the gate is still there after all. Is that about it?"

"Your sarcasm does you no credit, Mr Cole," Dravid replied. "But you have summed up what I said more or less accurately."

"Miss Ashwood knew about this?" Matt said.

"Yes. As I explained to you, we share our knowledge. We have sworn not to reveal it. That's why she couldn't tell you anything when you met."

"But you've told us," Matt went on. "You said that the main reason for the Nexus was to help me with something I have got to do. But I'm still not clear what that is – or what any of this has got to do with me."

"I think you know."

"No!" Matt looked him in the eye. "You're wrong."

"Then you must meet the Nexus. The other members are

on their way back to London. They'll be here tomorrow night. I'll look after you until then."

"Forget it," Richard said. "We've got day-return tickets. We're going back to York this evening."

"That's the last thing you must do. It's vital you don't go anywhere near Lesser Malling." He turned again to Matt. "I don't want to frighten you any more than you have been already, but I believe you are in terrible danger."

"Why?"

"I've told you why Raven's Gate was built. It was a barrier between two worlds and it was closed and locked. But for many centuries there have been people who have been trying to open it again. Of course, they haven't found it easy. They've had to develop special knowledge ... special powers."

"You mean magic," Matt said.

"We are just two days away from the start of Roodmas," Dravid said. "It begins at sunset on the thirtieth of April. It is one of the most important days in the witches' calendar. A day when dark powers are at their strongest. When black sabbath is celebrated and evil has its way."

"Mrs Deverill..." Matt began.

"I have absolutely no doubt that she and the other villagers of Lesser Malling are involved in some sort of black magic. Of course you will sneer, Mr Cole. But black magic is still practised today all over the world. Yorkshire has a long history of witchcraft – and although the witches of medieval times are gone, their descendants live on.

"A black sabbath on Roodmas will require three ingredients, the same as you will find in any such ceremony. The first is ritual. Matt has already described the whispers that he heard. The second is fire. You saw the dogs rise out of the flames. But the third, of course, is blood. They must have a sacrifice, and the best sacrifice of all would be that of a child..."

Matt stood up. All the colour had drained from his face. "They brought me there to kill me," he said.

"I'm afraid so."

"We should go to the police!" Richard exclaimed. "You're talking about a bunch of lunatics, and the whole lot of them ought to be locked up..."

"Matt has already been to the police," Dravid reminded him. "Two of them ignored him. The one who didn't, died."

"Why me?" Matt asked. "Why did they choose me? Why couldn't it be someone else?"

"I think you know the answer to that," Dravid said quietly. He stopped and laid a hand gently on Matt's shoulder. "I'm sorry. I know how hard it must be for you to accept all this. But you'll have time. I'll put you in a hotel tonight. The Nexus will take care of the cost. And from now on, we'll look after you."

"Why? What do *you* want from me?"

"We just want you to be safe."

"I wish it wasn't so cold," Matt said.

The three of them left the study. They went along the corridor past a row of glass cases. Wax figurines of primitive

218

people stared out at them. The sound of their footsteps echoed against the ceiling, flapping about the air like invisible birds. Halfway down the main staircase, Dravid stopped. "The keys!" he said. "They're in my jacket! I'll need them to let us out."

Hastily he stumbled back up the staircase and along the corridor. Matt watched him. It was only now that he realized how vast the museum was. Professor Dravid was just a tiny figure, crossing a balcony high above them. They saw the door of the study open and the light go on.

"Listen, Matt," Richard said. "This is all just a bad dream. Nothing can happen to you."

Matt stepped back from him. "You still don't believe it!" he exclaimed.

"Yeah – sure I believe in it. Old Ones and gates and witches and blood sacrifice! Look around you, for heaven's sake! There are rockets going to Mars. We've got satellites beaming phone conversations all around the world. They've unlocked the genetic code. And you've still got throwbacks like Dravid going on about devils and demons. Well take it from me, Matt. These five kids saving the world with magical powers don't exist."

"Of course they exist," Matt said. And suddenly he knew. It was very simple. "I'm one of them."

There was a sound. Something invisible had been thrown – or had flown – through the air. Matt and Richard heard someone cry out and looked back at the stairs. Sanjay Dravid had appeared again. He was walking slowly, his footsteps uneven, as if he was drunk or drugged. His hand was clasped to his neck. He stopped and let his hand fall and, with a gasp of horror, Matt saw a terrible wound – a gaping, horizontal line, perhaps cut with a sword – across the professor's neck. Blood curtained down, soaking into his jacket and shirt. Dravid raised his hands feebly. He tried to speak. Then he toppled forward on to his face and lay still.

Richard swore. Matt tore his eyes away from the motionless figure and looked at the main doors on the other side of the gallery. It was colder than ever. Even without seeing it, he knew there was danger all around.

And the doors were locked.

BONES

For what seemed like an eternity Richard and Matt stood where they were, staring at the still figure lying at the top of the stairs. Blood was spreading around Dravid's head. But there was no sign of an attacker. The museum was as empty and silent as it had been when they first came in. And there was something else. The air was icy and seemed to have thickened. It had a white, smoky quality, like a bad photograph.

Richard was the first to recover. "Wait here!" he said, then bounded forward towards the stairs.

"Where are you going?" Matt called after him.

"The keys!"

He took the steps two at a time, not wanting to get any closer to Dravid but knowing there was no other way. The blood had reached the edge of the first step and was already trickling down. Richard knelt down beside the body, trying not to look at the horrible wound. Then suddenly Dravid opened his eyes. Miraculously he was still alive.

"Five…" The single word was all he could manage.

"Don't say anything. I'll get help." Richard didn't know

what else to say. He was lying. The professor was far beyond help.

Dravid extended a trembling hand, which clasped a ring of keys. Richard took them gently. For a moment the two of them looked into each other's eyes. Dravid tried to speak again but it was too much for him. He coughed painfully. Then his head fell back and his eyes closed.

Holding the keys, Richard stood up. He could see Matt below him, some distance away, and knew what he was thinking. Right now there was a killer inside the museum. Someone – or something – had attacked Professor Dravid and they would surely be next. But what were they up against? Why couldn't they see anything? Moving slowly now, Richard went back down the stairs, his every sense alert. The two of them were so small in this enormous place. He felt horribly exposed.

"Did you get them?" Matt asked.

"Yes." Richard held up the keys. "Let's get out of here."

"What about Professor Dravid?"

"He's dead. I'm sorry. There's nothing we can do."

"But what killed him?"

"I don't know." Richard gazed upwards, his eyes sweeping across the vaulted ceiling. "But let's not stay to find out."

He turned and at that moment there was a sudden whirl in the air. Matt threw a protective arm across his face and staggered into Richard.

"What's wrong?" Richard demanded.

"There was something…" Matt looked around him but

there was nothing there. "Something flew near my head," he insisted.

"Flew?"

"Yes."

"Did you see what it was?"

"No. But I sensed it. It came so close… I felt it go past."

"I can't see anything."

But then it dived towards them again, sweeping down out of the mist, and this time there could be no mistaking it, even if it took Matt precious seconds to work it out. Triangular and white, the creature was neither living nor dead, coming at them like something out of a hideous dream. It had eye sockets but no eyes, wings but no feathers, a bulging ribcage with nothing inside. Moving faster than ever, almost a blur, it shot down. Its claws were stretched out and its needle-sharp teeth were bared in an evil grimace. Matt fell back. He felt one of the wings shudder past his face and knew that if he had waited a second longer he would have been decapitated. Now he understood what had happened to Professor Dravid.

Richard reached down and helped him up. "Did you see it?" he muttered.

"Of course I did."

"You saw what it was?"

"Yes!"

"What?"

"I don't know." Matt had recognized it but he couldn't put it into words.

"It's a trick," Richard said. "It has to be a trick. It wasn't real."

They had been attacked by something that couldn't fly, that couldn't even exist. It was a creature that hadn't been seen on the planet for many millions of years. A pterodactyl. Except that it wasn't quite a pterodactyl. It was the fossilized skeleton of a pterodactyl, wired together and put on display at the Natural History Museum. It had been brought to life and now it was somewhere above them.

"Look out!"

Matt shouted the warning as the pterodactyl swooped down a third time, plummeting out of the gloomy heights of the hall and hurtling towards them. He had no doubt that the claws would rip his flesh away if he allowed them to make contact. The creature was as vicious as it had been when it had flown over the prehistoric world. It was being guided, being used as an impossible weapon. Its head and claws missed Matt by centimetres and he thought he had escaped. But as it went past, one of its wing tips brushed his face and he felt a searing pain as the bone cut into him. He gasped and put a hand to his cheek. There was blood on his palm. The pterodactyl performed an aerial somersault and soared back the way it had come. There had been no noise, no warning. Nothing. The museum was utterly silent.

"Matt…" Richard began. There was panic in his eyes.

"I'm OK," Matt said, his hand still pressed against his cheek.

"You've been cut."

"I don't think it's deep."

Richard craned his neck, staring up at the ceiling. "We've got to go."

Matt grimaced. "I wasn't thinking of staying."

He had barely spoken the words before the pterodactyl was back. This time Richard was the target. The outstretched wing slashed through the air. It was as sharp as a sword. Richard cursed.

"Richard..." For a dreadful moment Matt thought he'd been hit.

"It's OK. It missed me. It's gone."

"Yes. But what about the others?"

"What...?"

Professor Dravid had called it the most remarkable exhibition of dinosaur fossils ever seen in London. The pterodactyl was only one of them. There were dozens more all around them. Richard and Matt were standing in the middle of an X-ray version of *Jurassic Park*.

Even as Richard realized the true nature of the danger, there was an explosion as one of the display cases, just a few metres away from them, burst apart. There had been a skeleton inside it, held up by a steel frame, but now it broke free and came lumbering out. It was hard to see anything clearly in the mist and the darkness but Matt could just about make out something that resembled a crocodile, long and narrow, with short, squat legs holding it just above the floor. It had thrown itself forward, smashing through the glass in a sudden, silent frenzy. The one thing it couldn't do was roar. It had no lungs. But its feet – bones without flesh – made a bizarre sound as they clacked against the mosaic floor. It was charging at them, its mouth gaping, its black teeth snapping at the air. Its tail thrashed behind it, scattering the fragments of what had once been its home.

The pterodactyl dived for a fifth time, its pointed beak aimed at Matt's head. With a cry he threw himself on to the floor, then rolled over and over again, avoiding the crocodile creature that had accelerated towards him, its jaws snapping. How could it even see, Matt wondered, with eye sockets that were completely empty? But it didn't hesitate. It turned round and came at him again. Matt was on his back. In seconds the creature would be on top of him.

Then Richard acted. He had grabbed a chair and, holding it like a baseball bat, he swung it at the crocodile, using all his strength. The heavy wood and upholstery slammed into the creature, knocking it off course and causing one side of its ribcage to collapse. It lay on the ground, twitching and rattling, still trying to get back on to its feet. Its mouth opened and snapped shut. Its head thrashed from side to side.

"Move!" Richard shouted.

A second showcase blew itself apart. Glass crashed down. One by one the dinosaur skeletons were coming to life. Bone rattled against marble. Matt got to his feet, wondering how many exhibits there were in the museum. And what about the one they had seen when they came in?

The diplodocus.

Even as Matt turned towards the huge creature, he saw the bones begin to tremble and knew that it too was coming to life. The diplodocus was twenty metres long. Its dreadful tail was coiling and uncoiling, animated by whatever energy was flowing through it. One of its legs moved, each of the joints shuddering. Its head swivelled round, searching for its prey.

"The door!" Richard yelled, then cried out as something crashed into him. It was a giant lizard skeleton, walking on its two hind legs, its arms outstretched. It was made up of at least a hundred bones suspended from a long, curving spine, with vicious teeth jutting forward, snapping at his throat. Richard fell backwards, his arms flailing. Matt saw the keys leave his hands and arc into the darkness. The lizard leapt into the air. Richard hurled himself sideways. The lizard crashed down. If he had waited one more second it would have landed on top of him. "The door!" He screamed the words again. "See if you can find a way out."

The mist was getting thicker and Matt could no longer see from one end of the hall to the other. There were further explosions, one after the other, as more exhibit cases were destroyed from within and half-visible shapes appeared, flying, strutting or crawling towards them. Richard was searching blindly for the keys. But perhaps the doors would open another way. Surely there must be a fire exit, or some way out in case of emergencies.

227

Matt ran the full length of the hall and reached the front door. Sliding to a halt, he grabbed the handle and pulled. The door was locked. Frantically he tried a second door. That was locked too. Looking out through the glass, he could see offices and flats across the main road. The traffic was moving as usual. Ordinary life … but it could have been a thousand miles away. Both sets of doors had been locked for the evening. There was no emergency lever. They were trapped.

"Richard!" Matt called out. There was no sign of the journalist.

"Stay quiet!" Richard's voice came out of the mist. "They can't see you. Stay where you are and don't make a sound."

Was it true? Another lizard thing – perhaps an iguanodon – was stumbling towards him, towering over him. Matt froze. The dinosaur skeleton had stopped right in front of him. He could see through its eye sockets, all the way into its skull. Its mouth was open, revealing ugly white triangular teeth, each one coming to a vicious point. It wasn't breathing – it couldn't – but even so, Matt could smell its breath. It stank of sewage and decay. In the far distance he heard the clattering of feet, the rattling of bones. Richard was silent. The dinosaur craned forward. It seemed to be scenting him, or perhaps sensing the pulse in his neck. Now it was only centimetres away. Matt wanted to run. He wanted to scream. He was certain the creature was about to attack. Was he just going to stand there while it ripped out his throat?

"Matt? Where are you? Are you all right?" Richard's voice echoed from the other side of the hall and the lizard creature twisted away and lumbered off in that direction. So Richard had been right. The dinosaurs were blind. They needed sound and movement to find their victims.

"I'm OK!" Matt shouted back. He didn't dare add more.

"Can you get out?"

"No! I need the keys!"

The keys were lying on the floor beside the stairs. Richard peered through the mist and finally saw them and lunged for them. At the same time a squat, solid-looking creature charged towards him, a single horn protruding from its mis-shapen skull. Somewhere in the back of his mind Richard remembered the creature's name. It was a triceratops. Fortunately it was slower than the others and it was moving clumsily, slipping on the marble floor. Richard snatched up the keys before it could reach him. Overhead, a second ptero-dactyl had joined the first. The two of them were performing a ghostly dance, wheeling over one another, high in the air.

Matt was still by the door. Richard could just make him out behind the wall of mist, but for a moment he disappeared as more ghostly shapes drifted between them. It was impossi-ble to be sure how many of the creatures had been brought to life, but no matter how many of them there were, none was more dangerous than the diplodocus, which remained at the very centre, looming over the others. There was no way Richard could get past it. But he had to move. If he stayed here much longer, *something* would find him. It might fly down from above or lunge at him from behind. A sudden snap of teeth. The slash of a claw. Death was everywhere and he knew it would come for him very soon.

And then the diplodocus swung its tail. It moved almost lazily. The great mass of bones whipped through the air and Richard gasped as it crashed into one of the columns. Broken marble and masonry rained down in a billowing cloud of dust. It was only now that he understood the full horror of his situation. Although they were only bone, the dinosaurs were as strong as they had been when they were alive. If they wanted to, they could bring the whole museum crashing down.

"Richard!" Matt called out and the diplodocus turned, searching for him. The pterodactyls peeled apart and joined the hunt.

"Take the keys!" Richard cried. "Just get out of here!"

He raised his arm and, with all his strength, threw the key ring at Matt. The keys flew over the diplodocus and hit the ground on the other side, skidding the rest of the way. Matt leant down and grabbed them.

"Come on!" he shouted.

"Get out!"

"I'm not leaving without you!"

"Just open the door!"

Matt knew Richard was right. Maybe opening the museum would in some way short-circuit the magic that had brought the dinosaurs back from extinction. Maybe he would be able to call for help. There were six keys on the ring. He picked them up and forced the first into the lock. It wouldn't move. He jerked it out and tried the second, then the third. None of them worked. It was almost impossible to concentrate on what he was doing. His hands were shaking. Every nerve in his body screamed at him to watch out behind. He managed to insert the fourth key. But before he had time to try it, the tail of the diplodocus brushed against his shoulder, enough to send him flying. It felt as if he had been hit by a truck. Bruised and dazed, he staggered to his feet, lurched back to the door and turned the key. At once a bell began to ring and a red light flashed somewhere behind the writhing mist. He had set off the alarm! At the same moment the door swung open. He was free.

But where was Richard?

The journalist hadn't moved. He had heard the alarm and knew that the door must be open – but he was still trying to work out how to get past the huge diplodocus. The way forward was blocked. Could he escape upstairs? A second later he cried out as his ankle was gripped by what felt like a coil of barbed wire. He looked down and saw a tiny crablike thing, only fifteen centimetres high. It had caught hold of him with teeth like drawing pins. Richard swore and shook it free, then kicked at its head with all his strength, smiling as the bone disintegrated. The smile was wiped away as the creature's mother, ten times bigger, scuttled towards him.

He made his decision and began to run. Sure enough, the

diplodocus heard the sound and its great neck twisted round. Other skeletons lumbered out of the shadows, encircling him. But the door was open. The way ahead was clear.

"You can make it!" Matt shouted.

The diplodocus was still standing between the two of them but with a shudder of excitement Matt realized what Richard was planning to do. As he watched, Richard ducked underneath the tail of the diplodocus and ran between its hind legs and beneath its belly. The dinosaur was too big, too cumbersome, to stop him, and the other creatures couldn't get anywhere near him. A quick exit between the monster's front legs and he would be at the door. He would be safe!

Enraged, the diplodocus reared up. Its powerful head pounded against the upper balcony.

A gust of cold wind touched the back of Matt's neck. He heard footsteps approaching.

Richard had come to a halt beneath the diplodocus. He was staring at Matt, his face twisted in shock and disbelief.

The balcony had been shattered by the impact. The great arch split open and with a deafening crash the whole massive pile of stone and mortar, glass and steel, plummeted down. Unable to bear the weight, the diplodocus itself collapsed, its legs buckling underneath it.

Matt was about to run forward, back into the museum, when a pair of hands reached out and seized him by the neck. He cried out and twisted round.

Richard was almost invisible behind the dust and falling

stone. The curving ribcage of the dinosaur had become a cage of another sort for him. It was as if he had been swallowed alive. He was trapped inside it.

Matt couldn't move. Mrs Deverill was glaring at him, her eyes aflame. Noah was holding on to him, his hands tight around Matt's throat. Matt lashed out, trying to break free. He felt his knee drive into Noah's stomach but at the same time Mrs Deverill had produced a damp cloth and pressed it against his face. The cloth smelled sweet and sickly. He choked, unable to breathe.

Richard saw Matt taken. Matt saw the journalist, his face streaked with blood, on his knees in the ghastly prison. Richard raised an arm, trying to brush away the curtain of dust and rubble that was smothering him. The curtain thickened and he was obliterated. A steel girder slammed down into the pile. Matt heard Richard cry out one last time.

Unable to fight any more, Matt allowed the darkness to take him. The traffic rushed past. He heard the car engines, saw a traffic light turn from green to red. Everything was suddenly far away.

The world twisted, turned upside down, and he remembered nothing more.

ROODMAS

The clouds had rolled in over Yorkshire and the entire country-side seemed flat and colourless. Even the birds in the trees were strangely silent. It had rained all night and was still raining now, the water spluttering out of the rusty drainpipes, trickling across the windows, falling into puddles that reflected a grey and hostile sky.

Matt woke up and shivered.

He was back at Hive Hall, lying on a rusty, sagging bed. He had been moved to a room next door to Noah on the first floor of the barn. There was no heating and he had only one thin blanket. He looked at his watch. It was seven o'clock in the morning. He sat up very slowly. His neck ached, his shoulder was so bruised that he could barely move his arm, and he could feel a scar on his face where the wing of the pterodactyl had caught him. His clothes were torn, dirty and damp. He stretched his arms and rotated his shoulders, trying to work some warmth into his muscles. It was Saturday, April the thirtieth. Professor Dravid had given the day a name: Roodmas. Some sort of witches' festival. This was what everything had been leading to. In twenty-four hours it would all be over.

Matt got up and went to the window. It looked out over the farmyard, where a couple of pigs shuffled about in their sty. Otherwise, there was nobody in sight. This was his second day of captivity. He had only been let out of the room to use the toilet, with Noah standing guard outside the door. It was also Noah who brought him his meals on paper plates with plastic knives and forks. There had been no sign of Mrs Deverill, but he had seen lights going on and off in the farm-house during the night and knew she was close.

Richard had been killed. That thought hurt him more than anything. It seemed to Matt that anyone who had shown him any kindness had died, and now he was finally on his own. But he was determined to fight back. If Mrs Deverill thought she could just drag him into the wood and stick a knife in him, she had a surprise coming her way.

He had already started. He was getting out.

Matt listened carefully for any sound in the barn. There was nothing, apart from the grunting of the pigs. It would be at least an hour before Noah brought his breakfast. He pulled back the mattress and removed a piece of iron about ten centi-metres long and flattened at one end. Other than the bed, there was no furniture in the room, nothing he could use to break out. But the bed itself had provided him with a tool. The metal bar had supported one of the legs. It had taken Matt most of the first day to work it free and another two hours to squeeze one end flat – using his own weight and the bed legs – so that it now resembled a crude chisel. His first intention had been to prise out the bars on the window but he had soon discovered they were too strong. Instead he had turned his attention to the floor.

The bedroom floor was made up of parallel wooden planks, each one fixed in place with a dozen nails. Working during the night, Matt had managed to free nine of the nails on one plank. Three more and he would be able to lift it out. If he could make a hole big enough, he would be able to squeeze through and drop down to the level below. That was his plan.

He pulled back the old colourless rug that covered the floor and set to work. The makeshift chisel was a clumsy tool and it was almost impossible to get it underneath the heads of the nails. It had slipped several times and Matt's knuckles had crashed into the floor until his skin was broken and bleeding. He had to be careful not to make any noise. That was the worst of it. Working quietly meant working slowly and he was aware of time running out. He gritted his teeth and tried to concentrate on what he was doing. First one nail and then another came out. Almost an hour had passed since he had woken up, but at last the plank came free. He prised it out and looked through the narrow gap he had made.

He saw at once that his plan was hopeless. He was too high up. If he tried to drop down to ground level, he'd twist an ankle or even break a leg. He felt a wave of despair rise up inside him. Why did nothing ever seem to go his way? He fought it back. He wasn't going to give up now. Maybe there was another way.

His power.

The blind medium, Susan Ashwood, had told him what he already knew himself. *"I felt your power ... I have never felt such strength before."* That was what she had said just before he had left her house. And he remembered the way Professor Dravid had looked at him at the museum. For a moment he had wondered if the professor was even, in some way, afraid of him.

Matt *was* different. He had known that all his life. He had seen the death of his parents the night before it had happened. He had dreamt all the details, right down to the bridge and the blown-out tyre. He had sensed there was a security guard at the warehouse seconds before the man had actually appeared. He had smashed a jug at the detention centre. He had called Richard without even opening his mouth. And then there had been the dreams that were some-how more than dreams. Four children... Three boys and a girl calling to him.

With him, that made five.

He sat down on the bed and concentrated on the door. If he could break a jug, why couldn't he turn a lock? It was just a question of finding the power inside him and activating it. He remembered the last time he had tried this, the morning when he had woken up in Richard's flat. It hadn't worked that time – but perhaps he hadn't really been trying. This was a matter of life and death. Surely that would help.

He purposefully slowed down his breathing, staring straight ahead, trying to forget everything else. He focused on the keyhole, trying to visualize the metal bolts inside. He could move them. He could open the door with a key that existed only in his imagination. It was easy. He had the power.

He reached out with his hands, trying to make the energy flow through them. "Turn!" he whispered. "Turn!"

The handle turned.

The door opened.

Matt's spirits soared – but only for a second. He had been cruelly deceived. Noah was standing on the other side. The farm worker had unlocked the door to bring Matt his breakfast. He was holding a tray with a mug of tea and a single slice of fried bread. What looked like a sickle hung from his belt. It had a wooden handle and a hooked blade that had been recently sharpened. The edge was raw silver and vicious.

"Breakfast," Noah muttered.

"Greasy and disgusting," said Matt.

"You don't want to eat it?"

"I wasn't talking about the breakfast. I was talking about you."

There was a gap in the floor. Matt had been aware of it from the moment Noah came in. But the question was, would Noah notice it? He had to keep Noah talking.

238

Somehow he had to keep his attention diverted.

Noah set the tray down on the bed.

"I'd like a bath," Matt said.

"No bath."

"How about a shower? Or maybe you don't know what that is. From the smell of you, I'd say you've probably never had one either."

The taunt worked. Noah was gazing at him, his attention diverted from the rest of the room. For a moment he stood there, breathing heavily. He took the sickle out of his belt and held it up to his lips. Then he ran his tongue down the blade. "I'll enjoy watching you being killed," he breathed. "You'll scream like a pig. You'll scream and you'll cry, and I'll be there!" He tucked the sickle back and walked over to the door. "No more food today," he announced. "You can die hungry." He slammed the door and locked it again.

Matt waited until he was sure Noah had really left, then he gulped down his breakfast. The tea was cold, the fried bread soggy. But he didn't care. Hot or cold, the food would give him strength and that was one thing he needed. He was secretly glad that Noah wasn't going to bring him lunch. That gave him more time. It was obvious to him that he wasn't going to open the door by magic – or any other means. There was only one way out of here and that was through the hole he had already made. It just had to be bigger, and now he could work uninterrupted all day.

When Matt next looked at his watch it was just after

239

three o'clock in the afternoon. His knees were sore. His back was stiff. His fingers were covered in blisters and one of his thumbs was gashed. But two more floorboards were free and only seven nails remained before the hole would be large enough for his purpose. He couldn't jump down, or swing himself down at arm's length. But he had another plan – and he would have only one chance to make it work.

Six o'clock arrived and still the fourth plank refused to budge. Seven nails stood between him and success. Now he worked more feverishly, caring less about the noise. What would he do if this didn't turn out the way he hoped? He smiled grimly to himself. The chisel was hardly the most effective of weapons but it would have to do. If he could at least give Noah something to remember him by, he would go more cheerfully. Picturing that moment, he stabbed down with the flattened bar of iron. Another nail came free.

It was already dark when Noah returned. There was the familiar rattle of the key and the creak of the opening door. He stood on the threshold with the sickle tucked into his belt. There was no electricity in the room. He took out a torch and flicked it on.

"Time to go." Noah sang out the words. "They're all waiting for you."

He was answered by complete silence.

"What's the matter?" he hissed. "Are you playing games?"

From the far side of the room, where the bed stood,

there came a painful groan.

"What is it? Are you sick?"

Matt groaned again and coughed – a hard, rattling cough. Anxiously, Noah held the torch at arm's length.

"If this is some sort of trick," he threatened, "I'll make you wish you'd never been born. I'll—"

He took two paces into the room and stepped on to the rug.

The rug was covering the hole that Matt had spent the whole day making. Noah dropped the torch and disappeared without a sound. The rug went with him, sucked downwards like an animal trap. At once Matt sprang off the bed. The torch was lying on the floor and he snatched it up, then hurried out of the room, along the corridor and downstairs. The sight that greeted him at the bottom was not a pretty one. He had hoped the farmhand would knock himself out when he hit the ground. But somehow Noah had fallen on the sickle. It had gone through his stomach and out the other side. His face was distorted in an expression of pain and surprise. He was quite dead.

Matt ran out into the darkness. It was raining and he felt needles of water slicing into his face. The road seemed to have been churned up into puddles and mud that threatened to drag him down. Twice he stumbled and fell, setting the bruise on his shoulder on fire. But he didn't even hesitate. He ran headlong into the night, unaware of anything but the sound of his feet hitting the road, the drumming of his blood in his ears and the gasping of his breath as it emerged in fierce white clouds from his mouth.

He ran until every step made him wince and his legs shouted at him to let him rest. His mind was numb. He was no more than a machine. Rainwater streaked across his face and trickled down the back of his neck. At last he came to the end of his strength. He had to stop. He saw a bank of grass and collapsed on to it. He had no idea how far he had come. A mile? It could have been ten.

The headlights of a car appeared in the distance. Matt lifted his head and, moving like an old man, began to get to his feet. He knew it was dangerous but he had no choice. He had to stop the car and ask for a lift. Perhaps the driver would hand him to the police. But it didn't matter. It was Roodmas. Tomorrow he would be safe.

Staggering forward, he raised his arms. The car slowed down and stopped. Its headlamps lit up the rain, making it look like spilled ink. It was a sports car. A black Jaguar.

The door opened and the driver got out. Matt tried to move towards him, lost his balance and tumbled into a pair of outstretched arms.

"Good heavens!" Sir Michael Marsh said.

It was the government scientist he had visited with Richard. He tried to speak but the words wouldn't come.

"What are you doing out here in the middle of the night?" Sir Michael demanded. Then: "No. Don't try to speak now. Let me get you into the car, out of this rain."

242

Matt allowed himself to be carried to the car and slumped gratefully into the front seat. Sir Michael shook off the rain and got in next to him. The engine of the car was still running, the windscreen wipers turning. But the car didn't move. Sir Michael looked completely perplexed.

"It's Matthew Freeman, isn't it?" he said. "What on earth are you doing in this dreadful state? Have you had an accident?"

"No... I..."

"You look as if you've just escaped from a pack of bears."

"I'm very cold."

"Then we must try to get you into the warm at once. Don't you worry. It's very lucky I ran into you. Everything's going to be all right now."

He put the car into gear and they moved off. Sir Michael turned on the heater and Matt felt a cushion of hot air surround his legs. He was safe! Sir Michael Marsh would listen to his story. He had the power to see to it that Mrs Deverill and the other villagers were defeated. He would make sure that no more harm would come to him. The car sped on through the night. Matt relaxed in the soft leather seat. All he wanted to do was sleep. He had never been so tired.

But he couldn't. Something was wrong. Something was terribly wrong. What was it? He played back the words Sir Michael had spoken just a few minutes ago.

"It's Matthew Freeman, isn't it?"

He knew his surname.

243

When Richard had taken him to Sir Michael's house in York he had introduced him simply as Matt. Only Mrs Deverill knew his second name. Sir Michael couldn't have known it.

Unless…

Matt scrambled for the door handle and tried to open it, but it was locked. He turned to Sir Michael just as a fist with a gold signet ring on one finger crashed into the side of his head, throwing him against the window and stunning him. The old man was unbelievably strong. Now Matt remembered seeing the car before – at Hive Hall.

"Please don't try to move," Sir Michael said. "The doors are locked and there's nowhere you can go. I don't enjoy hitting children and I don't want to do it again, but I will if you try anything."

There was nothing Matt could try. Every last ounce of his strength had deserted him.

"We'll be there very soon. It won't take long. And you needn't be concerned. It will all be over very quickly and it won't hurt as much as you think."

The car left the road. The wheels bumped over a muddy, stony track. They plunged into the pine forest. Ahead of them the lights of Omega One shimmered in the rain. Matthew tried to throw himself at Sir Michael Marsh but the old man easily pushed him back.

They reached the gates of the power station and stopped. The night was suddenly cut apart by an immense guillotine blade of lightning. The villagers were there, with Mrs Deverill standing in front of them, Asmodeus curled around her leg. They were all waiting for him.

"No!" Matt shouted, the single word echoing all around.

Sir Michael got out of the car. "Take him!" he ordered.

The door was pulled open. Grey, dripping hands reached in and clamped down on him. Matt lashed out but it was too late. He was dragged out of the car and lifted into the air. A huge spotlight cut through the rain, blinding him. There was a crowd of people ... the entire village. This was the moment they had been waiting for and now they had him.

Squirming and shouting, Matt was carried above their shoulders and into the heart of Omega One.

DARK POWERS

It was like being in a nightmarish technological circus.

The reactor chamber was a great circle with silver walls and a domed ceiling at least thirty metres high. Instead of sawdust, the floor was covered with black and white squares, and the roof was made of steel rather than canvas, with red and blue gantries criss-crossing high above the ground. There was an observation window in front of what must have been a control room and a wide balcony that ran the whole way round. Seating for an audience?

Across the centre of the chamber two railway tracks ran parallel with each other and there was a massive tower – all platforms, railings, ladders and dials – mounted on wheels so that it could move backwards and forwards. The tower dominated the chamber. For the moment, it was still. A single wide corridor led out of the ring. If it had been a circus, this would have been the path along which the animals and the clown's cars would have entered.

The arena was lit by brilliant floodlights attached to brackets. Everything was spotlessly clean and even the air had a metallic, sterile taste to it as hidden ventilators filtered it with a constant hum.

This was the heart of Omega One. Matt knew that under the floor, protected by ten metres of reinforced concrete and steel, a dragon lay sleeping. Its every breath trembled with pent-up anger. When it awoke, its roar would have the force of an exploding sun. Such was the power contained in the fragile cage of the nuclear reactor.

Watched by the silent villagers, Matt examined his surroundings. For all its technology, the power station was not so different from any modern factory. What made it so fantastic was that, in stark contrast to the machinery, it had been filled with the trappings of an almost forgotten age. The twenty-first century forced into an unholy marriage with the Dark Ages. Inside the nuclear power station the ground had been prepared for a witches' sabbath – for the celebration of black mass.

Despite the electric lights, the chamber was decorated with thousands of flickering candles, all of them black, their wicks spluttering. Smoke twisted up and was whisked away into the ventilation system. The candles surrounded a circle that had been painted on the chessboard floor with a series of words, written in capital letters, going all the way round. HEL + HELOYM + SOTHER… They were foreign words that meant nothing to Matt and he gave up trying to read them. Inside the circle there were various symbols – arrows, eyes, five-pointed stars and spirals – that could have been the doodles of some demented child, except that they had been marked out in gold paint, seemingly with care.

His eyes were drawn to a slab of black marble in the very centre of the circle. The stone was the size of a coffin, with a single design engraved in gold at the foot:

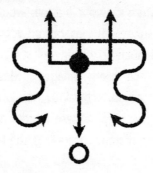

A wooden cross hung from above. But it was upside down. Directly beneath it, on the stone, lay a knife, its blade a twisted tongue of dull silver, its handle fashioned from the horn of a goat.

Matt shuddered. He knew what all the preparations were for. This was where his life was meant to end. The knife was for him.

The villagers closed in around him. More of them looked down on him from the window of the observation box. Mrs Deverill and her sister were standing next to each other. Matt recognized the butcher, the chemist, the woman with the pram… Even the children had joined in the ring, their faces pale, their eyes hungry. Nobody spoke. Nor did they force him on to the slab. They knew he had no choice but to surrender.

He had given them a run for their money. But he had lost and now it was time to pay.

"Matt…"

Somebody had called out to him. Matt looked past the villagers and saw a man standing outside the circle, his hands tied behind him to a metal railing. Matt ran over to him, everything else forgotten for a moment. It was the last thing he had expected. Richard Cole was still alive. His clothes were ragged, his face smeared with blood. He was helpless, a prisoner. But somehow he had survived the destruction of the museum and had been brought here too.

"Tell me I'm dreaming," Richard gasped as Matt reached him.

"I'm afraid not," Matt said. He was so surprised, he didn't know what to say. "I thought you were dead."

"Not quite." Richard managed a ghost of a smile. "It looks like Sir Michael Marsh is part of all this."

"I know. He brought me here."

"Never trust anyone who works for the government." Then Richard leant forward and whispered, "My left hand is almost free. Hang in there!" And Matt felt a surge of hope.

"So here we all are together!" The voice came from the one open door. The villagers turned towards Sir Michael Marsh as he entered the arena. "Shall we take our places? The end of the world is about to begin."

Two of the villagers had crept up behind Matt, and before he could react they had pulled him away. He struggled, but it was hopeless. The two men were huge and handled him as if he were a sack of potatoes. They dragged him over to the sacrificial slab, threw him on to his back and tied thick leather bands around his wrists and ankles. When they stepped back, he couldn't move. So this was where it ended. This was what it had all been for.

Richard was shouting. "Leave him alone! Why hurt him? He's just a kid. Let him go…"

Sir Michael held up a hand for silence. "Matthew is not 'just a kid'," he replied. "He is a very special child. A child we have been watching for almost half his life."

Mrs Deverill pushed her way forward. She was dressed in the same clothes she had worn in London, together with the lizard brooch, her eyes filled with hatred. "I want to be the one who cuts his throat," she rasped.

"You will do as you're told," Sir Michael replied. "I have to say, Jayne, you've disappointed me. You very nearly let him get away. A second time!"

"We should have locked him up from the start!"

"You're the ones who should be locked up," Richard cried. "You're all mad…"

"We're not mad." Sir Michael turned to him. "You know nothing. You live in your own cosy, mediocre world. You're completely blind to the greater things that are happening around you, like so many of your kind. But that will all change.

"I have dedicated my entire life to this moment. The preparations alone have taken more than twenty years, working night and day. Did Professor Dravid tell you about us? Did he tell you about the Old Ones?" Sir Michael paused but Richard said nothing. "I will assume that he did, and you probably thought that he was mad too.

"Let me assure you, the Old Ones exist. They were the first great force of evil. At one time they ruled the world until they were defeated – by a trick – and banished. Ever since then they have been waiting to return. That is what you are about to witness. Your friend Matthew is tied down on the very mouth of Raven's Gate." Sir Michael spread his hands. "That is where we are now. And the gate is about to open."

The villagers shivered with pleasure. Even Mrs Deverill forced a thin smile.

"The forces that created Raven's Gate knew what they were doing," Sir Michael continued. "The gate is unbreakable. Unopenable. Unmovable. Or so it seemed for centuries. Our ancestors tried as long ago as the Middle Ages. For hundreds of years from generation to generation they passed on their accumulated knowledge, their spells and rituals. But nothing worked until now. We are the chosen generation.

"Because we live in the twenty-first century. We have new technology. And there is a power that we can harness. The same power existed the day the world was created, but it only became available to us a short time ago. Nuclear power. The power of the atom."

He walked over to Matt, who strained upwards, trying to break the leather bands. He forced his shoulders off the sacrificial block – but there was nothing he could do. As Sir Michael approached, he slumped back.

"Do you really think it's so crazy to draw parallels between the power of the nuclear bomb and the power of black magic?" Sir Michael asked. "Do you really believe that a weapon capable of destroying cities and killing millions of people in a few seconds is so far removed from the Devil's work? To me it was obvious. I saw that the two different powers could be brought together and that, together, they could do what nothing had ever been able to do before.

"When Omega One was built I used my influence to ensure that it was built here, on the very spot where the ring of stones – Raven's Gate – had stood. The ancient stone circle would be contained right here, in this reactor room, if it hadn't been destroyed. Beneath us, the reactor has almost reached critical mass. It is as if a gigantic bomb has been buried in the heart of the gate, waiting to blow it apart and allow the Old Ones through.

"I built Omega One. I was also in charge of closing it down once the government had finished with it. I managed to dissuade them from actually razing it to the ground, and as soon as everyone had gone away, I set to work, quietly rebuilding it again. It took me more than twenty years, working with the villagers, the children of the children of the warlocks and witches who have inhabited Lesser Malling for centuries."

"But how did you get the uranium?" Richard shouted. "It's impossible! You told us so yourself. You'd never get the uranium."

"There was a time when it would have been impossible," Sir Michael agreed. "And it was still extremely difficult. But the world has changed. The collapse of the Soviet Union. Events in Serbia and Yugoslavia. Wars in the Middle East. There are mercenaries and terrorists crawling all over the planet, and finding ones we could do business with was only a matter of time. They too serve the Old Ones in their own way. We're all on the same side.

"For six months now we have kept the station going, feeding the reactor, priming it for tonight. Believe me when I tell you, the reactor works. Soon I will give the order for the last control rods to be lifted. This will raise the heat to critical levels. And the gate will melt and open."

"You'll all be killed!" Richard said.

"Only you will be killed. Because only you are outside the circle."

"That's what you think…"

"That's what I *know*." Sir Michael pointed to the symbols painted on the floor. "For centuries magicians have painted circles like this for protection. And they will protect us right now. If the radiation leaks, we won't be touched by it. The heat, no matter how fantastic, won't burn us. Only you will die."

"What about Matt?" Richard demanded.

"Professor Dravid didn't tell you?" Sir Michael smiled. "The three ingredients of the black sabbath. Ritual, fire and blood. We have inherited the rituals. We have created the fire. Now Matthew will supply us with the blood."

253

He picked up the knife and ran a finger along the blade.

"Blood," he continued, "is the most powerful form of energy on the planet. It is the very life force itself. Sacrifice has always been part of magical ritual because it represents a release of that power. There, once again, is the connection. The medieval witch splits throats. The twenty-first century witch splits atoms. Tonight we shall do both."

"But it doesn't have to be him!" Richard insisted. "Why Matt?"

"Because of who he is."

"But he's nobody... He's just a child!"

"That's what he thinks. But it has to be his blood. This is the moment that he was born for."

"That's enough!" Mrs Deverill hissed. "Let's get on with it."

Sir Michael looked at his watch. "You're right. It's time."

Matt couldn't move. The slab was cold against his back. The leather bands held him tight.

Inside the observation room a switch was activated. Far beneath the ground, electromagnets gripped the control rods and began to pull them upwards, centimetre by centimetre. The villagers joined hands, eyes closed. Slowly, the nuclear rods were sucked out of the nuclear pile. Sir Michael walked to the middle of the circle and stood above Matt, the knife in his hands.

It was twelve o'clock on the night of Roodmas. It was time to open the gate.

RAVEN'S GATE

So it came to this.

Matt was tied down, surrounded, helpless. In a few moments he would be killed. The ferocious heat of the nuclear reactor would weaken the gate, bringing it to the point when it could be finally smashed. And then the knife would plunge into his heart. Somehow his blood hitting the floor would be enough. At that moment Raven's Gate would open.

Richard couldn't do anything. Even if he managed to break free, he would never reach Matt in time.

But there was still the power.

Twice Matt had tried to find it inside himself. Twice he had failed to make it work. He had one more chance. But how…?

The villagers had begun to chant. It was a sound that Matt had heard before. They began with the same words that had haunted him when he had been alone at Hive Hall:

"NODEB … TEMOCMOD … EMANY … NEVAEH … NITRA."

But now that he was so close to them, Matt could make

out what they were saying. And suddenly he understood. He had assumed they were speaking in Latin or Greek but it was much simpler than that. It was an old witches' ritual. They were reciting the Lord's Prayer backwards.

Matt tried to ignore them. He was aware of the growing energy beneath him as the nuclear reactor reached critical mass. He knew he had to close his mind to all of it. Why hadn't he been able to break the vase in Richard's flat? Why couldn't he open the door when he was Mrs Deverill's prisoner? What was he doing wrong?

The murmuring filled the room, rising above the soft hum of the ventilation system. Sir Michael held the knife tightly in both hands, waiting for the moment when he would bring it down. Despite all his efforts, Matt found himself transfixed by the silver blade. This whole business had begun with a knife – the one that Kelvin had used to wound the security guard. It seemed that it would end with one too.

Think about the knife. Concentrate on it. Make it stop. Lying on his back, Matt tried to unlock the power that he knew was inside him. But it was no good. Sir Michael was in control. He was smiling to himself as he whispered the words of the invocation. Matt could see the sweat on his upper lip. He was going to enjoy this. His whole life had built up to it.

Far underneath the ground the control rods moved slowly upwards. As they left the core of the reactor, the neutrons rushed around the enclosed container, travelling at hundreds of miles per second, smashing into each other, releasing incredible heat.

And as the control rods rose, so did Raven's Gate.

Richard had managed to free one hand but the other was still trapped and he was fighting desperately with the rope. But seeing what was happening, he stopped, totally shocked.

The great stones, destroyed centuries ago, were rising out of the floor like monstrous plants. There were eighteen control rods. And there were eighteen stones, each one sliding up in the exact position that it had once occupied. They were ghosts, passing through the floor without touching it. But even as Richard watched, they shimmered, becoming more solid as they grew taller. Already they were towering above the villagers, forming a new circle behind them. In a few seconds they would be exactly as they had been. And Richard knew with a terrible certainty that it would be then that the knife would fall. The Old Ones would break free.

Matt saw all this and closed his eyes. The more he was drawn into the events around him, the less control he would have. Was there nothing he could do? He had smashed the jug of water. It hadn't been a dream. He had done it. But how? Desperately he tried to remember how he had felt when he was in the detention centre. What had made him different? Why had it worked then?

The whispers grew louder. Now something even more incredible was happening. The colour of the floor inside the circle had changed. The black and white checks had been washed away by a glow of red that seemed to be shining through, from underneath. The glow became brighter, the colour more vivid, until it was like a vast pool of blood. Suddenly a crack, deep and black, cut a jagged path across the reactor cap. The gate was breaking up.

Matt opened his eyes one last time. There was Richard, standing outside the circle, still struggling with the rope. There were Jayne and Claire Deverill, watching with something close to ecstasy. The ceiling – harsh, industrial lamps and silver pipes. The observation room with the villagers pressed forward, watching through the glass. The flames of the black candles, flickering and swaying. And the floor…

A speck of darkness had appeared in the red. Matt craned his neck so that he was looking down the length of his body and beyond. The floor had become transparent. He was looking through it, into another world. The speck moved. It was climbing, flying, swimming upwards, moving at an incredible speed. For a second he could make out a shape, some sort of creature. But it was too fast. The blackness welled up, blotting out the red, thrusting it aside in a chaos of swirling bubbles. A brilliant white streak seared across the surface of the pool. The black thing brushed it away and with a shudder Matt saw what it was: a huge hand. The monster that owned it must have been as big as the reactor itself. He could see its finger-nails, sharp and scaly, and he could make out the wrinkled skin of its webbed fingers. It had placed its fist against the barrier and the crimson bubbles were exploding around it

258

as it searched for the strength to punch its way through.

Matt closed his eyes. And suddenly, out of nowhere, the answer came.

The smell of burning.

That was what had triggered his power. He had smelled burning when he was sinking into the bog. The same smell had been there in the detention centre when he broke the jug. And even before that … long before that. Now he remembered. His mother had burnt the toast on the morning of the accident that had killed her. Somehow that tiny incident had become the trigger. He had smelled burnt toast the moment before the security guard had appeared in the warehouse. He had known what was about to happen.

He stopped trying to influence the knife. He stopped trying to turn something on inside himself. Instead he thought back to six years ago. He was eight years old again, sitting in a kitchen in a south London suburb. For just a second, a single frame in a film, he saw the yellow painted walls. There was the kitchen cupboard. The teapot shaped like a teddy bear.

And his mother.

"Come on, Matthew. We're going to be late."

He heard her voice and smelled it once again. The toast burning…

Inside the nuclear reactor the whispering had stopped. The great stones of Raven's Gate had returned. They stood, almost touching the dome of the power station. Their worn, flinty surface – thousands of years old – the metal plates, the pipes and machinery that surrounded them. Sir Michael Marsh raised the knife. His fists, clutching the hilt, tightened.

"No!" Richard shouted.

The knife plunged down.

It had less than an arm's length to travel. It would slice easily into the boy's heart. The tip reached Matt's shirt and it pricked his skin. But that was as far as it went. It stopped, as if caught by an invisible wire. Sir Michael uttered a strange, strangled moan, pulling down with all his might. He stared at Matt, knowing that the boy's power had finally awoken, and with that knowledge came the first whispers of fear and defeat.

"No…" he muttered in a broken voice. "You can't! Not now! You can't stop me now!"

Matt looked at the knife and knew that he was in total control.

Sir Michael screamed. The blade was glowing molten red. The hilt was burning the palm of his hand. His skin crackled and smoke rose, but he couldn't drop it. With a last effort he managed to bring his arms down and the knife tumbled uselessly to the floor. Whimpering, he spat on his wounded hands. At the same time the straps that had been holding Matt smouldered and snapped. Matt rolled off the altar and got to his feet.

He took a step forward and stood on the surface of the pit, daring the villagers to come close. Nobody moved. Even the creature beneath, although it was a hundred times his own size, cowered and backed away. A streak of poisonous green rippled outwards in a brilliant stain. Matt turned to face the villagers. Nobody tried to stop him. He broke through the circle and ran towards Richard. The metal railing behind the journalist snapped. Instantly he was free.

"Follow me!" Matt ordered in a voice that was barely his own.

Too stunned to do anything but obey, Richard followed him. By the time the villagers had absorbed what was happening, they had disappeared through the one door of the chamber that was still open.

Mrs Deverill recovered herself. With a howl of fury she launched herself after them. Mr Barker, the chemist, tried to follow her. But he had left it just too late. He had only taken three paces across the chamber when the ground in front of him broke apart, fragments of metal and concrete flying upwards. Orange flames roared and a dense cloud of white smoke poured out, smothering him. Screaming, he collapsed to the floor and lay still.

A siren wailed and lights set all around the dome began to flash. A radiation warning. The levels were already lethal and were rising with every second that passed. "Stay in the circle!" Sir Michael bellowed. He was sobbing, still cradling his ruined hand. "The radiation has broken free. But we're protected in the circle!"

The orange flames climbed up, higher even than the stones, licking against the ceiling. Smoke belched out, forming a living carpet. A sprinkler system had come on automatically and thousands of litres of water were showering down, soaking and blinding the villagers. Still, it wasn't enough to put out the fire. Not this fire. The flames leapt through the water, hissing and crackling. The whole building began to shake.

Claire Deverill was the first to break. With a panic-stricken cry she threw up her arms and ran between two of the stones, making for the same door that her sister had taken. But the moment she was outside the magic circle she was no longer protected. The heat of the flames blasted into her and her clothes caught alight. The smoke grabbed at her legs, dragging her down. She screamed and tried to scream again. But there was no air in the room, only smoke and fire. Her face contorted and her eyes went white. She fell and lay there, convulsing on the floor.

"Stay in the circle," Sir Michael repeated. "The doors are locked. They can't escape."

Beneath the floor the gigantic creature punched and punched again at the invisible barrier. But it couldn't break through. It had ritual. It had fire. But the blood of the child had been denied it, and it didn't have the strength.

And that was when Sir Michael noticed the knife. The tip had penetrated Matt's shirt and skin. Matt's power had stopped it, but not before it had drawn blood. There was a single red drop at the very tip of the blade. Sir Michael's eyes widened. With a cry of pleasure he leapt forward and snatched up the knife. The blood was still wet. It glistened beneath the arc lamps.

Sir Michael laughed and brought the knife crashing down towards the gate.

The power was surging through Matt and nothing could stand in its way. Locked doors were torn from their hinges as if struck by a tornado. Steel plates bent and crumpled as he approached. Omega One was a labyrinth but he seemed to know exactly where he was going. Down a flight of metal stairs, along a corridor, through an archway and on towards a set of automatic doors that hissed open as he approached. It was as if he had worked here all his life.

Richard was close behind him. The journalist no longer knew where they were going but he could tell that their general direction was down. Already they had to be well below ground level. The warning sirens were still sounding all around them, and lights flashed red and white at every corner. Steam hissed out of pipes. Water cascaded down from the sprinkler system. The whole power station seemed to be trembling, on the verge of breaking up, and he was worried that they were going to trap themselves. There couldn't be an exit under the ground. But he knew that this was no time to argue. He kept his mouth shut, following Matt in grim silence.

They passed through a room stacked from floor to ceiling with banks of machinery, then down another corridor. A door at the end flew open, beckoning them on.

It led to a metal gantry above a tank of water. But it was like no water that Richard had ever seen. Pausing to catch his breath, he leant over it. The water was blue – a fluorescent, unnatural blue – and it was crystal clear, without so much as a speck of dust on the surface. The tank was square and about three metres deep. At the bottom was a row of metal containers, each one stamped with a series of numbers. Half of them were empty. Half contained twisted bars of metal, packed tightly together.

Richard knew what he was looking at. This was where the radioactive waste from the reactor was stored to cool. It wasn't water in the pool, but acid. The boxes beneath the surface contained the deadliest substance in the world. With a shiver he stepped back. Matt was waiting for him, his face set with a strange determination. It was hard to tell if he was asleep or awake.

"OK. I'm coming," Richard said.

The blow took Richard completely unawares, crashing into the back of his head. If he hadn't been moving forward, it might have broken his neck. He fell to his knees. A woman brushed past him and stepped on to the middle of the gantry, facing Matt. It was Mrs Deverill. Richard tried to get to his feet but he was barely conscious. All the strength had drained away from him. He could only kneel there, helpless, as Mrs Deverill walked towards Matt, an iron bar clasped in her hands.

"He didn't listen to me," she spat. Her face was distorted by fury, her eyes livid, her mouth an inhuman grimace. "We should have locked you up, starved you, kept you weak. But

264

it's over now, isn't it? The power's gone. You don't know how to control it. Now I can kill you and take you back."

She raised the iron bar. Matt looked around him. He had nowhere to run. On one side there was a wall. On the other, a low railing to stop him falling into the tank of acid. The gantry was only two metres across. Mrs Deverill was standing between him and Richard. Even if he could have run away, it would mean leaving his friend at her mercy and he couldn't do that. He had no choice. He would have to fight.

She swung the bar through the air. As quick as a panther, Matt leapt aside, then lurched back as Mrs Deverill thrust the pointed end at his stomach. She was moving incredibly quickly for a woman of her age but her fury had lent her strength. Matt fell against the railings as she threw herself at him. There was nothing he could do. She was taller than him. She was armed. And she was quite mad. Grunting with anger and exertion, she pressed the bar against his chest, pinning him against the side with such force that Matt thought she would crack his ribs.

He wished he could use his powers against her, but she had been right about that too. The power was no longer there. He had exhausted himself getting this far. There was a faulty switch inside him and now it had turned itself off. He was an ordinary boy again. And she was beating him.

Mrs Deverill lifted the bar so that it slid over his chest and under his throat. Now she was using it to crush his windpipe. Her pinched face, with its jagged cheekbones, was very close

265

to his. Her eyes were burning with hatred and indignation. Matt felt the floor slipping away beneath his feet. He was being forced over backwards. The railing pressed into his spine and his neck bent back until he could see the pool behind him, upside down. With a gasp he brought his knee up, crashing it into the woman's stomach. Mrs Deverill screeched and stepped back. Matt twisted to one side.

The bar slammed down again. Matt ducked. A rush of air swept past his cheek as the bar smashed into the railing. Sparks flew up. Then he jumped behind her, trying to take her by surprise. But she had been expecting the move. She lashed out with one foot, tripping him up. Then he was on his back, staring up as Mrs Deverill raised the bar with both hands. She was going to use it like a spear, crashing it down into his chest.

"You're still mine!" she gasped. "I'll have your blood. I'll tear out your heart and take it back with me."

Her fingers tightened. She took a breath.

And then she pitched forward, crying out. The iron bar missed. Matt looked past her and saw that Richard had recovered enough to make one last effort. With all his strength he had pushed her from behind. Jayne Deverill had lost her balance. For a moment she tottered, then with a shriek she fell over the railing and toppled into the tank.

She sank like a stone, plunging into one of the crates. With bubbles erupting from her mouth, she tried to reach the surface. But it was already too late. The acid was eating into her. Richard peered down and saw that already much of her face had gone.

"Don't look, Matt," he warned.

Mrs Deverill was no longer recognizable. Her flesh was peeling away and her hair had come out. Richard closed his eyes. Witches had been burned in the Middle Ages, he knew, but it could never have been as ghastly as this.

Matt stumbled to his feet. "This way…" he said, quietly.

There was a door at the end of the gantry and another flight of steps going ever further down. The walls were suddenly different. Instead of the paint and smooth plaster of the upper corridors, these walls were cut out of solid rock and were covered with patches of damp moss. The iron steps were rusty, descending into darkness. Richard could hear the sound of rushing water. The underground river!

The steps ended at a small, triangular platform. Just below them, the black river swept through miles of underground caverns, beneath the woods. The cave system was like an underground pipe, filled almost to the roof with freezing water. There were no banks or towpath to walk on. There was no other way out.

"Hold on to me," Richard said. Matt hooked his arms around the journalist. "Just hold on."

They jumped.

The reactor chamber of Omega One was breaking up. The flames had burst through almost everywhere. The heat was so intense that the heavy pipes and platforms were melting. The ground was buckling and breaking. A crack had appeared in one of the walls and the night air was feeding the flames, fanning the smoke.

Sir Michael Marsh stood alone beside the altar, the wind and smoke curling around him. The villagers, mad with fear, had attempted to flee. But outside the protection of the magic circle they had been incinerated instantly, swallowed up by the inferno. Now the observation box exploded, shards of glass and metal splinters cascading into the chamber, a rain of death.

The metal tower at the far end of the ring wavered as a new spasm seized the floor. With a sickening screech and an eruption of sparks it keeled over, tearing through a wall. Another window burst, a fireball shooting through it like a bullet from a gun.

Sir Michael leant against the sacrificial slab. Beneath him, underneath the smoke and fire, the black hand of the creature that he had summoned hammered one last time against the gate. The ancient stones had almost gone. They were crumbling away, dust pouring out of the gashes that had formed in them. Omega One was in the grip of an earthquake of its own making, the walls vibrating, the metal ladders and platforms shaking loose and crashing down.

Then with one last cry, a cry such as the world had not heard for a million years, the creature, king of the Old Ones, broke loose. The gate shattered. A single drop of Matt's blood had been enough to weaken it. The hand stretched out.

"We've done it!" Sir Michael cried, his eyes widening. "You're here! You're free!"

The huge hand unfolded. All the light in the chamber was blotted out as the giant fingers stretched.

The hand was all around the scientist. He let out a thin scream of delight, which in an instant turned to terror as he realized what was about to happen. The hand closed on him and crushed him. Sir Michael Marsh died horribly, in the grip of the creature he had served all his life.

And then the reactor, pushed beyond its limits, disintegrated. A blinding, searing, fantastic light burst out, as bright as the sun itself: the light of an atomic explosion.

A huge mushroom cloud sprouted out of the ground. Man's most dreadful creation ran wild. Spiralling upwards, it rushed towards the night sky, carrying with it enough deadly radiation to destroy half of England.

But the gate was open.

The vacuum had to be filled.

The atomic energy recoiled, drawn back into the gate that it had itself helped to open. The mushroom had risen far above the ground but now it was pulled down again, while at the same time the smoke and deadly gases were dragged back into the chasm that had been broken between the two worlds.

The creature itself was engulfed, flailing helplessly as it was sucked down like a spider into a gigantic plughole. It was trapped in a torrent of pure light that swirled round and round it, forming a whirlpool from which there could be no escape. A curtain of molten red flooded across, then dimmed and died away. Slowly the black and white squares of the reactor floor shimmered and began to reappear. The creature was gone. The gate had been resealed.

Two miles away, Richard and Matt, coughing and shivering, were spat out of an underground cavern and, reaching the bank, pulled themselves on to dry land. On the horizon, a ripple of pink spread across the night sky as the sun began its climb over the edge of the world.

At last, it was over.

THE MAN FROM PERU

"*The Times*?"

"Nothing."

"The *Daily Telegraph*?"

"Nothing."

"The *Daily Mail*?"

"Nothing."

"The *Independent*?"

"Nothing."

"*Le Monde*?"

"I don't know. It's in French."

"There has to be something, somewhere."

Matt and Richard were sitting at the kitchen table in the journalist's York flat. Each had a pair of scissors and a mug of tea. More than a week had passed since their escape from Omega One, and both of them had changed. Matt carried a scar on the side of his face, a souvenir of the National History Museum, but he was looking a little less pinched and tired. Staying with Richard, sleeping late, watching TV and generally doing very little had obviously been good for him. As for

271

Richard, he was more optimistic, more organized. He still found it hard to believe that he had actually survived. And he was certain he was about to sell the greatest story ever written. It wouldn't just be a case of "hold the front page". His story would run on every page.

They were surrounded by newspapers and magazines that they had checked through, from first page to last. They had done this every day. And always it was the same.

"How many more do we have to read?" Matt asked.

"I can't believe this is happening," Richard said. "I mean, there must be a mention of it somewhere. You can't have a nuclear explosion in the middle of Yorkshire without somebody noticing."

"You've got that clipping from the *Yorkshire Post*."

"Oh sure!" Richard plucked a scrap of newspaper off the fridge door, where it had been held in place with a magnet. "Two column inches about a bright light seen over the woods near Lesser Malling. A bright light – that's what they call it! And they stick it on page three next to the weather reports."

For the past seven days Richard had been monitoring the news in the press, on the radio and on the television. He was completely bewildered. It was as if nothing out of the ordinary had ever taken place. Structural engineers were still investigating the damage done to the Natural History Museum. Millions of pounds' worth of dinosaur fossils had been destroyed – but nobody had mentioned Professor Sanjay Dravid, who must surely have been found dead in the mi

death or disappearance of Sir Michael Mar

who had once been an influential governmer

had received a knighthood. Yet there were no o.

comment, nothing. He might as well have never exist.

And what of Richard's story?

He had written it in the space of twenty-four hours. To start with he had kept it simple, confining it to ten pages, outlining very broadly what had happened. Matt had insisted that his name be left out. He knew what he had done but he still wasn't quite sure how he had done it... And the truth was, he didn't want to know. He had finally managed to find the power to stop the knife and to break out. But he remembered very little of it. One moment he was lying on the slab. The next he was fighting Mrs Deverill over the acid bath. What had happened was like a hideous dream. It was as if he had been taken over.

As far as Matt was concerned, he never wanted to mention Jayne Deverill or Raven's Gate again. And he certainly didn't want to end up on the front page of the world's newspapers. Some sort of superhero. Some sort of freak.

In the end Richard had agreed to give him a false name. It was the easiest way. He hadn't mentioned the LEAF Project either. It would have made it too easy to identify Matt – and anyway, it was something else Matt didn't want to see in print.

The ten-page story had been sent to every newspaper in

ndon. That had been three days ago. Since then, half of them had written back.

> Dear Mr Cole,
>
> The editor wishes to thank you for your submission, received on 4 May.
> We regret, however, that we do not feel it is suitable for publication.
>
> Yours sincerely...

All of them were more or less the same. Short and to the point. They didn't give any reason for turning him down. They simply didn't want to know.

Matt knew that Richard was frustrated and angry. He hadn't expected people to believe everything he had written. After all, a lot of it was beyond belief. But at the same time, somebody must have been asking what had happened at the museum and at the power station. There was a giant crater in the woods where Omega One had once stood. Lesser Malling was now empty. How could an entire village simply disappear overnight? There were a hundred questions hanging in the air – and Richard's article provided at least some of the answers. Why did nobody want to publish it?

There was also an unspoken worr between the two.

Matt knew that he was living on borrowed time. Mrs Deverill was dead and any minute now the authorities in London would take note of the fact that she had disappeared and wonder what had happened to him. The LEAF Project would reclaim him and he would be sent somewhere else. It was obvious that he couldn't stay with Richard much longer. Although there was enough room in the flat for the two of them, a fourteen-year-old boy couldn't move in with a twenty-five-year-old man he'd only known for a matter of weeks. Worse still, Richard was out of cash. He hadn't shown up for work for a week and as a result he'd lost his job on the *Gazette*. The editor hadn't even sent him a letter. His dismissal was simply announced on the front page: JOURNALIST FIRED. Richard couldn't help being gloomy. If he wasn't going to have an award-winning scoop, he would need to find work. He had mentioned that he might go back to London.

"You know what I think," Richard said suddenly.

"What?"

"I think somebody is doing all this on purpose. I think somebody's put a D-notice on the story."

"What's a D-notice?"

"It's a government thing. Censorship. When they don't want a story to get into the papers for reasons of national security."

"You think they know what happened?"

"Maybe. I don't know." Richard crumpled a newspaper into a ball. "All I know is that somebody should have said something and I can't believe that no one has."

The doorbell rang. Richard went over to the window and looked down.

275

"Postman?" Matt suggested.

"No. It looks like a tourist. He's probably lost." A lot of tourists went past the flat, but it was unusual for one to ring the bell. "I'll go down and get rid of him," said Richard, and left the room.

Matt finished his tea and rinsed his mug in the sink. At last he had begun to sleep properly again – and there hadn't been any more dreams. And yet, even so, he knew that they were still waiting for him, the four children on the beach. Three boys and a girl. With him, that made five.

One of the Five.

That was what this had all been about: four boys and a girl, who had saved the world once and who would return to do it again. At the museum, Matt had told Richard what he believed – that he was one of them.

Yet how could that be possible when they had lived thousands of years ago? Matt had some sort of power. That much was obvious. But it wasn't something he could control and, as far as he was concerned, he never wanted to see it or use it again. He sank his head into his hands. He had never been in control of his life … not for as long as he could remember. And right now he felt more out of control than ever.

Richard came back into the room, accompanied by a man dressed in a pale suit. He was certainly foreign, with very black hair, olive-coloured skin and dark eyes, but he didn't look like a tourist. He was carrying an expensive leather briefcase and appeared to be more like a businessman –

some sort of international lawyer perhaps.

"This is Mr Fabian," Richard said. "At least, that's what he says his name is."

"Good morning, Matt. I'm very glad to meet you." Fabian's voice was soft. He pronounced each word carefully, with a strong Spanish accent.

"Mr Fabian has read my article," Richard continued. "He's from the Nexus."

The Nexus. The secret organization that both Miss Ashwood and Professor Dravid had mentioned before Dravid was killed.

"What do you want?" Matt demanded. He'd had enough. He just wanted to leave this all behind.

Fabian sighed. "Do you mind if I sit down?" he asked.

Richard gestured to a chair.

Fabian took it. "Thank you, Mr Cole. First of all, let me say, Matthew, that I am very glad – indeed very honoured – to meet you. I know what you've been through. I hope you are fully recovered."

"You don't know the half of it," Richard growled.

Fabian turned to him. "You were, of course, at the Natural History Museum when Professor Dravid was killed," he said. "I would be interested to know how it was that you survived."

Richard shrugged. "It was the ribcage," he said. "I was trapped underneath a dinosaur skeleton. The ribcage protected me from the falling bricks, and Mrs Deverill dug me out." He stopped. "You say you've read my article. So maybe you can tell me something. How come nobody wants it?"

Fabian sighed apologetically. "As a matter of fact, that's the reason why I'm here, Mr Cole," he explained. "My organization has prevented your story from being published. It is our job to ensure that it never sees the light of day."

"What?" Richard stared at his visitor with anger and disbelief. "You're telling me that the Nexus—"

"I am really very sorry. I know it must be extremely frustrating."

"Frustrating! Are you out of your mind?" Richard cast an eye over the table and Matt was glad there wasn't a kitchen knife at hand.

"We can't allow your story to get into print, Mr Cole."

"Why not? And how did you stop me?"

"As to your second question, I'm sure Sanjay Dravid already told you. We have a great deal of influence. We know people … in government, in the police, in the Church. We advise them. And in this case we advised them not to publish your material."

"Why not?" Richard thundered.

"Please, Mr Cole." Fabian could see the fury in the journalist's eyes. "Let me try to explain." He waited a moment while Richard calmed down. "Let us start by admitting that your story is completely unbelievable. Witches and phantom dogs? Supernatural creatures called the Old Ones? A boy" – he pointed at Matt – "with some sort of magical power?"

"It happened exactly how Richard described it," Matt said, coming to his friend's defence.

"Did it? The police have been sniffing around for the last seven days and they have found precious little to support your version of events. It is true that the villagers seem to have packed their bags and gone. And Omega One is now in ruins. But, to give you just one example, if there really had been an explosion there, how is it that no sign of radioactive fallout has been found anywhere in the area?"

"I explained in the article," Richard said wearily. "We reckon that all the radioactive particles must have got sucked back into the gate."

"Ah yes. Raven's Gate. That's the most ridiculous part of all. You write that there was some sort of stone circle that nobody in the world had ever heard of…"

"Professor Dravid had heard of it," Matt said.

"Sanjay Dravid has gone."

"Wait a minute." Richard slammed a hand down on the table. "You're part of the Nexus. You know I'm telling the truth. So why are you pretending otherwise?"

Fabian nodded. "You're right. I thought I'd made that clear from the start. Of course I believe you."

Richard's head was spinning. "So why do you want to cover it up?"

"Because this is the twenty-first century and the one thing that people cannot live with is uncertainty. Where there is terrorism, people need to know that the police are in control. When new diseases appear, they expect science to find cures. We live in an age when there is no room for the impossible."

"But you believe in the impossible."

"Yes. But why do you think we have to keep our organization secret? Because people would think we were mad, Mr Cole. That is why. One of our members is a senator in the Democratic Party in America. He would be voted out immediately if he began speaking about the Old Ones. Another is a multibillionaire, working in the field of computer software. She supports us and believes in us, although her shares would plummet if that were known. I have a wife and children. But even they do not know why I am here."

He turned to Matt.

"Although you will not be aware of it," he said, "the LEAF Project knows that you are no longer in Mrs Deverill's care. We could tell them where you are. One word from us and you would be back in their custody."

Matt's heart sank. So it had happened, exactly as he had feared.

But then Richard surprised him. "Nobody's taking Matt anywhere," he snapped. "He's staying here with me."

"That is exactly what we have arranged." Fabian smiled for the first time. "You see? We have already spoken to the right people and it has all been dealt with. We can help you. And you can help us. We can work together."

"How can I help you?" Matt asked.

"I'm afraid your role in this is not yet over," Fabian replied. "Sanjay Dravid spoke about you. He thought your appearance was the single most remarkable event of his lifetime."

"Why?"

"Because he believed you were one of the Five."

And there it was again. *One of the Five.*

Matt sighed. "That's what you keep saying. But what does it mean?"

"Five children saved the world. Five children will save it again. It's part of a prophecy, Matt. What happened here in Yorkshire was only the start. The Nexus will be called together again and you will have to meet us all. Until then, we ask only that you remain here. And tell no one. We must keep these matters to ourselves."

There was a long silence.

"That's all very well," Richard said. "But how am I supposed to look after him? Since the Nexus knows everything, you may have noticed that I'm out of a job. And shouldn't Matt be at school? He can't just sit around here with me!"

"We can easily arrange a local school for Matt," Fabian replied. "Anything you need or want we can get for you." He produced a business card and slid it across the table. "As for your living expenses, we can look after that too." He clicked open the briefcase and took out a thick envelope, which he handed to Richard. The journalist glanced inside it and whistled. "That's five thousand pounds, Mr Cole. Think of it as a first payment. When you need more, you only need to call."

Fabian stood up. He held out a hand to Matt, who shook it unwillingly.

"I cannot tell you what a great pleasure it has been to

meet you," Fabian said. "We will meet again in London very soon." He seemed to be about to leave, but then he turned back and his eyes were troubled. "Perhaps I shouldn't tell you this," he said. "But you will have to know eventually and I think my friend Professor Dravid would have wanted me to tell you." He took a breath. "We believe there may be a second gate."

"What?" Matt was stunned.

"I live in Lima. In Peru. It is the reason why I was chosen to visit you today. There is evidence that another gate exists in my country. It may be that I will have to invite you there."

"You must be joking," Matt said. "I've done my bit. I don't want to know any more."

"I can understand that, Matt. Just remember – the Nexus is on your side. We exist only to be your friends." He nodded at Richard. "Please don't get up, Mr Cole. I can show myself out."

For ten minutes neither of them spoke.

"Well," Richard said at last. The cash was spread out on the table in front of him. "At least that solves the money problem."

"A second gate…" Matt had gone pale. He looked suddenly tired.

"It's got nothing to do with you," Richard said.

"It's got everything to do with me, Richard. I know that now. I thought it was all over when the power station was destroyed. But I was wrong. It's like that man said – it was just the start."

"No way," Richard said. "I mean, think about it for a minute. Do you really believe there's another circle of stones? And that maybe some other crackpot has gone and built a nuclear power station in the middle of it? It's got nothing to do with you, Matt. He's talking about South America. Thousands of miles away!"

"They'll make me go there."

"They can't *make* you do anything you don't want to do. And if they try, they'll have to get past me."

Matt couldn't help smiling. "Thanks for sticking your neck out for me."

"That was nothing. Actually, I didn't even mean to. It just sort of happened."

"Well, now it looks as if you're stuck with me."

Richard nodded. "I suppose so. It's a pain in the neck. On the other hand, I haven't got a job. I might as well play babysitter to you."

"I don't need a babysitter."

"Yes, you do. And I still need a story. So what it really boils down to is, we're stuck with each other."

"A second gate…"

"Matt, just put it out of your mind. I haven't got the faintest idea what's going on any more but I'll tell you one thing for certain. We're not going to Peru."

THE POWER OF FIVE

BOOK TWO

"Hair-raising, spine-tingling, satanic stuff." *The Times*

EVIL STAR

ANTHONY HOROWITZ

It began with Raven's Gate.
But it's not over yet.
Once again the enemy is stirring.

Turn the page to read a short taster...

BOOK TWO

The old man's eyes burned red, reflecting the last flames of the fire. The sun had already begun to set and the shadows were closing in. Far away, a huge bird – a condor – wheeled around in a lazy circle before plunging back down to earth. Then everything was still. The night was just a breath away.

"He will come," the old man said. He spoke in a strange language, and one known to very few people in the world. "We have no need to send for him. He will come anyway."

He got to his feet, supporting himself on a walking-stick carved from the branch of a tree, and made his way to the edge of the stone terrace where he had been sitting. From here he could look down into a canyon that seemed to fall away for ever, a fault line in the planet that had occurred perhaps a million years ago. For a time he was silent. There were a dozen men behind him, waiting for him to speak. None of them moved. Not one of them dared interrupt him while he stood there deep in thought.

At last he turned back.

"The boy is on the other side of the world," he said. "He lives in England."

One of the men stirred uneasily. He knew it was wrong to ask questions but he couldn't stop himself. "Are we just going to wait for him?" he demanded. "We have so little time. And even if he does come, how can he help us? A child!"

"You don't understand, Atoc," the old man replied. If he was angry, he didn't show it. He knew that Atoc was only twenty years old, barely more than a child himself, at least in his old mind. "The boy has power. He still has no idea who he is or how strong he has become. He will come here and he will arrive in time. His power will bring him to us."

"Who is this boy?" someone else asked.

The old man looked again at the sun. It seemed to be sitting, perfectly balanced, on the highest mountain peak. The mountain was called Mandango ... the Sleeping God.

"His name is Matthew Freeman," he said. "He is the first of the Five."

BIG WHEEL

There was something wrong about the house in Eastfield Terrace. Something unpleasant.

All the houses in the street were more or less identical: red-brick, Victorian, with two bedrooms on the first floor and a bay window on either the left or the right of the front door. Some had satellite dishes. Some had window boxes filled with brightly coloured flowers. But looking down from the top of the hill at the terrace curving round St Patrick's church on its way to the Esso garage and All-Nite store, one house stood out immediately. Number twenty-seven no longer belonged there. It was as if it had caught some sort of disease and needed to be taken away.

The front garden was full of junk, and as usual the wheelie bin beside the gate was overflowing, surrounded by black garbage bags that the owners had been unable to stuff inside. This wasn't uncommon in Eastfield Terrace. Nor was it particularly strange that the curtains were permanently drawn across the front windows and, as far as anyone could tell, the lights were never turned on. But the house smelled. For weeks now there had been a rotten, sewagey smell that had seemed at first to be coming from a blocked pipe but that had rapidly got worse until people had begun to cross the street to avoid it. And whatever was causing it seemed to be affecting the entire place. The grass on the front lawn was beginning to die. The flowers had wilted and then been choked up by weeds. The colour seemed to be draining out of the very bricks.

The neighbours had tried to complain. They had knocked on the front door, but nobody had come. They had telephoned, but nobody had answered. Finally, they had called the borough council at the Ipswich Civic Centre but of course it would be weeks before any action was taken. The house wasn't empty. That much they knew. They had occasionally seen the owner, Gwenda Davis, pacing back and forth behind the net curtains. Once – more than a week ago – she had been seen scurrying home from the shops. And there was one other piece of evidence that there was still life at number twenty-seven: every evening the television was turned on.

Gwenda Davis was well known in the street.

She had lived there for much of her adult life, first on her own and then with her partner, Brian Conran, who worked occasionally as a milkman. But what had really set the neighbours talking was the time, six years ago, when she had inexplicably adopted an eight-year-old boy and brought him home to live with her. Everyone agreed that she and Brian were not exactly the ideal parents. He drank. The two of them argued. And according to local gossip, they hardly knew the boy, whose own parents had died in a car accident.

So nobody was very surprised when the whole thing went wrong. It wasn't really the boy's fault. Matthew Freeman had been a nice enough child – everyone agreed – but almost from the moment he arrived he had been in trouble. He had started missing school. He'd been hanging out with the wrong company. He became known for a whole range of petty crimes, and inevitably the police had been involved. And finally there had been that robbery at a local warehouse, just round the corner from Ipswich station. A security guard had nearly died and Matthew had been dragged out with blood on his hands. After that, he'd been sent away on some sort of fostering programme. He had a new mother, somewhere in Yorkshire. And good riddance to bad rubbish. That was the general view.

All this had happened about three months ago. Since then, Gwenda had gradually disappeared from sight. And as for Brian, no one had seen him for weeks. The house had become more and more neglected. Everyone agreed that soon something would have to be done.

Now it was half past seven one evening in the first week of June. The days were stretching out, holding on for as long as they could. The people of Eastfield Terrace were hot and tired. Tempers were getting short. And the smell was as bad as ever.

Gwenda was in the kitchen, making supper for herself. She had never been a very attractive woman, small and dowdy with dull eyes and pinched lips that never smiled. But in the weeks since Matt's departure, she had rapidly declined. Her hair was unbrushed and wild. She was wearing a flowery dress and a cardigan which, like her, hadn't been washed for some time and hung off her, almost shapeless. She had developed a nervous twitch, constantly rubbing her arms as if she was cold or perhaps afraid of something.

"Do you want anything?" she called out in a thin, high-pitched voice.

Brian was waiting for her in the sitting room but she knew he wouldn't eat anything. She had preferred it when he'd had his job down at the milk depot, but he'd been sacked after getting into a fight with one of the managers. That had happened just after Matt had been sent away. Now Brian had lost his appetite too.

Gwenda looked at her watch. It was almost time for *Big Wheel*, her favourite television programme of the week. In fact, thanks to satellite, she could see *Big Wheel* every night. But Thursdays were special. On Thursday there was a brand new programme – not a repeat.

Gwenda was addicted to *Big Wheel*. She loved the bright lights of the studio, the mystery prizes, the contestants who might win a million pounds if they got enough questions right and dared to spin the wheel. Best of all, she loved the presenter – Rex McKenna – with his permanent suntan, his jokes, his perfect white smile. Rex was about fifty years old but his hair was still jet black, his eyes glimmered and there was a spring in his step that made him seem much younger. He had been on the show for as long as Gwenda could remember, and although he hosted two other quiz programmes as well as a dancing competition on the BBC, it was in *Big Wheel* that Gwenda liked him best.

"Is it on yet?" she called from the kitchen.

There was no reply from Brian. He hadn't been talking very much lately, either.

She reached into a cupboard and took out a tin of beans. It wasn't exactly what you'd call a feast but it had been a while since either of them had earned any money and she was beginning to feel the pinch. She looked around the kitchen for a clean plate but there weren't any. Every surface was covered with dirty crockery, a tower of soiled plates and bowls rose out of the sink. Gwenda decided she would eat the beans out of the tin. She plunged her hand into the brown, filthy water and somehow managed to find a fork. She wiped off some of the grease on her dress and hurried from the room.

The lights were out in the sitting room but the glow of the television was enough to show the way. It also showed the mess that the room had become. There were old newspapers scattered across the carpet, overflowing ashtrays, more dirty plates, old socks and underpants. Brian was sitting on a sofa that had looked ugly and second hand the moment it had left the shop. There was a nasty stain on the nylon cover. Ignoring it, Gwenda sat down next to him.

The smell, which had been bad throughout the house, was worse in here. Gwenda ignored that too.

It seemed to her that everything had gone wrong since

Matt had left. She didn't quite know why. It wasn't as if she had actually liked him. On the contrary, she had always known there was something weird about the boy. Hadn't he dreamt that his mother and father were going to die the night before the accident actually happened? She had only taken him in because Brian had persuaded her – and of course, he'd only wanted to get his hands on the money that Matt's parents had left their son. The trouble was, the money had gone all too quickly. And then Matt had gone too, taken away by the police as a juvenile delinquent, and all she'd been left with was the blame.

It wasn't her fault. She'd looked after him. She'd never forget the way the police looked at her, as if she was the one who'd committed the crime. She wished now that Matt had never come into her life. Everything had gone wrong because of Matt.

"And now, on ITV, it's time once again to take your chances and spin ... the Big Wheel!"

Gwenda settled back as the *Big Wheel* theme tune began. Fifty-pound notes twisted and spun across the screen. The audience applauded. And there was Rex McKenna walking down the flashing staircase with a pretty girl holding onto each arm. He was dressed in a bright, sequinned jacket, waving and smiling, happy as always to be back.

"Good evening, everyone!" he called out. "Who knows who's going to win big-time tonight?" He paused and winked straight at the camera. "Only the wheel knows!"

The audience went wild as if they were hearing the words

for the first time. But of course Rex always began the show the same way. "Only the wheel knows!" was his catch phrase, although Gwenda wasn't quite sure if it was true. The wheel was just a big piece of wood and plastic. How could it know anything?

Rex came to a halt and the applause died down. Gwenda was staring at the screen in a kind of trance. She had already forgotten her baked beans. Somewhere in the back of her mind, she wondered how it was that the television still worked when the electricity in the house had been turned off two weeks ago because she hadn't paid the bill. But the back of her mind was a very long way away and it didn't really matter. It was a blessing. How would she get through the nights without *Big Wheel*?

"Welcome to another show where the spin of the wheel could mean a million pounds in your pocket or a return ticket home with absolutely nothing!" Rex began. "And what a busy week I've had. My wife woke me up at six o'clock yesterday morning to remind me to put the alarm on. The alarm went off at seven and it still hasn't come back!"

The audience roared with laughter. Gwenda laughed too.

"But we've got a great show for you tonight. And in a minute we're going to meet the three lucky contestants who are competing for tonight's big prizes. But remember. If you want to get your hands on a million quid, what do you have to do?"

"You have to spin to win!" the audience yelled.

Brian said nothing. It was beginning to annoy Gwenda, the way he just sat there.

"But before we can get started," Rex went on, "I want to have a quick word with a very special lady, a real favourite of mine..." He stepped closer to the camera and, as his face filled the screen, it seemed to Gwenda that he was looking directly at her.

"Hello, Gwenda," he said.

"Hello, Rex," Gwenda whispered. It was difficult for her to believe that he was actually talking to her. It always was.

"And how are you tonight, my love?"

"I'm all right..." She bit her lip and folded her hands in her lap.

"Well, listen, my darling. I wonder if you've given any more thought to what we talked about. Matt Freeman. That guttersnipe. That little creep. Have you decided what you're going to do about him?"

Rex McKenna had started talking to Gwenda two months ago. At the beginning, it had puzzled Gwenda. How could he interrupt the show (watched by ten million people) just to speak to her? Somehow he even managed to do it in the repeats, and that couldn't be possible because some of them had been recorded years ago. At first it had worried her. When she'd told Brian about it, he'd laughed in her face and said she was going mad. Well, Rex had soon put her straight about Brian. And now she didn't worry about it any more. It was bizarre but it was happening and the truth was, she was flattered. She adored Rex and it seemed he was equally fond of her.

"Matt Freeman made a fool of you," Rex went on. "He came into your house and he ruined your relationship with Brian and then the boy got into trouble and everybody said it was your fault. And now look at you! No money. No job. You're a mess, Gwenda…"

"It's not my fault," Gwenda muttered.

"I know it's not your fault, old love," Rex replied. For a moment the camera cut away and Gwenda could see the studio audience getting restless, waiting for the show to begin. "You looked after that boy. You treated him like a son. But he's pushed off without so much as a by-your-leave. No gratitude, of course. Kids these days! He's cock of the walk now and you should hear the things he says about you! I've been thinking about it and I have to say … I believe the boy ought to be punished."

"Punished…" Gwenda muttered the word with a sense of dread.

"Just like you punished Brian for being so rude to you." Rex shook his head. Maybe it was a trick of the studio lighting but he seemed almost to be reaching out of the television set as if he was about to climb into the room. "The fact of the matter is that Matt is a very nasty piece of work," he said. "Everywhere he goes, he causes trouble. You remember what happened to his parents."

"They died."

"It was his fault. He could have saved them. And there are

other things you don't know about. He upset some very good friends of mine recently. In fact he more than upset them. He killed them. Can you believe that? He killed all of them. If you ask me, there's no question about it. He needs to be punished very severely indeed."

"I don't know where he is," Gwenda said.

"I can tell you that. He goes to a school called Forrest Hill. It's in Yorkshire, just outside York. That's not so far away."

"What do you want me to do?" Gwenda asked. Her mouth was dry. The tin of beans had tilted forward in her hands and cold tomato sauce was dripping into her lap.

"You like me, don't you, Gwenda?" The television presenter gave her one of his special smiles. There were little wrinkles in the corners of his eyes. "You want to help me. You know what has to be done."

Gwenda nodded. For some reason she had begun to cry. She wondered if this would be the last time Rex McKenna would talk to her. She would go to York and she wouldn't come back.

"You go there on the train and you find him and you make sure that he never hurts anyone again. You owe it to yourself. You owe it to everyone. What do you say?"

Gwenda couldn't speak. She nodded a second time. The tears were flowing faster.

Rex backed away. "Ladies and gentlemen, let's hear it for Gwenda Davis. She's a lovely lady and she deserves a big round of applause."

The audience agreed. They clapped and cheered until Gwenda left the room and went upstairs.

Brian remained where he was, sitting on the sofa, his legs slightly apart, his mouth hanging open. He had been like that ever since Gwenda had stuck the kitchen knife into his chest. Brian had laughed at her. He had said she was mad. She'd had to teach him a lesson that he wouldn't forget. Rex had told her to do that too.

A few minutes later, Gwenda left the house. She'd meant to pack, but in the end she hadn't been able to find anything worth taking apart from the axe that she used to chop wood. She'd slipped that into the bag that dangled from her arm.

Gwenda locked the door behind her and walked away. She knew exactly where she was heading: Forrest Hill, a school in Yorkshire. She was going to see her nephew, Matt Freeman, again.

He would certainly be surprised.

WELCOME TO THE DARK SIDE OF
ANTHONY HOROWITZ

THE POWER OF FIVE

BOOK ONE
He always knew
he was different.
First there were
the dreams.
Then the deaths began.

BOOK TWO
It began with
Raven's Gate.
But it's not over yet.
Once again the
enemy is stirring.

BOOK THREE

Darkness covers
the earth.
The Old Ones
have returned.
The battle must begin.

BOOK FOUR

An ancient evil
is unleashed.
Five have the power
to defeat it.
But one of them
has been taken.

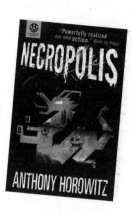

BOOK FIVE

Five Gatekeepers.
One chance to
save mankind.
Chaos beckons.
Oblivion awaits.

www.powerof5.co.uk   www.facebook.com/thepoweroffive   www.walker.co.uk

Alex Rider – you're
never too young
to die…

High in the Alps,
death waits for
Alex Rider…

Sharks. Assassins.
Nuclear bombs.
Alex Rider's in
deep water.

Alex Rider has
90 minutes to save
the world.

Once stung,
twice as deadly.
Alex Rider wants
revenge.

He's back –
and this time there
are no limits.

Alex Rider
bites back…

Alex Rider –
in the jaws
of death…

One bullet.
One life.
The end starts here.

ANTHONY HOROWITZ

"KILL ALEX RIDER"

RUSSIAN ROULETTE

THE DEADLY PREQUEL TO THE
BESTSELLING ALEX RIDER SERIES

OCTOBER 2013

Author photo by Des Willie

ANTHONY HOROWITZ is the author of the number one bestselling Alex Rider books and The Power of Five series. He has enjoyed huge success as a writer for both children and adults, most recently with his highly acclaimed Sherlock Holmes novel, *The House of Silk.*

He has won numerous awards, including the Bookseller Association/Nielsen Author of the Year Award, the Children's Book of the Year Award at the British Book Awards, and the Red House Children's Book Award.

Anthony has also created and written many major television series, including *Injustice, Collision* and the award-winning *Foyle's War.*

You can find out more about Anthony and his work at: www.anthonyhorowitz.com